Nowhere to Turn

Turn

~A Ryan Turner Novel~

By Jorrell Otoño Mirabal

The events and characters in this book are completely
fictitious. Any similarities to real persons is not intended by
the author and is only coincidental.

The scanning, uploading, and selling and distribution of this
book without the author's permission may be labelled as
theft.

JM Publishing
Jorrell Mirabal
PO Box 1168, Magdalena, NM 87825
jorrellmirabal@yahoo.com

ISBN-13: 978-1986558402

For my family. To those who are still with me, and those who have passed away from this life. I love you all.

NOWHERE TO TURN

CHAPTER ONE

February 5, 2017

The coffee was strong, black, and scorching hot, just how Ryan Turner liked it. Steam rose from the mug, and the cup's heat soared through Ryan's hand but, severe heat and all, he guzzled it down like cold lemonade on a sweltering summer day. It surprised people at times how fast and easily Ryan could drink a hot cup of Jo, yet he usually would reply with a smirk, followed by another swig of coffee. After a lifetime of being a coffee drinker, his taste buds were non-existent. He loved the burning sensation he received as the hot coffee poured down his throat and into his stomach.

"Sir, are you ready to order?"

Ryan pulled the mug away from his lips and looked up at the waiter standing next to his table.

"Ah, yes," Ryan said, "let me see here."

Ryan set his cup on the tabletop in front of him, wiped his mouth with the back of his hand, and opened a menu. Leaning back in his chair, right leg crossed over his left thigh, he looked intently at Mongolies' Italian menu in front of him.

Ryan pointed at a dish listed on the menu. "Yes! There we are. I'll take this right here."

The mustached waiter looked over Ryan's shoulder at the menu.

"Ze toasted panzanella?" the waiter asked in a strong Italian accent.

Ryan nodded and flipped the menu closed. "Yes! Thank you, kind sir."

The waiter nodded, took the menu from Ryan's hands, and left for the kitchen. Ryan glanced down at his watch. *10:01 p.m.*

It's after 10...where is Kyle?

Ryan began to scan the restaurant when, as if on que, a second waiter approached him.

"*Wi, Wi,*" the six-foot-tall, black-haired, blue-eyed, ladies' man of a waiter said.

Ryan tried to keep from laughing at the man's failed attempt at an Italian accent.

"*Ze* name is Pablo," the waiter said, taking a slight bow. "Do you need anything, sir?"

Ryan smirked. "As a matter of fact, I do, Kyle...I mean Pablo. I must speak with your manager as soon as possible."

"Monsieur Mongolie?" Kyle asked shaking his head. "E-e-e, he is in a meeting at *ze* moment, but his son is in *ze* back if you wish to speak with him?"

Ryan scratched his chin. "I guess he'll have to do."

"Well, *andiamo*, monsieur," Kyle said, motioning toward the kitchen.

Ryan stood and began to follow his "waiter".

"For the record," Ryan said, "your Italian is pathetic...Monsieur is French."

Ryan laughed as Kyle casually threw him the middle finger as they entered the hectic kitchen.

Dodging frazzled waiters, waitresses, and cooks, Kyle and Ryan weaved their way through the kitchen until they came across a little office in the far-right corner. The door to the office was closed and Kyle tapped on the long window next to the door. The man sitting at the desk inside didn't even bother to look up from his computer, but motioned for Kyle to come in. Kyle did so, followed by Ryan.

"Mr. Mongolie," Kyle said, "I have a customer here who needs to speak with you."

Paulie Mongolie Jr. disgustedly shook his head and asked, "Why? What is it?"

Ryan stepped forward with his hands behind his back. "Sir, I need to speak with your father. It is urgent."

"He's in a meeting, get out of my office," Paulie stated bluntly.

Ryan didn't budge.

"Umm, sir, did you not fully understand the part where I said that it was urgent?"

Paulie stood up, trying to act intimidating, while he pointed his finger at Ryan's chest. "Do you not understand English? Get out of my office before I make you get out! You…Pablo, get this fool out of here."

Kyle stayed put while Ryan whipped out his FBI badge and shoved it in Paulie's face.

"Maybe this will better help you understand. I am Agent Ryan Turner, FBI. This here is one of my partners, Kyle Harrison, and I need to know where your father is NOW!"

CHAPTER TWO

Paulie flopped back down into his chair and folded
his arms across his chest.

"I don't know where he is."

Kyle jumped in this time pulling out a Glock from inside
his black vest.

"You listen, and you listen good," Kyle said shoving his
pistol in Paulie's face.

Ryan reached back and closed the window blinds.

"We know who you are," Kyle continued. "We know all
about you and your father's involvement with Cybris Caine.
We know Caine is here in New York City. So, it does you no
good to play dumb."

Paulie fidgeted and avoided looking Ryan or Kyle in the
eye.

"I can't say anything," he said.

Ryan reached over the desk and with both hands,
grabbed Paulie by the shirt, and dragged him across the desk,
sending papers flying and the computer crashing to the floor.
Ryan tossed the little man to the floor and drew a Glock of
his own.

"Where is he!?" Ryan yelled out.

Paulie crawled into a ball, whimpering. "You don't
know Caine like I do. You have no idea! He'll torture me.
He'll hurt my family."

Kyle kicked Paulie in the ribs. "Snap out of it and grow
a pair," he growled.

Ryan rolled his eyes at one of Kyle's favorite phrases.

Kyle went on. "When Caine has a bullet in his head
there is no way he can hurt you or your family. But when you

have one in *your* head, there is no way that you can help or provide for your family."

Paulie took a deep breath and sat himself up, holding his side.

"The fridge…there's a hidden door behind it."

Ryan and Kyle each looked over toward the corner of the room where Paulie was pointing. There in the far-left corner of the office was a restaurant-sized refrigerator up against the wall. Ryan and Kyle approached it and suddenly the door behind them flew open. Both agents spun around to see Paulie sprinting out of the office. Kyle started to take off after him, but Ryan grabbed him by the back of the shirt to stop him.

"Let him be," Ryan said. "Kuron will deal with him."

Ryan then put his hand up to his ear. "Hey, Kuron! Mongolie Junior thinks he's slick and is headed your way."

Ryan listened to Kuron's reply through his hidden earpiece. Ryan heard his reply and smiled.

"Yeah, Kuron's got it covered."

CHAPTER THREE

Kuron Taylor sat next to the entrance, on a sofa in the waiting area of Mongolies. He had his arms spread out over the top of the couch. Kuron Taylor was African-American and had a massive build. Detective Taylor stood 6-feet-7-inches tall and weighed a solid 250 pounds of pure muscle. He had a massive, bulging neck and chest. His arms were huge and cut and the veins in his arms stuck out of his dark skin. He was quite intimidating on the surface and although he was tough as nails, he had a soft, caring heart. Kuron sat upon the waiting area sofa, his long legs crossed out in front of him. He took a drag from the cigarette that hung out of his mouth. He wasn't a frequent smoker, but there were times out in the field that he'd keep a cigarette pressed between his lips to calm his nerves. Kuron watched as the young hostess came over to him for the third time that night.

"Sir?" she asked politely.

Kuron smiled at the blonde girl. "Yes, ma'am?"

She put on her fake grin and leaned closer to Kuron asking, "Are you sure everything is alright? And once again, before you dine, you must get rid of that cigarette. There is absolutely no smoking past this sitting area."

He understood her concern and was honestly surprised that she had not contacted law enforcement yet. He was a big, intimidating guy dressed in street clothes, who had been sitting in the fancy restaurant lobby for over an hour now.

Kuron stuck out his bottom lip and nodded, gazing through the glass entrance doors.

"Umm, yeah…I believe so. My boys probably got caught up in the wonderful New York City traffic."

Kuron pulled his cell phone out of his pocket and peeped at it, pretending to read something on the screen.

"Yup, they should be here any second now, ma'am."

The hostess nodded. "Lovely, sir, but I'm sorry to inform you that in a few minutes we are going to have to ask you to leave. I'm sorry."

Kuron then heard some commotion from the dining area and smirked as he saw a little man swiftly walking in his direction, bumping into tables as he went along.

"Ma'am, would you mind taking a seat for a second?" Kuron asked.

The blonde girl looked puzzled as Kuron stood up.

"I insist," he said as he grabbed her by the arm and pulled her down onto the sofa.

She looked distressed, but Kuron ignored her. He kept his eyes on the little man scampering toward him. The little Italian was clear of all the dining tables and began to jog now. Kuron looked down at the hostess for a split second.

"Please don't be alarmed. My name is Kuron Taylor, FBI."

Just as he finished his sentence, Kuron turned and grabbed Paulie Mongolie by the throat as he passed by. Kuron felt Paulie's body go stiff as he scooped him off his feet with both hands and threw him down roughly onto his back. Paulie landed with a thud, knocking the air out of him.

"Where do you think you're going?" Kuron asked.

Paulie Mongolie's mouth hung open as he gasped for air.

"Sit down, man," Kuron said. "Stay a while."

He plopped the Italian down onto the sofa and squeezed himself between Mongolie and the hostess. The girl sat there speechless, with eyes as big as saucers.

Kuron turned to the woman. "You can get back to working now if you want."

Hurriedly, she got to her feet and scampered away.

"So, buddy," Kuron said as he put his arm around the pale Paulie Mongolie, "where were you headed in such a hurry?"

The little man's chest heaved in and out as he was finally able to catch his breath.

"Excuse me, I didn't quite get that."

Mongolie still said nothing. Kuron patted the little Italian on the shoulder.

"You're neck deep in some serious stuff. You know that, right? With the intake and massive outpouring of illegal drugs and weapons here in this restaurant? We know all about it…and have known for quite some time now. But, we decided to keep an eye on you, hoping you'd give us a lead on Caine. And what do you know? Here we are about to put a wrinkle in your father and Caine's rendezvous tonight. So, the whole lot of you is done for. There's no point in being a hard ass…so let's talk. Let's have a friendly little conversation here."

Paulie smirked and Kuron wanted to knock the stupid look off his face.

"Well," Paulie began, "how is your night going thus far, Agent Taylor?"

Kuron was taken aback by the man's comment and glared down at him.

"You know who I am?"

Now Paulie was acting like the cool and confident one.

"Of course, you sort of stand out, you know."

Kuron scratched his chin with the hand that wasn't grasping Paulie's shoulder.

"How do you know who I am?" Kuron spat out.

Paulie chuckled then placed his right leg over his left and leaned back in his seat.

"When you work for someone like Caine," Paulie began, "you know things. We knew who you three were, and we know that you had been onto us for quite some time now. I mean, let's be honest here, Agent Harrison's 'waiter' disguise was pretty good, but the Ryan Turner guy? I recognized him the moment he walked into my office. Our guys recognized him the moment he came into the restaurant tonight, as did they recognize you. We knew you'd be here tonight, Agent Taylor."

Kuron was stunned. He was speechless.

"So, Agent Taylor," Paulie continued, "I'm pretty sure you've got it all backwards. You are the one in some serious trouble, not me."

Kuron punched Paulie square in the face.

"What are you talking about?"

Paulie grinned as a slight stream of blood ran out of the corner of his mouth.

"What am I talking about? There are five of Caine's men, who are dining here tonight. They are armed and more than willing to die. There are only three of you. Check. Your friends? They're walking straight into a trap. Once they hit the bottom of the stairs down that passage, they are not going to find what they are expecting. There was no meeting between my father and Caine. My father is dead. He was weak-hearted, so Mr. Caine had him eliminated. Your two buddies are fixing to find him tied to a chair with quite an impressive set of explosives on his lap, which are set to go off here at any moment. When they go off, a whole set of explosives strung throughout this restaurant are bound to go off too. Check-mate, Agent Taylor. And me? I was supposed to shut the passage door behind them, I didn't. Whether you kill me, or whether I am absolutely incinerated, it does not matter to me. I messed up, and Mr. Caine isn't going to let that slide. We are both dead men, Kuron Taylor."

Kuron was completely shocked.

"You've got to be kidding…!"

Grinning, Paulie interrupted him.

"Hail, Caine!" he spat out just before Kuron punched him across the face once more, knocking him out cold.

"Ryan, Kyle, get out of there now! I repeat, we need to leave now! We were set up!" Kuron said with his hand pressed against his ear.

He then whipped his Glock out and kept his eyes peeled for any of Caine's men. He didn't know what was about to happen, but he knew the next few minutes were about to get very interesting.

CHAPTER FOUR

Stealthily, Ryan and Kyle tip-toed down the hidden passage's spiral stairway. As they finally approached the bottom they could see a door. Ryan still had his gun out, and the closer they got to the door, the more his stomach churned. Something felt off. Besides, he was only feet away from the most wanted man in the world. He was feet and seconds away from *the* Cybris Caine. Caine was dangerous, so very dangerous.

For years, Ryan and his team had been trying to bag Caine and this was the closest they had ever gotten; however, as much as he wished it didn't, the whole situation scared Ryan. Caine himself had decapitated the Prime Minister of England. For years he has been the driving force behind the assassination of FBI, CIA and government figures. He was the world's most powerful criminal drug lord. He had his own "army" that spread across the entire globe. Every continent and every country worldwide contained people who followed him. He had an empire…the most widespread empire in the world. And here Ryan was, possibly moments away from finally catching up with or putting an end to Cybris Caine.

Ryan took a deep breath. Standing in front of the door now, he could picture Caine. Caine's parents were originally from the Congo. His skin was dark as night. He had perfect white teeth that shone when he smiled his signature smile. Caine had dark brown, menacing eyes that were almost black. He was of average height but built like a rock. Cybris Caine was a fitness fanatic and it was easy to see. It would be no surprise if his system was altered with muscle-enhancing drugs as well. Ryan took a deep breath and with both hands on his Glock, he aimed at the door ready for anything. He motioned toward the door with his gun. Kyle slowly reached for the doorknob and began to turn it.

Ryan started to get shaky. His heart felt as if it was going to beat out of his chest. Beads of sweat formed on his forehead. Just as Kyle was about to throw open the door, their earpieces erupted. It was Kuron.

"Ryan, Kyle, get out of there now! I repeat, we need to leave now! We've been set up!"

Ryan was stunned and lowered his Glock just as Kyle threw open the door. Inside was a dimly lit room with nothing but a wooden chair in the middle of it. Tied to the chair was none other than Paulie Mongolie Sr., with his throat slit and his shirt drenched in blood. Strapped to his lap and chest were explosives. Ryan knew it the moment he saw them. He looked up above Mongolie to see more explosives strung-out across the ceiling. Ryan and Kyle both began to take steps back.

"Kuron…" Ryan said, "what in the world is going on?"

"Guys, we need to leave. This whole place is about to be blown sky-high. Caine set it all up. They knew we were going to be here tonight. There was never a meeting between Mongolie and Caine. We need to get these people out of here. And heads up, Caine's got men here, armed. Five of them, I believe."

Ryan and Kyle made eye-contact, and then sprinted back up the stairway.

CHAPTER FIVE

Kuron wasn't sure what to do. He had to get all the people out of the restaurant and at the same time keep an eye out for the five men Paulie had mentioned…*IF* he was telling the truth. Kuron stood to his feet and motioned the hostess over to him. He looked at the girl's nametag.

"Whitney?"

The girl nodded.

"We need to get these people out of this place immediately. We are all in danger…but we need to be subtle about this. Go table to table. I'll help you."

Confused, Whitney slowly nodded her head and quickly walked over to the nearest table. Kuron then began to approach tables himself. At the first table he came to, sat a bald, Caucasian man. Instantly, Kuron spotted the gun tucked into the guy's pants' waistband underneath his shirt. Kuron sat down in the chair next to him and shoved his Glock into the man's side.

"Where are the rest of you?" he whispered into the man's ear.

The bald man grinned. "And why should I tell you?"

Kuron pressed the gun harder into the man's side. "To keep me from killing your worthless self."

The man continued to flash his yellow teeth at Kuron. "We're all fixing to die here in a second anyway, so what difference does it make?"

Kuron hated it, but he was afraid the man next to him just might be right.

CHAPTER SIX

Ryan threw himself out of the door at the top of the stairway and sprinted out of Paulie Mongolie's office and into the kitchen.

"Hey!" he yelled. "Everyone, get out of here now! There is a bomb threat! We all need to leave immediately!"

Stunned cooks, waiters, and dish washers all froze for a second then all at once dropped what they were doing and rushed out of the kitchen. Everybody scattered, leaving the kitchen in a hurry; all except one woman. Ryan spotted her right away. She was short, Hispanic, and wore a tall chef's hat. It was not her extreme lack of height that caught his eye, but that she hadn't moved a muscle and was reaching for something at her waist. It was moments like these that Ryan was made for. His instincts and ability to never miss a detail was remarkable, and his friends and colleagues always referred to him as having a sixth sense. Time seemed to stand still. He felt that he knew the woman was pulling a gun, but he had to be sure. Every motion that she made progressed slowly in Ryan's eyes.

Her hand came up from her waist and in it was what he instantly recognized to be a hand gun. Before the woman could point the gun in Ryan's direction, he had unloaded two rounds into her chest. Kyle had already begun to leave the kitchen and Ryan followed close behind. The moment they burst through the kitchen doors and into the dining room, Ryan's sixth sense kicked in again. Even through the absolute chaos, he could make one of Caine's men holding an Uzi submachine gun. In the direction of the gun, Ryan could see Kuron sitting next to a bald man, both with their backs to the gunman. Ryan whipped his Glock in the direction of the gunman and fired, hitting the man in the head and dropping him to the ground as the Uzi erratically sprayed bullets around the room.

Two down.

Ryan then heard shots to his left and found that Kyle had taken out another one of Caine's henchmen.

Three down.

"Oh, no," Ryan said as he looked over in Kuron's direction to see that the Uzi had done considerable damage.

The bald man Kuron had been sitting with now lay dead, face-down on the table. Kuron was kneeling on the floor over a woman. A small, crying child stood next to Kuron's side. Ryan sprinted over to Kuron.

"Is she okay? Are *you* hit?"

As Kuron helped the woman to the sitting position, he said, "Baldy over there got a bullet to the head, good riddance, and she's hit in the thigh. Not her heart or head, which is good, but I think she's hit in her femoral artery. It's bleeding bad."

BANG, BANG!

Ryan spun around to his left to see Kyle holstering his Glock as he trotted toward Ryan.

"That's four," he stated.

"And baldy here makes five," Ryan said, motioning to the dead man sitting at the table next to him.

Ryan jerked a white tablecloth from a nearby table and used it as a tourniquet, tying it tightly above the wound on the woman's leg. The woman grimaced and cried out. "Okay," Ryan said, "that should hold up for now. Kuron, grab her. We need to get her to a hospital. I'll take the girl."

Kuron did so, and Ryan lifted the hysterical little girl into his arms and the group sprinted toward the big glass doors at the entrance.

"What about Paulie?" Kuron asked. "He's crashed out on the couch here."

"Kyle," Ryan ordered, "grab him. He might be of some use, even though I'd rather leave him here."

Kyle didn't skip a beat and swooped Paulie off the couch as he ran by. The group busted through the doors and out into the New York City streets. They turned to the right and headed down Parson's Boulevard, all three agents yelling at nearby people to run.

"Lucky for us, the hospital is straight down Parsons…MOVE, GET OUT OF THE WAY! RUN!" Ryan yelled as they ran through the crowds.

He glanced at the little girl in his arms. She continued to cry, and Ryan's sleeve was already wet with tears.

"What's your name?" Ryan asked. "How old are you?"

She sniffled. "K-K-Kayleen," she replied. "I'm four."

Ryan continued to run and dodge people along the crowded New York street.

"That is a beautiful name, Kay…"

BANG!

Ryan was suddenly thrown off his feet and fell into a heap on the ground. His ears were ringing, and he couldn't hear a thing. He laid flat on his back with Kayleen on his chest. Her eyes were bulging, and tears streamed down her cheeks. Smoke began to fill the streets and was already starting to burn Ryan's eyes. He struggled to his feet, lifting Kayleen up with him. Looking around him, he saw Kuron getting to his feet, pulling the screaming woman up with him. Next to him was Kyle, who was kneeling on one knee and covering his ears with both hands. People all around Ryan were yelling and screaming, but he couldn't hear anything aside from the sharp ringing in his ears. With Kayleen in his left arm and using the palm of his right hand, he struck his ear hard, straining to regain his hearing.

With the bleeding woman cradled in his arms, Kuron yelled at Ryan. Ryan couldn't hear a single word Kuron was saying. He pointed to his right ear and shook his head. Kuron responded with what Ryan could make out as a four-letter word beginning with an "sh" and ending with a "t". Kuron motioned for them to go and began to run down the crowded sidewalk once again. With Paulie Mongolie flung over his shoulder, Kyle followed behind Kuron. Ryan slapped his ear a few more times, and then trailed his two best friends and colleagues down Parsons Boulevard, toward Queens Hospital.

Ryan kept his eyes on the woman in Kuron's arms as she slipped in and out of consciousness. He knew she didn't have much time left. He stopped in his tracks, pulled out his cell phone, and quickly dialed 911. As he lifted the phone to his now partially functioning ear, Ryan was suddenly filled with a sense of relief. Headed down the road straight toward them was a flurry of ambulances, fire trucks, and NYPD cars. Instantly, he removed the phone from his ear and waved down an ambulance. Kyle and Kuron had also realized what was going on as they too ran to Ryan's side. Watching an ambulance pull up to the curb near him, Ryan realized everything would be all right.

CHAPTER SEVEN

Ryan sat in a leather chair in the waiting room of
Queens Emergency Facilities. On his lap laid Kayleen
Johnson, who was sound asleep with her head on his chest.
Over the past few hours they had spent together in the
hospital, he had quickly become quite fond of little Kayleen.
She was a sweet girl and very talkative and grown-up for a
five-year-old. She also went by the nickname of Kay and her
absolute favorite color was purple. Her mom's name was
Laura and she was a nurse at "Mont Sinee Hospal", which
Ryan translated into "Mount Sinai Hospital".

Kayleen didn't have a father and she and her mother
lived in a house in Jamaica, New York, that Kayleen's
grandparents had once owned and raised Laura in. Kayleen
loved eating ice cream, playing soccer, and watching Tom
and Jerry. She constantly reiterated to Ryan how much she
loved her mother. Although Ryan had continued to tell her
that her mother was going to be okay, Kayleen continued to
be extremely upset and worried. Eventually, she had cried
herself to sleep.

Explaining what had happened to J.J. Mauer, Head of
the Bureau, was rough. Mauer had seen what had happened at
Mongolie's on the evening news. Although he was relieved to
hear his three agents were alright, he was fuming. Ryan gave
him the rundown of what had happened and told him about
the predicament he was in with Laura and Kayleen. Mauer
allowed Ryan to stay at the hospital with the little girl, while
Kuron and Kyle took Paulie Mongolie to FBI headquarters.
Mr. Mauer said he'd call FBI Director, Trey Felix, right away

to discuss what had happened and what to do with Paulie Mongolie.

"Ryan Turner?"

Ryan had begun to doze off and lifted his head at the sound of his name being called. Standing in front of him was a short, plump nurse.

"Yes?" he replied.

The nurse clasped her hands together. "Room 214, she is awake and alert now. The procedure went well, and she is going to be okay."

Ryan smiled. "Thank goodness."

He stroked Kayleen's hair and asked, "May we go in there now?"

The nurse beamed, "Of course, of course!"

Ryan nodded and thanked her. He slowly stood up and lifted Kayleen with him. She awoke abruptly and rubbed her eyes. She muttered a few words then laid her head on Ryan's shoulder and fell back asleep. Ryan followed the nurse to room 214 and she opened the door for him.

"There you are," she said motioning Ryan into the room.

"Thanks," he replied.

As soon as he and Kayleen entered the room, the woman lying in the hospital bed turned her head toward them and smiled. Ryan's heart stopped. She was gorgeous. Her natural beauty radiated. Laura was jaw-dropping, head-turning, naturally beautiful. Through the chaos and nonsense at Mongolie's, Ryan hadn't really put too much notice into her. She had high cheekbones, beautifully tanned skin, long jet-black hair, long eyelashes, and stunning blue eyes. She had a perfectly shaped mouth and nose, and straight, pearl white teeth. Ryan couldn't help but smile back at her.

"How are you doing?" he asked.

Laura sat up in her bed a bit.

"I'm alive," she said. "It was only a little bullet, Mr…?"

Ryan took a seat in the chair that was next to the head of the bed.

"Ryan, Ryan Turner."

Laura stuck out her hand and Ryan shook it gently.

"I'm Laura Johnson."

Ryan smiled. "Pleasure to meet you. Sorry about what happened earlier, that was a mess."

Laura's eyes enlarged, and her mouth fell open. "Wait…sorry? Are you the one that shot me?"

"No, no, no, that is not it at all! I'm just saying…" Ryan stopped short as he realized that Laura was laughing.

"Take it easy, Agent Turner, I'm messing with you. Are all of you FBI people this uptight?"

Ryan couldn't help but smile again. "Do all nurses aspire to be comedians?"

Putting her hands up, Laura teased, "Wow, Mr. Agent, you barely came across me a few hours ago and already know my entire backstory, huh?"

Ryan nodded his head. "Oh, of course. I'm the real deal."

"Let me guess," Laura said, "my little Kay told you?"

Ryan looked down at the sleeping girl. "She sure did. She is quite the talkative little girl."

Laura held her arms out and Ryan carefully handed Kayleen over to her.

"Are you sure you're okay holding her?" Ryan asked.

"Oh, I'll be fine," Laura replied. "She's a sweet, sweet girl and an easy sleeper. She won't hurt me. The way you handled her, you must be a great father."

"To be honest," Ryan said, "I'm not a dad. I've never even had a little brother or sister. I mean, I had a little brother once, but we were separated when we were young."

Laura nodded her head. "Oh…" she said.

Ryan shrugged. "I know, I know. Twenty-nine-years-old with no children. It's kind of sad."

Laura rolled her eyes. "Well, guess what? I'm twenty-eight, raising a girl on my own. That's kind of sad too."

"Well," Ryan said pointing to Kayleen, "it seems to me that you have done a fine job."

Laura smiled as Kayleen nestled up against her. "Thank you! That means a lot." Laura stroked her daughter's long hair. "So, you're a hot shot FBI agent?"

Ryan laughed. "I guess you can put it that way."

"What brought you to the Big Apple?" Laura asked.

Ryan settled in his seat. "I live here actually."

Laura scrunched up her nose and eyebrows. "No way, I thought you were all headquartered in DC?"

"Yes, but agents are spread all across the country," Ryan said. "And actually, a few years back, we had a headquarters established here in New York City too. With the ever-growing agency, the Bureau's higher-up guys decided it would be best to have another base."

"Wow!" Laura exclaimed. "That's interesting. I had no idea…so if I may ask, and hopefully I'm not killed off or anything if I do," Laura winked, "but what was the deal at the restaurant tonight?"

Ryan shook his head. "Mongolie's has been a major spot for illegal drug and weapon trade for quite some time now. They did so through a man by the name of Cybris Caine. We were supposed to intrude on a meeting between Paulie Mongolie Senior and Caine himself, but we found out that we had been set up. Our mission had been compromised. We and everyone in that restaurant are lucky to have gotten out of there alive."

Laura nodded slowly. "That is some serious stuff…sorry, I shouldn't have asked. It's really none of my business."

"Oh, no, you're fine," Ryan said. "It isn't that top secret, and I'm pretty sure I can trust you."

The two locked eyes.

"You think so? You know, I could be some serial killer, or terrorist or something, and you wouldn't even know."

Ryan smiled. "I'm good at reading people, it's partly why I make the big bucks," he joked. "You're a good person. I can tell. You especially don't look like the typical terrorist. However, if I'm wrong, you do realize I'll have to make you disappear."

Laura chuckled. "Even if I was some kind of terrorist, I'd be too good, and you'd never catch me." Laura winked again. "But, you're not too bad yourself, I mean I'm not an FBI agent, or a psychic or anything like that, but you seem like a great guy, Mr. Turner, and I can't thank you enough for everything."

"Well, it's no problem at all," Ryan said.

Just then, the plump nurse Ryan had spoken with earlier, shuffled into the room.

"Hello, again," she said. "Sorry if I am interrupting anything, but I just need to check your vitals."

"You're fine," Laura said with a smile.

Ryan glanced at her.

Oh, that smile!

Ryan felt like a star-struck, dumb teenager again. He hardly knew Laura, yet something about her made him feel something inside that he hadn't felt in years.

"Everything is great," the nurse reported. "You're doing wonderful and I've got to say, you all have a beautiful family. You truly do."

Ryan and Laura exchanged glances then looked at the nurse at the same time. They were both unable to spit out a rational sentence.

"We…I'm…we aren't…" Laura muttered.

"What we are trying to say is, we aren't exactly a family," Ryan said.

"Oh?" the nurse noted with a surprised look on her face. "Well, then, whatever you have going on, it's working. You do look great together. I'll leave it at that. I will be back in a while to check on you, dear."

Laura smiled at the nurse again. "Thank you, ma'am."

The nurse left as quickly as she had come in. Laura giggled, and Ryan blushed.

"Well, quite the family we have here, huh?" Laura teased.

Ryan chuckled. "Oh, most definitely. I'm just glad Kayleen got her mother's looks".

Now Laura was the one who was blushing. Ryan stood to his feet.

"I better get going, Laura," he said. "I'm going to have quite a mess at the office here in a few hours. Are you sure that you two are okay? Is there anything I can do?"

Laura didn't reply, but instead leaned over to the other side of the bed and grabbed a napkin and pen off the small bedside table. She quickly scribbled something down on the napkin, folded it up, and turned back toward Ryan. She reached out her hand and placed the napkin in his palm.

"We'll be okay, thank you so much," she said. "Now, you better not lose that." She motioned to the napkin in Ryan's palm. "I don't want some New York City hobo or someone finding it on the street and deciding it would be a clever idea to call or text me."

Ryan smirked and stuck the napkin deep into a pocket in his pants.

"I definitely won't lose it."

Laura stuck out her hand once again and the two shook hands.

"Thank you again," she said. "I really can't thank you enough, Mr. Turner."

Ryan nodded to her and grinned. "Call me Ryan."

Laura smiled her heartwarming smile. "I'll see you around, Hot Shot."

CHAPTER EIGHT

November 12, 2017

"Daddy, daddy! Let's go-o-o-o-o-o! Come on sleepy head!"

Ryan rolled over in his bed to see Kayleen at his bedside, tugging at his sheets. Ryan rubbed his eyes.

"Kayleen, do you know how much sleep I got last night?"

Kayleen put her hands on her hips.

"Plenty," she said with a smile.

Next to Ryan, Laura Johnson Turner tossed and turned then sat up in bed.

"Kay, honey," she said, followed by a yawn, "your dad had a long day and night. It's only 6:30, let him get some sleep."

Kayleen stuck her lip out and with a defeated look on her face said, "Okay, okay, I'm sorry."

As she finished her sentence, Kayleen started walking out of the room.

"Kay?" Ryan said, bringing Kayleen to a halt. "Are you really going to go out with me in your soccer pajamas? You want everyone thinking that you are homeless?"

Little Kayleen spun around, looked down at her onesie pajamas and began to say something but stopped herself short. Her eyes lit up. Her face beamed with growing joy.

"I mean, I guess if you really want to. Whatever floats your boat," Ryan said.

Kayleen grinned, spun on her heels and took off running out of the bedroom.

"I love you!" she yelled, running to her room.

Laura punched Ryan on the shoulder.

"You need some rest," she said.

Ryan kissed his wife on the cheek. "I promised her that I'd take her to Cold Stone and the Pet store today. I'm going to do just that."

"But Ryan…"

Ryan held a finger up to his wife's lips. "I'll be fine, I mean it…you sure you don't just want to skip work and go with us? It's going to be fun-n-n."

Laura rolled her eyes and punched Ryan in the arm again.

"Rub it in why don't you?" Laura muttered. "I almost would, but I better sleep a little bit. I've got a hefty schedule at work this next week. Besides, daddy-daughter time is always good."

Ryan put his arm around her. "I know, you better enjoy these next two days off."

He kissed her softly then pulled himself off the bed. "I love you, sweetheart. I'll see you in a while."

Laura nestled up under the covers.

"I love you too," she said.

Ryan quickly got dressed, left his bedroom, entered the hallway, and headed into the living room. Across from him in the living room was Kayleen. She was sitting on the floor next to the front door of the house, with her pink leather purse slung over her shoulder.

"Wow," Ryan said as he took a right into the kitchen, "someone is sure excited."

Kayleen put her arms out to her sides and shrugged.

"Duh-h-h," she said.

Ryan made a cup of coffee while Kayleen tirelessly urged him to hurry up. Within minutes the two were out the door and walking down 158th Avenue toward Cross Bay Boulevard.

"Why, good morning, my dears."

It was Shirley Shamble, their next-door neighbor.

"Good morning, Mrs. Shamble, how are you doing?" Ryan replied.

"Morning!" Kayleen chirped in.

Shirley grinned as she walked over to the garden within her yard, a small gardening hoe in hand.

"I'm doing well," the kind, elderly woman replied. "Where are you two going this fine morning?"

Ryan stopped walking and leaned himself against Shirley's fence.

"We are on our way to get us some Cold Stone," he said.

"And see the puppies!" Kayleen chipped in.

"Oh my, that sounds like fun!" Shirley said. "What flavor are you getting, sweet girl?"

Kayleen grasped the top of the fence and peeked over it.

"Cotton Candy with gummy bears! I like your hair, Mrs. Shamble," Kayleen added.

Shirley Shamble grinned and placed one hand on her hip and ran the other through her hair.

"Well, thank you," she said. "I got it cut and permed last night. I have to do what I can to help this dead white hair look somewhat decent."

Kayleen flashed a thumbs-up and said, "It looks very good, Mrs. Shamble!"

Shirley blushed. "Gosh, you're just a doll. Well, you two have fun now!"

"Have a wonderful day," Ryan said, "and tell Mr. Shamble hello for me."

Shirley nodded. "I will as soon as Gerald gets his old bones out of bed."

Ryan chuckled, took Kayleen's hand, and the two continued on their way.

CHAPTER NINE

They walked hand in hand down the sidewalk playing "I Spy". Once they reached Cross Bay Boulevard and took a left, Ryan glanced down at Kayleen and smiled. He had never been happier in his life. He had a job that he loved, the woman of his dreams, an amazing little girl, and a wonderful home in Jamaica, New York, rather than the old apartment he used to live in. Life was just plain good. He felt it couldn't get any better.

Aside from a drug bust the day before and lots of paperwork, work had been fairly laid back, giving him lots of time with his new family over the past few months. Ryan rubbed the wedding band on his ring-finger and thought back to the day he proposed to Laura. It was July 10th, 2017, in Paris, France. Yes, "the" Paris, France. Ryan had been sent there to meet with MIB agents to discuss Cybris Caine and his whereabouts. They met, talked, exchanged classified files, and then went their separate ways. J.J. Mauer allowed Ryan to stay an extra few days and gave him two extra plane tickets. With those tickets, he took Laura and Kayleen and they stayed at *Le Royal Monceau* for three nights. The hotel was amazing. The proposal happened the second night as the three of them ate out at Epicure and took a moonlight walk alongside the Seine River. In a clearing, Ryan fell to one knee and proposed. Laura broke into tears and said yes. It was the greatest night of Ryan's life.

"Finally, we're here!" Kayleen cried out.

"Yes, we sure are," Ryan replied, opening the front door of Cold Stone.

Kayleen stepped inside, barely able to contain her excitement. After some contemplating, Ryan decided on a "Love It" sized bowl of mint ice cream with fudge and Oreos mixed into it. Kayleen got her usual Cotton Candy ice cream with gummy bears in a "Like It" sized bowl. They found an open table and sat down to devour the ice cream.

"I'm going to beat you this time!" Kayleen said as they both took a seat.

Ryan raised his eyebrows. "Oh? Is that right?"

"Sure is," Kayleen said as she dug her spoon into the cotton candy ice cream.

Ryan then slowly went at his too and grinned at his little girl as she hurriedly ate up her bowl of ice cream.

"Done!" she exclaimed as she finished licking her bowl clean and threw her hands in the air. She excitedly clapped and stood from her seat to take a bow. Ryan slumped his shoulders and stared down at his bowl containing the remaining mint ice cream.

"You're just too good, Kay," he said.

Kayleen folded her arms across her chest. "Thank you, thank you very much."

Ryan shoved the rest of his treat into his mouth. "Let's go see some puppies, what do you say, Champ?"

Kayleen hopped to her feet and grabbed Ryan by the hand.

"Let's go, let's go!" She shouted, trying to pull Ryan out of his seat. "Come on!" she urged as Ryan licked off his spoon and disposed of his trash.

"I'm coming," he said. "Take it easy."

The two exited Cold Stone taking a right down the sidewalk. In little to no time they were in front of Petco. Kayleen threw open the door and she and Ryan walked in.

The store smelled strongly of animals. Kayleen let go of
Ryan's hand and ran to the back of the store where the sound
of barking dogs was coming from.

"Slow down, Turbo," Ryan said, calling after Kayleen.

"Come on, Grandpa!" she answered back.

Ryan laughed and hurried after her. Kayleen stopped at
the first enclosure she came to and leaned up against the
glass. Inside was a three-legged, black, dachshund puppy
curled up against the window.

"Aw-w-w!" Kayleen exclaimed as she tapped on the
window with her finger tips, causing the puppy to lift its head
up and yawn.

The dog tilted its head to the side while looking intently
at Kayleen. She giggled and put her palm up against the glass.
The puppy barked and licked the glass where Kayleen's hand
was.

Kayleen squealed with delight. "See! She wants to go
home with us, Daddy!"

Ryan shook his head. "I don't know about that,
sweetheart."

Kayleen put her nose against the glass and the puppy
barked again while licking at the glass.

"Dad?" Kayleen asked sweetly, looking up at Ryan now.
"It needs us. Look at her, she's missing a leg and needs a
good house. And, Daddy, our house is a good house! Please
can we have her? Pretty please?"

Ryan rubbed the back of his neck. He really didn't want
to deal with a new dog in the house.

"Don't break the girl's heart," a voice chimed in.

Ryan looked over his shoulder to see a Petco employee
standing behind him.

The gray-haired woman smiled at him. "Come on now, sir."

Ryan shrugged. "I don't know, I don't think a puppy is a good idea right now."

Below him, Kayleen stuck out her bottom lip, then her face lit up and she opened her purse. From her purse she pulled out a one-dollar bill and handed it to Ryan.

Ryan smiled. "We would need a lot more of those to get a dog, Kay. Good try though."

Kayleen stuck her lip out again and lowered her head.

"Okay," she said in defeat.

"Actually," the Petco lady said, "that is just the right amount for this puppy, young lady."

Ryan stared at the woman in disbelief. "Are you serious?"

"Serious as can be," she answered. "Now do you want this little pup or not?"

Ryan took a deep breath, knowing he had just been played like a fiddle. "We'll take it."

Kayleen screamed and hugged Ryan's leg.

"Thank you, thank you, thank you!" she exclaimed as Ryan hugged her back.

"Now let's find a carrier, food, bowls, and a collar and leash, I guess."

Kayleen did a fist pump in the air. "Yes! Yes! Yes!"

The Petco woman retrieved the puppy and handed the small dog to Kayleen.

"Thank you so much!" Kayleen said while she hugged the Dachshund.

Ryan and Kayleen wandered through the store and picked up the needed puppy supplies. Within minutes, they were walking out of Petco with a small canine in its carrier.

The moment they stepped back out onto the street, Ryan's phone began to vibrate and ring inside his pocket. Ryan set the dog carrier down next to his feet and withdrew the phone from his pants' pocket. He swallowed when he saw who was calling. It was Mr. Mauer.

"Hello," Ryan answered.

"Morning, Turner," Mauer responded.

He was a man of very few words and was always short and straight to the point.

"Good morning," Ryan said. "How are you doing?"

There was a pause.

"Just fine," Mauer replied. "Are you busy?"

Ryan knew what that meant. "No, sir, not at all. What's up?"

Another pause.

"Meet me at headquarters as soon as you can."

Ryan picked the carrier back up. "Yes, sir, I will be there shortly."

With that, the line went dead.

"Who was that, Daddy?" Kayleen asked as then began to walk again.

Ryan took a deep breath. "It was my boss, and he wants to talk with me."

"The big jolly guy?" Kayleen asked.

Ryan laughed. "Yes, J.J."

"Oh," Kayleen said, "I like him. He's funny."

"Well, Kayleen, I think that's the first time J.J. has ever been described as funny."

CHAPTER TEN

Ryan kissed Laura and Kayleen goodbye then hopped on his black Harley and left his house. Yes, the New York traffic was no joke and it would usually be easiest for him to take a bus, cab, or subway, but he loved his bike. He loved the freedom and isolation his motorcycle provided. At 1:30 p.m., Ryan parked in his personal spot in the parking garage located under the Empire State Building. The FBI headquarters was underground and very few people knew where it was located. Ryan stepped off his Harley, kicked the kickstand down and stuffed his keys into his pocket. He walked over to a pair of metal doors. The doors were solid, thick, and shiny but had no knobs or handles. To the right of the doors was a keypad and a retinal scanner above it.

Ryan leaned over to allow the scanner to read his eyes. The laser traveled across Ryan's eyes twice then there was a beep and the keypad lit up. Ryan typed in the password he knew from memory and the doors slid open.

"Welcome, Agent Turner," said the computerized voice.

Ryan stepped through the doorway and the doors closed behind him.

He walked down a long, narrow hallway until he came to a door on his right that had a plaque next to it. The plaque had his name printed on it.

"I guess I could check my email before I go give Mauer a visit," he said aloud to himself.

Ryan turned the door handle and entered his office. He took one step inside and instantly came to a stop. Straight across from him sat a very, very…very large man behind Ryan's personal desk. It was J.J. Mauer, Head of the Bureau.

CHAPTER ELEVEN

J.J. Mauer was a massive man. Mauer was six-feet-four-inches tall and weighed an impressive 350 pounds. He had a big round head, cheeks that jiggled whenever he spoke, a bulging belly, huge shoulders and hands the size of boulders. J.J. Mauer sat there, leaning forward in the chair with his hands clasped in front of him on the desk. Ryan was surprised to see Mr. Mauer in his personal office.

"Um…um…" Ryan stammered. "Mr. Mauer? How, how are you doing?"

"I'm good," the big man answered.

Ryan nodded slowly. "I'm surprised to find you here."

"Yes, I'm sure."

Ryan took a couple of steps into the room. "Is everything okay?"

J.J. Mauer nodded one solid nod. "Yes," he said simply.

Ryan restrained himself from rolling his eyes. He hated conversing with Mr. Mauer. J.J. Mauer was a good man and Ryan liked him just fine, but he was incredibly hard to carry out a conversation with. He was always very emotionless and spoke as if he had a limit on the number of words he was allowed to say every day.

"Well?" asked Ryan. "I'm here. What's up?"

Mauer unclasped his hands and began to pick at a hangnail on his right thumb. For over a minute there was complete silence in the room.

Finally, Mauer spoke. "Please close the door."

Ryan let out a breath and turned around to do so. J.J. Mauer clasped his hands together again then hid them on his lap.

"I'm retiring," he said plainly.

Ryan waited for a longer explanation but got none.

"You're retiring?" Ryan asked.

Mauer nodded. "Yes, yes, I am."

Ryan was puzzled. "Why? I mean, why so sudden?"

"I spoke with Director Felix," Mauer said. "He respects the decision."

Ryan folded his arms across his chest. "Okay, and any decision you make I too respect."

There was another period of total silence.

"Ryan," Mauer said, leaning further forward, "you are to take my place as Head of the Bureau."

Ryan's mouth fell open. He stared at his boss.

"Are you serious? I don't know about that…"

Mauer put up his hand. "Listen, I have been in this business for thirty-some odd years. I'm a sixty-five-year-old man. It is my time. It is my time to go. Director Felix and I had a long, heartfelt, in-depth conversation. I've done what I can to serve this country. I have left it all out there. It is time for new leadership, new views. You are young, Ryan, but you are experienced. You have seen things and done things that very few people ever have or ever will see and do in their lifetimes. You are one of the best agents the Bureau has ever seen. You've been the FBI's go-to man ever since you stepped into the agency. Nobody is more qualified for this position. Felix and I both strongly believe that you are the man for the job. So, Agent Turner, do you accept this offer?"

Ryan let everything he'd just heard sink in. That was the most he had ever heard Mauer say in one sitting. Never would Ryan have expected this conversation to be happening, at least not now, so random and so unexpectedly. Ryan slowly shook his head from side to side.

"Sir, with all due respect, and in all honesty, I wasn't expecting this at all. I'm not going to lie. I don't really know what to say…like you said, I agree, I feel that I'm a very good field agent. I've made solid contributions for years and feel I still can."

Mauer nodded and his cheeks jiggled. "I know this must be unexpected. You have been, like I said, such a strong asset as an agent, but as Head of the Bureau, you can also do remarkable things and even bring the agency to heights it has never reached. You and the Director can and will do remarkable things together. I know it. You have a new family, Ryan. This will benefit them and you both. This will be a much better situation for your family. You will be Head of the Bureau, versus a field agent whose life is constantly at risk. Plus, the pay is so much better. This will be better for you all the way around. I do want that for you. I've never really been able to talk with you like this, or say a lot of things, but I like you, Ryan. I truly care about you and now that you have a little family of your own, I care for their well-being too. You are a great friend. One of the few I've ever had."

Ryan swallowed. This was crazy, insane. Mr. Mauer was right. It was the perfect situation for he and his family. Ryan bit his bottom lip and pondered everything over. It was too much to take in at once.

"Okay," he said. "I'll talk with Laura about all of this."

"Sounds good," Mauer responded. "Now, Ryan?"

"Yes, sir?"

"I'm going to be completely honest with you," Mauer said in a more hushed voice, "this world is not what it used to be. People are twisted. The world in general is a twisted place. My job has only become harder as the years have gone by and I can't take it anymore. We are in very dangerous times and I feel things may only get worse. The Bureau needs you, Ryan. Really, I'm not just leaving because of my old age, or because it is 'my time'. I am leaving because the FBI, this country, the world, needs *you*. Yes, it may sound a little extreme, but it really isn't. You are a *great* man. One of the best. It will take someone like you to turn things around. It won't be easy, things may get nasty, things will get messy; however, you will make a difference. You will make the difference this agency needs right now."

Ryan was more shocked and even more confused.
What exactly is he inferring?

In general, the world was a bad place...but something told Ryan it wasn't that simple, and that Mauer meant something deeper than that.

"What exactly do you mean?" Ryan ventured.

J.J. Mauer took a deep breath in and exhaled. "Six o'clock. Meet me at my home at six tonight for dinner. We will discuss this some more, and we will go over the official paperwork necessary for you to take my place. Have a great rest of the day, Ryan."

Mauer stood from his seat, walked over to Ryan, shook his hand, and waddled out of the office, leaving Ryan there still stunned.

CHAPTER TWELVE

Ryan closed the door to his office and wandered over to the seat behind his desk. He decided he would stay there the rest of the day to work on some things and process everything he had just heard.

I need to talk with Laura.

Ryan withdrew his cellphone from his khaki shorts' pocket and dialed his home phone number. After continuous ringing there was no answer. He waited a few minutes, then tried a second time, getting the same result.

Where are they?

Ryan tried Laura's cell phone and got no answer. He strummed his fingers on the desk top in front of him.

"Where are you?" he said aloud.

He decided to call his neighbors, the Shambles, to see if they knew of Laura's whereabouts. After a few rings there was an answer.

"Hello?" an elderly woman said.

Ryan pumped his fist in the air. "Yes! Hello, Mrs. Shamble, this is Ryan Turner."

"Ryan," Shirley Shamble said, "what is it, dear?"

Throwing his feet up on his desk and crossing them, Ryan asked, "Do you happen to know where Laura and Kayleen are?"

"As a matter of fact, I do," Shirley said. "Now, Laura? She went to the hospital. There was an emergency there and she had to fill in for the day."

"And Kayleen?"

"Gerald just returned from taking her to Day Care. The kind woman there, Dora, I think it is, told Ger that if you or

Laura were not able to return before they closed, she would take Kayleen home with her until either of you got back."

Ryan sighed with relief. "Sounds good, thank you Mrs. Shamble. I'll be home later tonight. Thanks again!"

"Oh, of course," Shirley said. "Have a good rest of the day, Ryan"

Ryan smiled. "You as well."

Laura was at work; she wasn't going to be able to give Ryan her opinion and consent. Ryan started up his computer and sighed. He was bummed that he wouldn't be able to speak with Laura today, and with that, told himself he was going to end up making the decision himself. Deep inside, he knew what that decision was going to be. Ryan Turner was soon going to be the new Head of the Bureau.

CHAPTER THIRTEEN

6:00 o'clock. He had to be there before then. Right before. He had to make it there as close to six o'clock as possible and get out before the clock struck six. He was shooting for 5:45. That was his goal. He had plenty of time though to get everything done that he needed. It was November 12th, 5:00 p.m., when he darted out of his office and hopped onto his motorcycle. He did a little wheelie as he pulled out of the parking lot. He loved messing with his new bike. He later pulled his Harley Davidson into a nice driveway that he had pulled into many times before.

He stepped off his bike and looked over his left shoulder. He saw an elderly woman tending to her garden. He smiled. He liked that old woman a lot. She was one of the sweetest souls he knew. The woman pulled a couple of weeds and then glanced over at him and grinned.

"Why, hello. Back from work so soon, Agent?"

He smiled back at the woman. "Yes, I've got a quick meeting with the boss at 6:00. I have to grab a few things from here."

The woman smiled the biggest smile. "Well, you have fun now."

He walked up to the door and turned back to the old lady in the garden. "Thank you, have a good one, Mrs. Shamble."

Then he walked through the door and into the kitchen. He helped himself to a bowl of macaroni and cheese, went into the living room, and flipped on the television.

He watched a good five minutes of the ESPN channel. On the screen, a sports reporter was commenting on the "MLB play of the year" from a few weeks earlier when the

New York Yankees were battling the Boston Red Sox in the conference finals of the playoffs. The rising star C.J. Yates had hit a walk off home run in the 14th inning of game 7, for the Sox to win the game and earn their spot in the World series. The Yankees were his favorite team, but they had a very up and down season. He felt they should've beaten the Red Sox in four games. It made him mad. Furious, even. He finally pushed the power button on the remote and walked down the hallway and into the master bedroom.

He entered the cozy bedroom and approached the closet. He rummaged through the large walk-in closet, digging through shirts and coats which he had worn many times before. Finally, he found what he was looking for. The man carefully removed a plastic bag from his pocket and pulled out a pair of latex gloves from inside of it. He pulled the gloves on, then grabbed a Glock 47 pistol from a jacket pocket and discharged the clip.

"Perfect," he said.

The clip contained three bullets. He shoved the clip back up into the gun and holstered the Glock into the holster at his waist. He looked down at the watch on his wrist. He had time, plenty of time.

He pulled off his gloves and walked out of the front door and over to his motorcycle. His hands grasped the handlebars and he pulled himself onto the bike seat. His right hand reached down to the key, starting the ignition with a simple turn. He put the jet-black Harley Davidson into gear and took off down the road.

CHAPTER FOURTEEN

The man pulled up to a little house. It was a nice place; not too big, not real small. He walked up to the front door and knocked. He glanced at his watch. He was right on time. The door swung open. A huge, jolly man stepped up to the door's threshold.

"Oh!" the big man exclaimed. "Well, come in, come in and make yourself at home."

The visitor helped himself through the door and straight into a large living room, which contained a brown leather couch and two light-brown leather recliners on each side of a fireplace. Above the fireplace hung a large flat-screen television.

"Sit, sit down and make yourself at home."

"Ok, thank you, sir," the visitor said in reply.

The visitor walked over and sat in the recliner on the right-hand side of the couch facing the tv. He glanced around the room and saw the remote sitting on the other recliner. He thought about flipping on the television, but immediately thought better of it. There was no need for television. This was going to be short and sweet.

"Would you like anything to drink, my friend?" the jolly man asked from the kitchen.

"I'll take a coffee, if you have it," the visitor replied, and glanced over his shoulder at the kitchen only to see the enormous man waddling into the living room.

He waddled over to the visitor and handed him a mug.

"Be careful," The big man said. "It's quite hot."

As the visitor grabbed the cup, coffee sloshed over the sides of the mug, and splashed onto the visitor's hand.

"OW!" he cried out.

He quickly rubbed the burning coffee onto the arm rest of the seat he was in.

"Sorry about that!" the heavyset man said as he waddled over to the unoccupied recliner in the room. He sat down, a cup of coffee in one hand, a pile of papers in the other.

"So, are you still up for everything that is going on?" the owner of the house asked.

"Yes, I'm definitely ready. This is all going to be good."

The overweight man gave a nod with his head, making his giant cheeks shake.

"The meeting today didn't scare you too bad earlier, did it? Maybe I should have just called you into my office instead."

The visitor shook his head and threw his hands up slightly. "Oh no, no, it was fine. I didn't mind it. I'm excited."

"Okay," the big man said. He shifted his weight causing the seat beneath him to creak. "Would you like to fill out the paperwork now? We still have some time."

The visitor got up out of his seat. "May I use the restroom, because…"

"Oh yes, yes, go on ahead. It's in the hallway directly behind me."

"Ok, thanks," the visitor said and walked around the first recliner, behind the couch, and past the giant man in the seat.

The visitor started down the hall but stopped in his tracks.

"Oh, and I was going to say, Mr. Mauer, I do have plenty of time. But you on the other hand…" The man spun on his heels, and pulling on a second pair of gloves, approached the back of the J.J. Mauer's recliner. "You don't"

The visitor pulled out the pistol from his pocket and put the muzzle to the back of J.J. Mauer's head. With one smooth motion of his finger, he pulled the trigger. One shot was all that was needed. Blood and brain matter splattered across the living room, showering the floor, fireplace, and television.

CHAPTER FIFTEEN

It was exactly six o'clock. Ryan stood over J.J. Mauer's dead body, checking for a pulse. There wasn't one. Smack dab in the center of J.J. Mauer's forehead there was a giant, bloody hole. On the back of his head was a smaller hole. The living room was a wreck. There was blood all over the floor and blood seeping off Mauer's body and into the seams of the recliner. Pieces of skull and brain matter were also scattered around the wood floor. He was dead as can be.

Ryan looked around and as he stared down at the 47 Glock in his hand, he heard two very familiar sounds. The first sound was the sound of police sirens in the distance and the second was a man's voice.

"Come out with your hands up! This is the FBI! We've got you surrounded!"

Ryan froze, his hand still grasping the pistol.

No…no. It couldn't be.

He looked out the living room window directly across from him and made eye contact with the FBI agent standing outside. It was Kyle. Kyle Harrison. And he was aiming an M14 directly at Ryan.

Ryan could almost feel the red dot sight dancing around on his chest. He had never been in this situation before. He had *always* been the good guy.

Do I just turn myself in?

He asked himself the question but knew he couldn't do it. He knew all the overwhelming evidence was against him…Ryan raised his hands up over his head, dropped his gun and tried to think. It's all he could do. He stood there with his hands in the air, facing the window. Kyle slowly approached the large window, gun in hand, still aiming at Ryan's chest.

"Stay where you are, or I'll shoot. Cooperate with me. Nice and easy."

Kyle kept moving toward the window.

"I am going to come through the door now! Stay where you are."

As Ryan stood there, a few thoughts flashed through his mind. First off, he wasn't surrounded, Kyle was all alone. That was obvious. Second, Kyle wouldn't shoot him. It was hard to see the inside of the house from outside and Kyle couldn't know for sure who was standing over J.J. Mauer's body. Third, there was a door out back. Mauer had a back porch and back yard that contained a garden and a lawn. At the back of the yard was a fence that separated Mauer's property from another residence. Fourth, those neighbors had a car. A fast car. Last, but not least, he had to get out of there. He knew he was in a bad spot. He knew evidence upon evidence was now stacked against him. He knew he had to think fast.

Kyle was 20 feet from the window now, keeping his slow pace.

"Stay where you are! Stay where you are! I am going to come through the door…!"

Kyle had been screaming every time he spoke, so Ryan would be able to hear him through the closed window.

Ryan began the count in his head.

Three…two…one…now!

The moment Kyle turned toward the front door, Ryan dove to his right. Just before he hit the floor, Kyle fired his M14. The window before him shattered, sending shards of glass flying. The front door of the house flew open.

"Ryan? Is that you?"

Ryan hit the floor and rolled over, jumping back onto his feet as quickly as possible. Ryan sprinted through the kitchen, then took a right turn into Mauer's utility room. He threw open the back door and took off in a dead run toward the back fence. He got a few feet away from it and leapt through the air. He cleared the fence easily but landed on the other side in a heap. He got back on to his feet and kept running. He ran right up to the house's driveway and opened a red Porsche's front door. Just as he hoped, the key was in the ignition.

Man, these people are careless.

He turned the car on, screeched back in reverse, and took off down the jam-packed road.

Ryan knew New York like the back of his hand, which made it easy to escape out of the wretched city. As he made his way out of NYC and reached the freeway, his left arm suddenly went limp and Ryan almost went off the side of the road. He regrouped himself and got back into his lane. A horn blared behind him.

"Ugh!"

The pain came unexpectedly.

Ryan's whole left arm began to shake uncontrollably. He unbuttoned his left sleeve and gasped. His arm was drenched blood. A bullet had gone straight through his arm. Skin and muscle hung limply off his forearm and bicep. Ryan pulled over to the side of the road and heard more horns honk in his direction. He grimaced while searching the car for some sort of tourniquet. In the back seat he found a thin sweatshirt. He tried to piece his arm back together and wrapped his shirt tightly around it to slow the blood flow. He then headed back down the road. He didn't think the injury was life-threatening, but knew his arm was probably going to need attention. He decided that he needed to give Gerald Shamble a visit.

CHAPTER SIXTEEN

The killer drove. Not fast, not slow, he just drove. He was already covered in blood. He didn't need to be asked questions. He didn't need to get caught. And that is why he just drove the fast, low-riding machine beneath him. Not fast, not slow, he just drove. He knew exactly where he was going. He was a very smart man. He turned to the left and suddenly came to a halt in front of a gas station. He looked around and saw the usual: drug addicts, hobos, tourists, normal everyday civilians and men and women on their way home from work.

He removed a bandana from his pocket and tied it around his neck, then pulled it up over his nose and mouth. He then placed a black beanie atop his head. He removed himself from his vehicle and jay-walked across the road. He made it to the other side and stopped on the sidewalk. Reaching down, he pulled his pant leg up. Wrapped around his shin and calf was a small holster. The killer always carried an extra firearm. He was careful, precise and always prepared. The man pulled the pistol out and took off the safety. He stuffed it into the holster at his hip, looked around him at his surroundings and began to walk toward Gerald and Shirley Shamble's door.

The killer pulled the bandana off his mouth and nose and knocked twice. In no more than a few seconds, the door opened a crack and Gerald Shamble's beady eyes peered through the crack.

"Ryan?" he said, pulling open the door.

The killer said nothing.

"Oh! Why hello again, what are you…?"

"I need your attention, Dr. Shamble," the killer said, cutting Gerald Shamble's sentence short.

"What can I do for you?"

"I was shot. I need your help. I don't think it is too bad. I just don't want to waste my time going to the hospital. I trust you more than anyone there, anyway."

"Well, come on in."

Gerald Shamble stepped to side and opened the door a little wider. The killer walked in and Gerald gestured toward the right of the entrance.

"Go lay down on the bed in there. I'll be there in a second."

The killer nodded in agreement as he walked to the bedroom. He moved inside and stepped out of his black dress shoes, then pulled himself onto the bed. He sat at the foot of the bed with his feet dangling off the side and waited.

Five minutes later, Gerald T. Shamble walked into the bedroom carrying a small, rectangular, forest-green box.

"I assumed you needed me to possibly remove a bullet, and you might need stitches. Am I correct?"

"I think you're right," the man on the bed answered.

"Okay, where were you shot?"

Shamble set the box on the bed and opened it up. The killer began to pull off his shirt but stopped short.

"May I have a glass of water first…if that's okay?" asked the killer.

"Um," Shamble began, slightly confused, "yes, I guess so."

Shamble paused for a second, leaned over the bed and looked past the living room and into the kitchen.

"Shirley! Please bring me a glass of ice water."

There was a second of silence then Shirley responded, "On my way, Ger."

Within seconds, she was trotting across the living room with a glass of water in her grasp.

"Here you go," Shirley said, passing the glass over to her husband.

"And how are you, sweetie? What happened?"

"I'd rather not talk about it," the killer said.

Shirley gave a shrug and began to walk back out the bedroom door.

"Oh, Mrs. Shamble," said the man on the bed.

Shirley stopped and turned around. "Yes?"

The killer popped his neck and stared into Shirley's eyes. "You don't know what happened to me, but it'll be fairly easy to tell what happened to you."

Before she could react, two bullet holes appeared between Shirley Shamble's eyes. The pistol in the killer's hands had a silencer on it, so there was very little sound. The gun was now aimed at the back of Gerald Shamble's head. He was shaking from head to toe as tears poured down his face, but no sound came from his mouth. He cried silently. He cried and stared off toward the doorway and at his dead wife lying limp on the carpeted floor.

CHAPTER SEVENTEEN

"Stand up Gerald," the killer said firmly.

Dr. Shamble didn't move. He sat there shaking.

"I said GET UP!"

The killer shoved the muzzle of his pistol into the side of Gerald Shamble's head. He slowly got up and kept his eyes on the dead body in front of him. The killer got to his feet too.

"Lead me to your office!"

Shamble didn't move.

"Now!"

The man punched Dr. Shamble in the back of his head and his knees crumbled beneath him. The killer grabbed Shamble by the back of his neck and stood him up.

"Go!"

Gerald Shamble walked out of the room and took a right. He walked with robot-like motions. He stared blankly ahead. The killer followed, still holding the gun to the back of Shamble's head.

"Sit down," he ordered.

Shamble did what he was told and sat on the rolling-chair in front of the computer, which sat on a big wooden desk.

"Get a pen and paper and do it quickly before I get trigger happy!"

Shamble retrieved a pen and paper from a desk drawer and began to write word for word what the killer told him to write down. He began at the top left corner on the first line of the paper and wrote the first words: "Dear Laura."

For another three minutes, Gerald Shamble wrote. He had just about finished another page when the killer told him to stop.

"Why did you make me…."

The killer shot Gerald in the right hand and the bullet went through his hand and into the desk, sending splinters and debris flying.

"AGH!!" Shamble cried out. "But, why…."

The killer shot Shamble's left hand.

"AGH!!" Shamble cried out again.

"I'll take it from here, Doc."

Gerald stared down at the letter he had just been forced to write. The killer aimed the gun at the side of Shambles head and pulled the trigger. Shamble fell limp, but the killer caught him before his head hit the desk. He didn't want blood on the letter. It was for Laura. It needed to look nice. He tried to ignore the blood splatter across the wall and floor. He rolled the chair out of the way and Shamble fell out of it, face down onto the floor. The chair tipped over on top of him. The killer looked down at the letter written to the woman he loved. He pulled a black pen out of his pants' pocket and signed the bottom of the letter. He signed his signature and marveled at it.

"Yours Truly, Ryan Turner," it read.

He loved these people, but they had to die. He had no choice. What killed him inside was that they loved him too. He looked in the direction of the wall by the door and saw Gerald Shamble lying in a pool of his own blood. He looked away immediately. He had to keep it together. He wouldn't let himself fall apart. He turned his attention back to the letter.

*Should I leave it here and let someone find it or put it in
an envelope and take it to the house next door?*

He thought about the good and bad of both situations. In
the end he left the letter as was. He didn't want to take any
chances of getting caught again. If he kept playing it smart,
he knew he could maybe get out of this mess…or had he
already let his sentimental side take over him by writing this
letter? No, if it came down to it he would be able to plead not
guilty. Killing Mauer had been a close call. It had been risky,
but he had done it. He was here at step two now. The question
was, when would he decide to execute step three?

He walked out the door, placed the pen in his pocket,
and the gun back in his holster at his waist. He avoided
looking down at the doctor. He made his way into the living
room. Then he made his mistake. He glanced toward the
guest bedroom and there he saw the old woman lying
lifelessly on the carpeted floor. Her flowery, purple dress and
the white carpet were stained red. His whole body started to
shake and shiver. He had killed her. He wanted to put his
pistol to his own head and end it here. He had taken her life,
and for what? He knew that he had to do it. He had no choice.
They were the only people who saw him earlier that day,
right before he had killed Mauer.

He had needed that letter written to Laura too. He had
seen many deaths before. He had been responsible for many
before. He had to compose himself, but he didn't. He
couldn't. He fell to his knees right before the front door,
cupped his face in his hands, and started to cry.

The tears came easily, and he let them pour out. He
didn't care anymore. He'd held it in for way too long. He had
to let it out. He sat there with his face in his hands for what
seemed like ages. He knew he was wasting time. Finally, the

killer removed his hands from his face and pulled his sleeve back looking at the time. It was 8:50 p.m. Laura would be home in ten minutes.

CHAPTER EIGHTEEN

The man in the overalls had watched it all happen. He couldn't believe his eyes.

He was crouching behind the bar in the Shamble's kitchen watching the killer carefully. The killer looked at his watch and stood back up onto his feet. The man in the overalls shifted his weight. He needed to do something fast. He kept watching the man who now stood in front of the door. He was unsure of what to do. Then he knew. He knew what he had to do the instant he saw it. The killer pulled his right pant leg up and scratched his ankle. In that split second, the man in the overalls saw what he needed to see. He caught a glimpse of a skull tattoo on the killer's ankle. The guy in the overalls had been around for a long time. He knew what that tattoo meant. This man had killed some of the people he cared dearly for. He wasn't going to let it slide. He glanced around the corner at the killer, only to see his right hand reaching for the doorknob. He leapt to his feet and charged the killer, a blade held in his hand.

The killer knew he had to go. He reached down, pulled his pant leg up, pulled his black sock down a bit and scratched his ankle. He then paused for just a second as he stood back up. A slight sound made his head turn toward the kitchen.

It's nothing...I'm just going crazy.

Then he reached out for the doorknob to leave. Out of the corner of his eye he saw him. A man about 6 feet and 4 inches tall and weighing well over 200 pounds was running straight for him, wielding a blade in his hand.

He was stunned. Baffled. He couldn't move. Before he knew it, the man in the overalls was throwing himself at him. The knife soared at the killer's throat. The killer reacted just in time. He was hit hard with brute force as the man tackled him. But as soon as the man in the overalls made contact with him, the killer threw his forearm out in front of his own throat to block the knife's blow. The knife sunk into his arm and he could feel it scrape bone.

"Ugh!" he screamed out in pain.

He hit the ground hard, the huge man on top of him. There was rage in the man's eyes. The killer was pinned to the floor, the knife still in his arm. He didn't want the other man to pull the knife out. The guy in the overalls was stronger than the killer and a whole lot heavier. The man who had attacked the killer threw a hard punch at the murderer's nose, but the killer countered it with his free arm. Then, with the arm that had been stabbed, the killer punched the attacker on the side of his head with all his might.

The attacker became disoriented for a second which gave the killer just enough time for his next move. He placed his hands flat on the floor and pushed his shoulders forward, head butting the attacker square in the nose. Blood began to pour out of the man's nose. The killer then jerked the knife out of his own forearm and shoved it into the man's stomach. The killer twisted the knife in all different angles, causing the man in the overalls to jerk in pain. However, the man came back at the killer with more punches. This time he landed them. He kept the killer underneath his weight and threw a left then a right swing at the killer's face. The left swing hit him in the mouth and the right hit him square in his nose.

Both men's faces were now covered in blood and each
of them were yelling and screaming at each other. The killer's
vision was blurred. He pulled the knife out of the man's
stomach then stabbed him again. This time the blade
penetrated through the man's throat and the tip came out the
back of his neck. The man in the overalls froze and a gurgling
sound came out of his mouth. His eyes looked to almost pop
out of his head as the killer pulled the knife downward,
slicing down toward the man's sternum.

Blood seeped out of the man's mouth and ran down his
chin and onto the killer's chest. Blood poured out of the
man's throat. The killer jerked the blade out of the man's
neck and pulled himself out from under the weight of the
body. The killer rolled the dead man over onto his back and
examined him. He knew the man. The light brown hair and
the long scruffy beard…his name was Johansson Chame. He
had retired a year ago and had done yard work for the
Shambles' ever since. He'd once been an outgoing, talented
FBI agent. Now he was a dead man; only a corpse with blood
soaking his beard and white T-shirt.

The killer peeked out the door and glanced over to his left.
He saw her. Laura. He froze. He slammed the door and
ducked back into the house.

What if she comes over to visit Gerald and Shirley?

The killer sprinted to the guest bedroom window
hopping over Shirley's dead body. He carefully opened the
curtains and watched Laura. She was leaning into the back
seat and seconds later came out holding little Kayleen on her

hip. She looked around her, walked up to her door, and entered her home. That was close, too close.

The killer peeked out the door a second time and saw that it was clear. There was hardly a soul to be seen. He pulled the bandana back up and over his face. He power-walked to the sidewalk and then sprinted across the road. He must've been an odd sight to the bums and drug addicts hanging around. He was covered in blood. There were spots of dark red blood in his hair and across his chest. His nose was broken and swelling, his face bloodied. The man in overalls had thrown things off. The attack was so unexpected. He kept his head low and shielded his face the best he could. He was lucky to be alive. He was lucky she didn't make her usual visit to the Shambles as she normally did when she first got home. He was lucky Johansson hadn't taken pictures of the attacks. He was lucky Johansson hadn't called 911. Now, he hoped he was lucky enough that no one around recognized or could identify him.

CHAPTER NINETEEN

Ryan put the sports car into drive and pulled out of the gas station parking lot. He pulled the car out onto the busy road. He looked in the passenger-side mirror and saw her. Laura was holding Kayleen's hand and they were skipping toward the Shamble's front door. Ryan's heart stopped. He swerved into the left lane and was almost rear-ended by a little blue car. He jerked the wheel back to the right and looked in the mirror again. Ryan turned his gaze back toward the road and didn't look back.

Laura fought back the vomit coming up from her stomach into her throat. Johansson was dead, she knew that much and that was enough. She hadn't even taken a step into the house and knew that Johansson wasn't the only dead body in that home.

She was on her knees bawling. Kayleen stood next to her with concern in her eyes.

"What's wrong Mommy?" Kayleen asked hugging Laura's waist. "Why are you so sad?"

Laura caught her breath and hugged her little girl back. "It's…" Laura sniffled. "It's nothing, sweetheart."

Laura stood up on her wobbly legs and wiped her eyes with the back of her hand, still staring at the door.

"Let's go back to our house."

Laura held Kayleen's hand. Her whole-body shivered. They went inside their house and Laura immediately walked

Kayleen to her bedroom. Laura picked her daughter up and set her on the bed. Then she walked over to the base of the bed and flipped on the TV. Dora the Explorer was on and Laura left it as is.

"Stay here okay, Kay? Don't come out of your room until I come and get you, okay?"

"Okay, Mommy."

Kayleen crawled on her hands and knees over to her pillow and pulled her bed's covers over herself.

Laura halted in the doorway, a smile on her face. Kayleen was the greatest thing to ever happen to her. It didn't matter the situation, she always managed to cheer Laura up.

"I love you, Kay."

Kayleen stopped in mid-song with Dora and said, "Love you more, Mommy."

She almost thought about knocking but chose not to. Instead Laura twisted the handle and stepped into Gerald and Shirley's home. She crossed the threshold and closed the door. She glanced down at Johansson Chame lying flat on his back, his beard soaked in blood, eyes bulging, white shirt and overalls bloody, and mouth wide open. She bent down into a crouching position over Johansson's dead body and examined him.

Out of habit, Laura checked for a pulse. There was none. A gaping hole was at the base of Johansson's neck and a small gash was at the back of his neck. Someone had shoved a blade into his throat and sliced a huge gash in it. That was why the hole was so large and gruesome. A pool of blood covered the floor. She felt Johansson's face. His nose was broken It was one of the worst breaks she had ever seen. Laura shook her head and walked over to the kitchen. Right away she noticed that a kitchen knife was missing from its place. She had cooked there many times before. She couldn't find the missing knife anywhere and guessed the killer had taken it. Her husband was rubbing off on her. She noticed the details.

She walked out of the kitchen and for the first time investigated the guest bedroom. Her heart broke in two. There in the doorway was a body. Shirley Shamble was lying there, two bullet holes right between her eyes. Laura staggered over to the bedroom and looked down at her old friend. There wasn't much to examine. Shirley's hair was covered in her own blood and two small bullet holes were directly between her two hazel-colored eyes.

Silent tears welled up in her eyes as she continued to the next room. She entered the doorway into the office and computer room and that is where she found the third body. A yard from her left foot, against the wall was Gerald Shamble. He lay flat on his face with an office chair on top of him. She knelt beside him and pushed away the office chair. She rolled her old friend onto his back and got back up right away. She saw what she needed to see. Gerald had been shot once in each hand and twice in the side of the head. It didn't matter that there was blood on his face, Laura still kissed Gerald on the cheek.

Laura stood and backed up and for reasons unknown to her, she walked over to the Shamble's computer. She had a strange feeling to approach that direction. There was blood as well as a computer, pen, and a letter on the desk. Laura gasped when she saw who it was written to.

"Dear Laura," it read.

She continued to read:

"Dear Laura, I'm sorry this had to happen. I loved the Shamble's too."

Wait, what?
It was Gerald's handwriting.
Why...?
She continued to read the letter:

"But they had to die. It hurts me to have to do this to them. They were wonderful people. As good as they came. I've always loved you. From the day I laid eyes upon you at Mongolies."

The letter continued to tell of the writer's profound love for Laura and she turned the page over to the back and the talk of the profound love for her continued. She finally got to the last paragraph:

"I'll always love you. Give Kay a big hug for me. She has always had a special place in my heart. She is an amazing little girl.
Yours truly, Ryan Turner"

Laura couldn't breathe. Her legs stopped supporting her and she almost fell to the floor but caught herself on the desk. She read the last part of the letter one more time:

"Yours truly, Ryan Turner."

No, No! It can't be. This isn't happening...
Laura wouldn't let her mind accept what she had just seen.

"Yours truly, Ryan Turner."

The four words repeated over and over in her head. Ryan didn't do this. He didn't. He couldn't have. Laura heard the sirens as she walked out of the Shamble's home. There was no need to hurry and call 911 now. They were already on their way. Gerald's neighbors, the Tooks, must have heard the commotion and alerted law enforcement, or maybe Johansson had... The sirens were close, so Laura ran back over to her house. She didn't want any part of this.

She walked in and shut the door behind her then approached Kayleen's bedroom. She was sound asleep, arms wrapped around her teddy bear.

"Yours truly, Ryan Turner."

The four words wouldn't leave her. She walked into the living room and threw herself onto the couch. The remote was already there to her right. She flipped on the television and switched from ESPN to Channel 2. The news. The first thing she saw was her husband's face filling up the TV screen.

CHAPTER TWENTY

The words came to her again.

"Yours truly, Ryan Turner."

She stared at the screen, listening to the voice come from the screen.

"This man, Ryan Turner, is wanted for the murder of the Head of the FBI, J.J. Mauer. He is the prime suspect, although no one is for sure that he is guilty. We take you to the scene earlier today." Ryan Turner's face disappeared and now a woman standing in front of a house came into view. "We are here at the home of J.J. Mauer. Around 6:00 p.m. tonight, he was shot in the back of the head by one of his own men. I am here with Agent Kyle Harrison, who watched the whole thing go down."

The camera moved to a handsome face.

"I have no comment," Kyle said, trying to avoid the camera's gaze.

"Please, sir, what did you see happen?"

Kyle stared at the woman now. "This is what I hate about the media. You always jump to conclusions and get your nose in the middle of things. You always need to have a story. We lost an amazing man today. This is a day of mourning. You say Ryan Turner is responsible…"

"Well is he not? Were you not here? We overheard you discussing it," the woman said, cutting off Kyle.

Kyle looked to be frustrated. "There is no way of knowing that Ryan did this. To everyone out there watching, J.J. Mauer was not killed by Ryan Turner. He was not. We know very little about what happened here. End of story."

Kyle put a hand up against the camera-lenses and walked away.

The camera moved back to the reporter. "I'm Gina Grayman, live from the scene, back to you Jason."

Laura stared at the screen as the weatherman began to talk about rain chances.

"Yours truly, Ryan Turner."

Ryan was a murderer. Ryan had written that letter.

"Yours truly, Ryan Turner."

It was his signature, his words. Laura became light-headed, cupped her face in her hands, and cried.

CHAPTER TWENTY-ONE

It had been a long day for Kyle Harrison. It had been a long, mixed up, emotional day. His boss was dead, and his best friend was being hunted down, but he kept himself together. He kept himself calm and composed. He had to. He just had to.

Kyle decided to leave the scene. He'd seen enough. J.J. Mauer was dead and Ryan had killed him. There was so much evidence against Ryan now. His prints on the doorknob, his pistol lying in Mauer's living room and Kyle had seen Ryan standing over Mauer's body, pistol in his grasp. Kyle backed his car out of J.J. Mauer's driveway and started down the road.

Kyle drove in the direction of his home down the traffic packed New York City roads. Kyle Harrison lived six blocks past Mongolies...or what used to be Mongolies. Kyle kept reminding himself of that. It was 9:42 p.m. when Kyle took a sharp right turn and parked in from of a decent-sized house. The house's lights were all turned on. He walked up to the front door and knocked three times. Halfway through his third knock, the door swung open and he was almost knocked off his feet as Laura Turner threw herself into him, wrapping her arms tight around his waist.

"Is it true...?" Laura was in tears.

Kyle hugged her back.

"I'm so sorry," was all he could manage to say.

Laura told Kyle to come inside and they walked into the enormous kitchen. The two sat at the table which was placed in the middle of the kitchen. They sat across from each other and Kyle looked Laura in the eye. She had dark circles under her dark blue eyes. There were streaks of mascara down her cheeks and her black hair was a mess. Laura was the first to speak.

"Why?" was all she asked.

Kyle shook his head. "I really don't know. I've known Ryan for so long and he's a wonderful friend. I don't know what caused him to do this, but I have a few theories."

Laura remained quiet. Kyle took a deep breath.

"Pay. He wasn't getting paid too much. None of us really were. Mauer made good money. The Head of the Bureau always has. Ryan is, well was, second in charge. He was right behind Mr. Mauer in the pecking order. We all knew that if Mauer were to pass away or retire that it was likely Ryan would take his place. Maybe, just maybe, Ryan wanted that position for himself. He was very sneaky about killing Mauer. If I hadn't stopped by and seen it happen, I don't think we would ever have found out it was him. With Mauer dead, Ryan would have most likely moved up into his position as Head of FBI Operations, increasing his paycheck and eliminating the stress of being an agent. I don't know how logical it is because I don't think Ryan would do it for that, but that's one theory."

Laura said nothing.

Kyle took another deep breath. "He was threatened. Someone could have threatened Ryan. Someone could have made Ryan do what he did by threatening him, saying they'd kill you and Kay…someone like Cybris Caine. Cybris could have seen the skill and smarts Ryan possessed when we raided Mongolies. Ryan was a threat to Caine. Caine might have felt he had to get rid of Ryan and Mauer at the same time. But, what gets me is, why wouldn't Caine put away

Ryan and Mauer himself? It's not like he isn't capable. I don't know, those are just theories of mine."

There was an uncomfortable silence that lasted for several minutes. Then Laura finally spoke.

"Pay? That doesn't really make sense? Ryan was happy with his job. Between the two of us, we were doing just fine financially. I guess it could've been the stress of being under Mr. Mauer and always having to put his life on the line, but I don't know. I just don't understand."

Kyle nodded. "Like I said, they're…."

To Laura it was as if Kyle wasn't there. She could hardly hear the words coming out of his mouth.

"Cybris, or someone like Cybris Caine being involved in that way? I don't understand that one either. If that was the case, then why did he run from you? He could've just stayed put and turned himself over to you. He would've had a valid excuse."

Laura kept her eyes fixed on the table. Her face was expressionless.

Kyle said, "I see where you're coming from Laura. I completely understand, but, like I said, they're just theories. I'm leaning toward the Cybris Caine one though. Caine might've told Ryan to not get caught or else he'd kill you and Kayleen anyway. Cybris Caine is a horrible man. One of the worst this world has ever seen. Who knows what he told Ryan; if that is the correct theory. But trust me Laura, I'm going to get to the bottom of this for you, for Kayleen, for me, for the FBI, and especially for Ryan."

Laura kept her eyes on the table. "Four questions."

"Okay, what are they?" Kyle asked.

"One, how do you know for sure that Ryan killed Mr. Mauer?"

Kyle sighed. "Well, first off, I was an eye witness. I saw it firsthand. Plus, we…."

"Did you actually hear the gunshot or see Ryan shoot him?"

"No, I didn't see it, but I heard it. I pulled my motorcycle up to the house and heard the shot go off, then I saw Ryan standing over the dead body with a pistol in his hands. I pulled my M16 out of its case and told him that it's the FBI and he was surrounded. I told him to freeze and stay where he was, and I approached him. As I got closer I realized it was Ryan. He looked terrified. Guilty. Unexpectedly, he dove to the side and I didn't see him again. That's suspicious, in itself. Later, I and our team found Ryan's pistol in the living room. Around half an hour ago, I was informed that the bullet that killed Mr. Mauer had come from Ryan's personal handgun."

Laura kept her eyes on the table. "Two, what would you do?"

Kyle was puzzled. "What do you mean?"

"What would you do? How would you feel if one night you came home to find three dead bodies in your neighbor's home and how would you feel to have everyone saying that your spouse was the murderer? How would you feel if you flipped on the TV and saw Cindy's face on the screen, reporters saying she was wanted for murder?"

"I haven't really put much thought to that."

Laura stayed silent.

Kyle continued. "But I presume that I'd be feeling the same way you feel right now. If I was told that Cindy was a murderer, I would be baffled, stunned, not able to believe it. I would do whatever I possibly could to find the truth. I'd do whatever I possibly could to ensure myself that she wasn't a cold-blooded killer…and what are you saying about three dead bodies in your neighbors' home? What in the world are you talking about?"

Laura didn't take any notice to Kyle's last question. "Three, who killed Mr. Mauer?"

Kyle shrugged. "We've been through this already, Laura."

"Who killed Mr. Mauer?" Laura repeated.

Kyle tried to keep from getting annoyed. "Well…I don't want to believe it, but…Ryan. I'm pretty sure Ryan did."

"Four, who killed Gerald and Shirley Shamble?"

CHAPTER TWENTY-TWO

Kyle ran out the door as soon as the words left Laura's mouth. Laura remained seated at the table; eyes fixed on the table top. The clock read 10:10 p.m. Laura waited. The conversation with Kyle played in her mind over and over again.

Why did Ryan do this?

She played with the fingers rhythmically on the table.

What has my husband done?

Kyle threw open the Shambles' front door and instantly spotted the dark shape of a body lying on the floor. He switched on the lights. Immediately, Kyle recognized the body. It was his old friend, Johansson Chame.

Kyle shook his head. He knelt over Johansson's body. The man had been stabbed in the throat. Kyle staggered over to the Shambles' kitchen and retrieved a dish towel. He made his way over to Johansson and placed the violet colored rag over the dead man's face.

Now, where are Gerald and Shirley? thought Kyle.

He decided to check the master bedroom. His heart sunk when he walked into it. Lying on the floor dead was the sweet woman, Shirley Shamble. A tear escaped Kyle's eye. He grabbed a small gray blanket off the bed and laid it over Shirley's lifeless body. Kyle was already shaken up. He had cared about the Shambles and Mr. Chame. He was becoming sick to his stomach.

He searched the bathroom next to the master bedroom. No body to be found there. Kyle did stop inside the bathroom and fell to his knees and vomited into the toilet. He pulled himself up onto wobbling legs, forcing himself to stand. Kyle exited the room and made his way to the office. There he found Gerald Shamble. Kyle dropped to a crouching position in the doorway. Dried blood covered the floor and Gerald lay lifeless in a heap against the wall. Kyle moved into a sitting position and put his back against the open door. He removed his cell phone from his pocket and dialed the FBI Director's number.

After a few rings there was an answer. "Hello, Harrison."

Kyle pulled his knees to his chest. "Hello, Mr. Felix."

Director Felix coughed, then said, "How may I help you?"

"Director," Kyle said, "I've found some more bodies…"

Kyle stood up and approached the desk and froze. On the desk was a letter. It was written to Laura and signed by Ryan Turner.

"Harrison?" the Director asked somewhat frustrated.

Kyle snapped out of his daze. "Ryan's neighbor's, the Shambles, they're dead, along with their caretaker."

The Director exhaled. "Wow, the elderly folks? The husband was a doctor, correct?"

"Yes, sir," Kyle answered.

"What happened?" Felix asked.

"The Shambles were both shot and the caretaker, Johansson Chame, was stabbed to death."

After a short silence, Felix said, "Johansson was an honorable man. Harrison? Who did this?"

Kyle rubbed the back of his neck. "I have reason to believe that it was Ryan, sir."

"Turner?"

"Yes."

The Director said nothing. Kyle patiently waited for Felix to take it all in.

"This is bad," Felix said. "Have news outlets covered Mauer's death?"

"Yes," Kyle answered.

"Oh, no, the whole country probably knows by now. We need to hush this. We must keep all this within the Agency. This is going to leave a nasty scar on us. We must keep all this from the public. Ryan has allegedly killed four people today, one of which was the Head of the Bureau. We cannot afford to look like this in front of our people. We cannot exploit this baggage. I'll make sure the news stations are informed that Mauer was killed by a thug. The thug was killed tonight by our own agents. End of story."

Kyle nodded. "Yes, sir, Mr. Felix."

"Harrison?" Felix said, while breaking into another coughing fit. "You and Agent Taylor find Turner. I'm leaving this up to you. The two of you were Ryan's closest friends and colleagues, so the two of you must be the ones to find him. He is dangerous. He must be captured and put into custody. And Harrison…you are in charge. With Mauer and Turner both out of the picture, you must be the leader there in New York until we figure some things out."

Kyle was somewhat surprised at Director Felix's instructions but felt honored.

"I won't let you down, Mr. Felix."

"Good," the Director answered. "Get the Shambles' home cleaned up and get to work as soon as you can. Good luck, Harrison."

Before Kyle could reply, the phoneline went dead.

The clock read 10:25 when Kyle came back into Laura's kitchen. He had tears in his eyes and kept shaking his head. Laura said nothing. Kyle stopped once he was inside the front door and spoke.

"I'm so sorry Laura. They were as good of people as they come. I loved them. I can't imagine all the mixed-up feelings you must be having."

"So," Laura said, "who killed them?"

"Ryan," Kyle replied still shaking his head. "Ryan did."

Laura said nothing.

"Again, I can't say how sorry I am. Good night Laura."

As he finished his sentence, Kyle Harrison walked out the door. In time, Laura fell asleep right where she sat. She laid her head down upon the table, closed her eyes and fell into a deep sleep. She didn't hear the police and ambulance sirens blaring half the night.

CHAPTER TWENTY-THREE

The phone rang on the night stand at exactly 6:00 a.m. A sleepy hand reached out of the hotel bed and picked up the cell phone. He man put the phone up to his face. It was ringing, and the screen was flashing, indicating that someone was calling him, but the screen was blank, not showing what number was trying to contact him. He knew exactly who it was though. The person who had called was careful. The caller's cell phone number never showed up when he placed a call. The man lying in the bed looked down at the ringing phone and lifted it up to his ear.

The man on the other end of the phoneline was sitting at a table in a restaurant located in Rome, Italy. It was his favorite place to eat in the world. It was extremely expensive, but money was never a problem for him. He had the money to leave a $250.00 tip every time he ate there. Plus, he owned the place. Literally.

"Hello?" the man in the hotel answered.

The man in the restaurant smiled and reached with his free hand to pick up his fork. He cut off a piece of meat and shoved it into his mouth. He slowly chewed. *Delicious.* He loved this place.

He swallowed, licked his lips and asked, "How's it going?"

The man in the hotel shifted uncomfortably and sat up with his feet hanging off the side of the bed.

"Good. Everything has gone according to plan so far. To be honest, I had one hiccup."

"Yes, I know," the man in Rome answered.

The man on the bed shivered. The voice on the other end of the phoneline scared him to death. That deep, cold voice sent chills down his spine.

The man in Rome waited for an answer and eventually the hotel man asked, "How do you know I messed up?"

"I'm a powerful man, you know this," he said as he took another bite of cooked meat. "I have my people. I have my ways of knowing."

Once again, the man on the hotel bed shivered. "It won't happen again, I promise."

He waited for an answer but heard only deep, raspy breathing. After a long pause an answer finally came. "I don't know. It was a costly mistake. You should have been out faster, but instead…you hung around and you were spotted. Such a costly mistake." The man on the bed was now cold, his teeth chattered, and his hands shook.

Struggling to keep the phone still against his ear he said, "I'm sorry, I promise it won't happen again. I promise you that. I've been around for a long time. I don't make mistakes like these. You know that."

He continued to shake, straining to hear an answer from the caller. A minute passed by, then two. The man sitting on the bed began to wonder if the caller had hung up when he finally heard, "Mistakes don't sit well with me."

The man on the hotel bed shivered again. "I'm telling you, please, I…"

"You have three days."

"Three days for what, sir?" the man on the bed asked.

He heard the man in Rome slowly chewing then take a deep breath and say, "To kill her. You have three days to kill Laura."

CHAPTER TWENTY-FOUR

Ryan stood at the front desk and checked out of the Hampton Inn at exactly 11:00 a.m. He was exhausted, physically and emotionally. The woman at the front desk kept looking at him, not knowing if she should call the police or call an ambulance. As Ryan handed her his room key, she finally spoke.

"Umm, Mr. Lloyd? Would it be rude if I asked what happened to you?"

Ryan looked at the short, blonde, tattooed woman.

"It's a long story. I was kind of beat up last night by a gang. Not fun."

He had showered but was still covered in blood. His black pants had a few splatters of dried blood on them. His long-sleeved shirt was as wrinkled as it could possibly get, and it reeked of blood, sweat, and grime. He had lost a large amount of blood. He was able to rest last night and drank massive amounts of water out of the bathroom sink. Still though, his head throbbed, and his ears rang. He was alive though, and he was safe. For now, at least.

"You never went to the hospital for help?" the woman asked.

"Does it look like I've been to a hospital?" Ryan snapped back.

The woman lifted an eyebrow. "Point taken. Let me grab you a hoodie. One of my coworkers has some in the back. He's a jerk, so I'll be more than happy to give you one."

The woman went through a door behind the counter and later came out holding a generic gray hoodie. Ryan thanked the woman and exited the hotel.

The first thing that caught Ryan's eye when he walked
out the front door was that his car had been totaled. The
passenger seats were lying in the middle of the parking lot,
his windshield and driver-side window were shattered, and all
four tires were flat. He approached the car, which sat in a
parking spot directly across from the entrance.

Who did this and why?

He looked in through the broken driver-side window and
reached under the seat. The keys were gone.

*Whoever this person or persons were, why didn't they
just steal the car?*

Ryan unlocked the door, pulled his arm out, and swung
the door open. He squatted down on his haunches and
reached under the seat a second time to search more
thoroughly for the keys. He didn't find them.

Ryan stepped out of the car and pondered his next move.
He turned around and stared at the airport across from him.
Just then, cars peeled into the hotel parking lot. Some were
NYPD police cars, others were solid black. He immediately
recognized two of the men in the black cars.

FBI.

Ryan turned and ran. He ran with his back to the
entrance of the hotel, got to the back of his car and leapt
through the air. Ryan landed upright on the side of the hill
leading down to the JFK airport, and took off sprinting down
the hill, running across jam-packed roads, and ignoring
furious road-raged drivers.

The FBI cars came to the Hampton Inn parking lot and
screeched to a stop, one on each side of the stolen Porsche.

The three NYPD cars pulled into random spots in the parking lot and the occupants hopped out with pistols drawn. Out of the first FBI car came a 6-foot-tall agent holding an M16 rifle and out of the other car came a six-foot and seven-inch tall, 240-pound man, wearing Oakley sunglasses on his face, and a holding Glock 19 in his hand.

Along with Kuron, Kyle Harrison walked to the back end of the torn-apart sports car. Side by side, the two men gazed on toward the airport. Kyle took his rifle off safety and Kuron began to nod his head.

"You think that's him?" Kuron asked.

"No," Kyle answered. "I *know* that's him."

The two agents began to run down the hill toward the airport, chasing down a man, who was now tearing across the airport parking lot toward the airport terminal.

Ryan was halfway through the airport parking lot when he looked over his shoulder. Behind him, two familiar men had just made it to the base of the hill and were running after him. He had 200 yards on Kyle and Kuron and he didn't want them to get any closer than that. Ryan ran as fast as his legs could go. After what seemed like a lifetime, Ryan finally arrived at the drop off area and sprinted through the automatic doors into the airport terminal.

He ran past the luggage checkout and metal detectors, flashing his badge as he went by. He sprinted by food stands, waiting areas, and empty terminals. Then after he made his way up three sets of escalators, he saw what he needed to see. Ahead of him were eight different flights on each side. Sixteen in all and he had to choose one of them. Ryan looked at the different flights many times as he stood at the top of the escalators. He wasn't worried about destinations, he was worried about timing. Thirteen of the sixteen flights were scheduled to lift off between an hour and two hours from now. Two flights were scheduled for lift off in 15 to 30 minutes which left one flight. Ryan didn't even look at the sign above the doors heading into the boarding area that led into the plane; he just saw a short line of five people pulling tickets out of their purses and pockets, getting them checked by the two airport security men standing at the entrance. Ryan darted to the line, his badge held in his right hand. The line was now down to three people. A pretty brunette in her early thirties was first in line and was in deep conversation with the ticket agents. Behind her was a wiry man in a business suit holding a small briefcase. Last in line was an elderly man with thin white hair, a wrinkled face, and worn callused hands. He wore a blue and white button up plaid shirt that hung down just below his waist. He wore light khaki shorts and shiny white tennis shoes. On his face he had a big smile that showed crooked, yellow teeth. Ryan decided he'd be his target.

Ryan jogged over to the man and tapped him on the shoulder.

"Sir?"

The old man turned around and looked up at Ryan.

"Yes?"

Ryan showed him his FBI badge. "Alec Terino, FBI."

The old man nodded, examining Ryan's face.

"Good to meet you, young man, but I'm sorry, I've got a plane to catch."

He started to turn around as the airport security urged him to hurry and board the plane, but Ryan reached out and grabbed the man by the forearm.

"About that…" Ryan started to say.

"Sir, we must check your ticket and get you on the flight now…as in right now," one of the cocky airport authorities said, cutting Ryan off.

"Carry on," the old man told Ryan.

Ryan breathed in and exhaled. "May I get on this flight? Can I use your ticket to board this plane? I know it sounds terrible to ask an elder…"

The man held the ticket out to Ryan. "Of course, agent!"

Ryan was stunned at how easily the man had agreed to what Ryan had asked of him.

"Go on, don't be shy. Take it."

Ryan grabbed the ticket from the kind man. "Thank you, you have no idea how much this means to me. You're literally a life saver, sir."

Ryan reached out and shook hands with the man, but when he attempted to let go, the man kept hold and placed his free hand on Ryan's shoulder.

"I'm a retired FBI man. People don't realize the things you go through," the man said, looking directly into Ryan's eyes. "I will get another flight out in the morning. I am in no hurry. Good luck with whatever it is you have going on, young man."

With that, he walked past Ryan and headed for the escalators.

CHAPTER TWENTY-FIVE

Ryan stood there frozen in place, the ticket held loosely in his hand. The man was right. People had no clue what those in the FBI go through.

"Well, well, some piece of work FBI puke did just enough mooching to get a ticket from that poor old man? What a guy!"

The taller of the two airport workers snatched the ticket from Ryan's grasp then punched a hole in it. Ryan walked through the opening that lead into the plane and out of the corner of his eye saw the two men start to close the door.

The annoying airport security man spoke again. "Have a nice trip, Mr. Agent, sir."

Kyle and Kuron had searched what seemed like the entire JFK airport, but they never saw any sign of their friend Ryan.

"He got on a flight," Kyle said stopping after taking three escalators upward.

"Why do you think that?" Kuron asked.

"I've known Ryan for a long time, Kuron. He mooched a ticket off someone and got onto a flight."

"You sound like there is no doubt in your mind, man," Kuron said finally coming to a stop where people were watching two little known college teams playing on the screen.

"Just listen to the conversation between those two airport authorities over there. The little bit of conversing I've heard, they are talking about a ragged-looking FBI agent."

Kyle was pointing toward two young men dressed in white airport authority shirts. Kuron glanced in their direction.

"Then let's go give them a little talking to," he said.

The two agents stopped a couple of steps from the men and pulled out their badges. Kyle spoke first.

"Kyle Harrison, FBI. This is my partner, Kuron Taylor. I overheard you talking about an FBI agent coming through here a second ago."

The bigger of the two airport authorities smirked. "Yeah, the piece of work mooched a ticket off some elderly man and hopped onto a plane. He looked like he had just been through world war three or something."

"Please," Kyle said, "can you let us on the plane?"

"Sorry to break it to you," the airport security authority said, "but that plane is long gone, fellas. So, you can walk your happy little selves right out of our airport."

Kuron finally spoke. "You guys show some dang respect. You work at an airport! An airport. We can do anything we want to! We have a thousand times the authority you two morons have! Seriously. Show some respect."

Kuron was now up in the man's face and was glaring down at the top of his head. The airport authority stepped back and raised his hands in the air.

"Whoa, easy Sasquatch! We don't want any problems, but we would like to ask you guys to leave. Listen, I have seen all the stuff on the news about the FBI for years, and all the conspiracy theories surrounding all you. I don't trust you, and I sure don't respect you. I let one of you by today when I shouldn't have. I am not obligated to give you the time of day. We need to go talk to our guys over there about today's new shifts."

The big man patted his partner on the back and the two airport authorities started to walk away.

"And where do you think you're going, man?" Kuron grabbed the cocky authority by his collar and threw him against the wall and got in his face once more. "I'll ask once. Tell me, where was that plane headed?"

Ryan sat at the very back of the American Airlines plane, looking out the window and trying not to make eye contact or let anyone see his face. He already looked and felt like crap as it was, and this already made him stand out. Ryan didn't need people putting two and two together and realizing that he was a wanted killer. There was a possibility Mauer's death hadn't been publicized, but he wasn't positive.

The plane had lifted off around ten minutes ago and Ryan already knew how extremely lucky he was. He was lucky that he decided to get a room at a hotel near JFK airport. He was lucky that the lady at the front desk had not watched the news and seen that he was wanted for the murder of four innocent people the previous night. Ryan was lucky that nobody in the airport realized who he really was. He was lucky that, even though he felt extremely guilty, the old man had believed in him and handed him his plane ticket. He knew the airport authorities wouldn't have allowed him to board the plane without a ticket even if he was an FBI agent. It was just the way it was. He was lucky the jerks at the airport *had* let him onto the plane. He was lucky that he had made it just in time to board the plane. Ryan knew he was lucky to be in a plane that wasn't overly full and that there was a pair of open seats and that he didn't have to sit next to or close to anyone. He was lucky he was on his way out of New York City. He didn't care what flight destination had been available to him. He was just happy he found one departing so quickly. A non-stop flight to Los Angeles was going to work just fine. Really, he couldn't have ended up with a better flight. As much as he had gone through and endured, Ryan felt that he was a very lucky man.

CHAPTER TWENTY-SIX

"Los Angeles," the airport security said. "The plane was headed to Los Angeles, California."

His mood had shifted. The young man no longer felt cocky and tough.

"Los Angeles?" Kuron said, loosening his grip on the white man's collar. "When is the next flight to LA?"

"Not sure," came the reply.

"Well, then," Kuron growled, "hurry up and find out."

Kuron let go of the man's collar and the man pulled a walkie talkie from his waistband.

"Mr. Murphy, do you copy?"

"This is him, what's up K.C.?"

K.C. pushed a button and raised the walkie talkie to his mouth. "I've got some FBI agents here wondering when the next flight to Los Angeles is."

There was a slight pause before an answer came.

"I'll check on that," replied Murphy.

After an uncomfortable silence lasting a minute or two, the walkie talkie came to life.

"K.C., do you copy?"

"Yup," answered K.C. "So, when's the next flight?"

"I don't know why but there is a long delay between flights to LA today," said Murphy. "The next flight is scheduled to leave at 5:45 tonight."

"Okay, thanks."

"You said that there were guys from the Bureau that were wondering about this flight?"

K.C. looked at the two agents in front of him. "Yes, sir, they're right here in front of me."

"Ask them why they don't just fly one of the Bureau's helicopters, or private jets, or something? I mean, I bet they have the means of transportation."

Kuron snatched the walkie-talkie from the man.

"Listen!" Kuron yelled into the device. "The head of operations, J.J. Mauer, was killed last night and we need to get to Los Angeles. We need to get there as soon as possible and you're blowing us off. We don't have enough time to find a pilot, find a chopper or jet, then fly to LA This is urgent…so, Mr. Murphy, when's the next flight headed to LA?"

There was a brief pause.

"I already told K.C., the next flight is at 5:30 and you can get on it then if you want. No charge."

Kuron shook his head and laughed out loud. "Let me say it again, Murphy, when's the next flight to LA?"

"I…" Murphy started, then paused. "We can get you on a private plane in around an hour or so. I can find a pilot here pretty quick."

Kuron smiled. "That's more like it, Murphy. Good doing business with you!"

Fifty-three minutes later, Kuron Taylor and Kyle Harrison were boarding a little plane with no luggage. They only had their firearms, the uniforms they wore, and the peace of mind that they were right on the tail of one of their friends, Ryan Turner, who had killed four people in the last 12 hours. Once inside the plane, the two sat across from one another in two of the six seats. Kyle sat by the window. Kuron set his hand on his friend's shoulder.

"We're going to get him, Kyle. We'll find him."

"I don't know about that," Kyle said. "Ryan is a smart man. I doubt that we will find him in LA"

CHAPTER TWENTY-SEVEN

The flight lasted a total of six hours. Ryan had slept every second he was in the air with his arms crossed on his lap and his forehead buried on his arms. It was a comfortable enough way to sleep while hiding his face. Ryan was the last to walk off the plane and he kept his head low, giving a slight nod to the flight attendant as he walked by.

While all the other passengers hurried to find their luggage, Ryan hurried elsewhere. He practically ran and got himself out of the airport in no time. He quickly ran down the first cab he spotted, beating various people to it. Ryan jumped into the back seat and told the driver to head to the nearest Wells Fargo Bank.

"You got it, mon," replied the Jamaican driver as they sped away into traffic.

The private plane landed softly on the runway at 6:08 p.m., and by 6:11, Kuron Taylor and Kyle Harrison were stepping off the plane and walking down a set of portable stairs. They hitched a ride on an airport security cart heading toward the terminal. They raced through the terminal and arrived at the airport entrance within minutes. The FBI agents found a bench and sat down. Kyle placed his elbows on his knees and cupped his face in his hands.

"If you were Ryan, Kuron, what would you do? Where would you go?"

Kuron placed his hands behind his head and leaned back against the wall.

"That's a tough one," he said, "but, if I were him, I would head into LA right away. I wouldn't think twice. He's low on money right now and won't risk using his credit or debit card anywhere. So, I'm guessing he'll find an ATM. The account that he likes to draw money out of is his Wells Fargo account. Then he'll get out of LA. He'll end up right back here and will get on a flight out of Los Angeles."

Kuron finished and still looked straight ahead, biting his upper lip in deep thought.

Kyle shifted in his seat and shrugged. "So, what do you think we should do then?"

Kuron got to his feet. "Find the closest Wells Fargo. There are ATM's in the airport, but we could give it a try. I mean, even if he used an ATM, we could get someone at the bank to look up his recent account activity. If my memory is right, there is a bank just outside the airport."

As if on cue, a taxi pulled up directly in front of the two agents. As a young couple headed toward the cab and reached for the door handle, Kuron placed his hand there first. He flashed his badge and pulled open the door allowing Kyle to jump in. The couple stood there stunned as Kyle and Kuron jumped into the cab. Kuron started to pull the door closed but stopped short.

"Sorry, ma'am, but we have a fugitive to catch."

"Where to, mon?" the dreadlocked driver asked.

Kyle answered, "To the nearest Wells Fargo Bank, and there is a two-hundred-dollar tip if you really step on it."

The wide-eyed driver looked at the agents in his rearview mirror.

"Dang, mon, in that case, 'I'm-uh' step on it good."

Kyle smiled to himself. "That might be a good idea, but the problem is, we're still sitting here."

The driver stepped on the gas pedal, causing the car's tires to screech and smoke as they pulled out away.

"Are you meeting a friend there or something?" the driver asked.

Kyle and Kuron looked at each other.

"No, why?" Kyle asked.

"Well, I just dropped off a man a second ago, who looks like you, mon. He looked a little rough, mon, but he had a badge just like you two."

Kyle's jaw dropped. "Where was he headed?"

The driver glanced in the mirror and said, "Told me the same you did, Mon, to go to the nearest Wells Fargo."

"How long ago did you drop him off?" Kuron chirped in.

The driver replied, "Eh, two, maybe three minutes ago. He was my last customer. The bank is not far from here."

Kyle's jaw dropped again. "You step on it, and we'll make that three-hundred-dollars."

CHAPTER TWENTY-EIGHT

6:15 p.m., and Ryan was walking away from the Wells
Fargo building with a wad of cash in his pocket. He had
withdrawn three-thousand dollars from his account and had
developed a plan. As he walked away from the bank, he made
his way to the large store directly across the street. Ryan
made it to the sidewalk and found his opportunity to jaywalk
across the road. He walked straight for the store, his mind
racing.

Now what?

Ryan made it to the main doors of the store and out of
the corner of his eye he saw something that made his blood
run cold. It was them. Kyle and Kuron. Ryan stopped in his
tracks and watched as the two agents leapt out of a taxi in
front of the Wells Fargo Bank. They looked around and Ryan
covered his face then turned to look at the men again. The
two men jogged straight up to the bank's entrance, guns in
one hand and badges in the other. Ryan entered the store.
They were here. They had tracked him to LA.

How? How did they get here so fast?

Ryan shook off the thought about Kuron and Kyle.
Instead, he began his search. He had a list in his head of
things he needed, and things he needed to do. He needed
every one of these things to get out of LA safely.

Kyle and Kuron rushed into the bank with guns drawn and
badges in plain view. Kuron was the one to speak first.

"Alright, listen up! I am Agent Kuron Taylor and this is Agent Kyle Harrison. We are with the FBI. We are here looking for a man by the name of Ryan Turner. He is a little over average height, looks a bit battered, and was last seen wearing a gray hoodie. Anyone seen him? Better speak up now if you have."

A short man from behind the counter spoke up. "We saw him. Black hair, just over six feet tall, probably. He looked a little ragged. Wore a hoodie."

Kuron and Kyle put their handguns into their holsters and this time Kyle spoke.

"Alright, now, how long ago was he in here? We don't have much time."

The short man looked at the clock and spoke again. "Um, three or four minutes ago, I presume."

"Thank you," Kyle and Kuron said at the same time.

"Where did he go? Where did he head to?" Kyle asked.

The man behind the counter shrugged his shoulders. "I have no clue. I really don't know." Then his eyes lit up and he pointed toward the door. "You can ask him though. Old Billy over there. See that bearded man over on the sidewalk? He might have an idea. He notices everything. He has quite the mind."

The agents glanced at each other and darted out the door, ready to do something neither of them had ever done before: interrogate a homeless man.

Kyle pulled a wad of cash out of his pocket. He walked up behind Old Billy and waved the bills in front of his face.

"Hi, there, Billy," he said. "Like what you see?"

The old man lunged forward attempting to grab the money, but Kyle pulled it away before he reached it.

"Now, Billy," Kyle said, "I will give you all of this, but I need you to help me. What do you say?"

Billy looked over his shoulder and gave the agents a dirty look. He was crouched down on his haunches. His cut off blue jeans reached to just above his knees. He wore an old, plain, brown T-shirt, and a plastic necklace hung around his neck. He had a to have been missing half of his teeth and he had a long gray beard that looked as if it had never seen a comb. He had bushy eyebrows and scraggly gray hair, which hung past his shoulders.

"Lie!" Billy said as he turned his back to the agents.

"No," Kyle said. "Not a lie."

He pulled another bill from his pocket which made a total of $60.00 that he held in his grasp.

"Now, Billy," Kyle said in a harsher tone, "what do you think of this?"

Kyle waved the cash in the old man's face. Billy looked over his shoulder again.

"I like. What you want?"

Kyle placed his hand on Billy's shoulder. "We are looking for a man who is about six feet tall, black hair, and is wearing a hoodie. He walked out of the bank just a few minutes ago. Have you seen him?"

Billy looked up at the blue sky and shook his head. "Actually, it was four minutes and twenty-five seconds ago and he made his way over there."

Billy pointed directly across the road at a store which had a sign above the entrance that read "Super-Mart".

"He went over that way, alright." Billy kept his eyes locked on the sky.

Kyle tossed the wad of bills on the homeless man's lap.

"Thanks Billy," Kyle said. "That wasn't so hard was it?"

Billy looked over his shoulder and moved his eyes between the two agents. "Five minutes, seven seconds. I'm guessing you want to catch him?"

Kyle shrugged.

"Well, I guess so," he said in an irritated voice.

Billy looked back toward the road and the supermarket. "Five minutes and twenty-one seconds, and you guys are still standing here."

CHAPTER TWENTY-NINE

Lucky for Ryan, the store had a changing room in the men's clothing section. He stripped off his shirt, threw off his shoes and unbuckled his pants. Once he was undressed, he began to rummage through the items he had purchased. He lifted and gazed at a blue Los Angeles Dodger's T-Shirt and put it on. It was almost too small, but it would work for now. He then picked up some blue and white Nike Basketball shorts that were a tad big, so he had to roll the waistband once over itself. Next, he pulled on some long white Dickies socks. Then he slipped on a pair of gray and white tennis shoes. He finished tying his shoes then reached down and grabbed a shiny silver necklace that had a good amount of bling to it. At the bottom of the necklace was a shiny "LA" symbol. He flung the necklace around his neck and reached into the bag to take care the finishing touch to his latest look. He grabbed a can of blue face paint and covered his face with it. He then retrieved a blue, afro-wig from off the floor. He placed the fake wig atop his head and looked himself over in the mirror. He had gone from the ultimate New York Yankees fan to being decked out in Los Angeles Dodger blue.

"What have I become?" he thought aloud.

He shook his head and almost let himself smile.

He put his hand in a bag and pulled out a cheap pair of NYS sunglasses. He then sat down on the chair inside of the room and pulled his cell phone out of his pocket. He had one text message. It was from Kyle.

It read: **Turn yourself in Ryan. We can help you.**

If you only understood.

Then it hit him. Laura hadn't called or texted. He felt horrible. He knew deep inside that all of this was killing Laura.

He had another thought.

How stupid can I be?

The FBI and CIA would easily be able to track his cell phone. Ryan cursed. He threw the phone into a grocery bag. As he did so, there was a loud knock on the dressing room door.

Ryan jumped. "Easy man, I'm almost done."

Outside of the dressing room, a man groaned. Ryan shook his head and thought if only the man knew that a wanted killer was in this dressing room. Ryan placed the sunglasses over his eyes and looked into the mirror.

Perfect!

He crouched down, scooped up all his old clothes and threw them into the grocery bags and tied the handles in a knot. Ryan lifted all the bags off the ground, unlocked the dressing room door, and stepped outside.

Ryan nodded to the short man waiting outside of the dressing room.

"Sorry for the wait."

He walked out of the men's clothing section, down a long aisle, past the checkout area and headed for the entrance of the Super-Mart.

Kuron and Kyle ran across the road and kept on running toward the store. Once they made it there, the pair of automatic doors slid open and a few people exited while the two agents entered. They stopped right inside the store and confronted three civilians. There were two women and one man. The two women were short; one was in her twenties and the other's hair was grayish-brown, making her look around fifty or sixty. The man was very eye-catching. He was decked out in blue. His face was painted blue and he wore a blue wig. He wore a large pair of sunglasses on his face. He wore a heavy gold necklace around his neck and an LA Dodgers long-sleeved shirt. The Dodger fan walked with a slight limp, his back looked bent, and his shoulders were hunched over. The two agents extended their arms and held their palms out.

"Hello, let me have your attention. We work for the FBI. I'm Agent Taylor. This is Agent Harrison. We're here looking for a man about 6 feet tall. He has dark hair. Fairly slender build. Last seen wearing a hoodie. Any of you seen someone matching this description?"

All three individuals shrugged and walked past Kuron and Kyle.

"Well," Kyle said, "welcome to friendly Los Angeles, Kuron."

Kyle remained at the entrance and Kuron entered further into the store to search for their friend, Ryan Turner.

That was a close one.

Ryan was proud of himself. His disguise was legitimate. Kyle and Kuron had thought nothing of it. They didn't even take a second glance at Ryan. To them he was just a crazed, all-out Dodger fan. For the first time in a long time, Ryan finally let a real smile spread across his face. Once he cleared through the doors of the Super-Mart, he looked to his left and found a large trash can sitting against the outside wall. He stuffed his grocery bags containing clothes, paint, and his cell phone in the can. He limped away, his back bent, a smile on his face.

Ryan made his way across the road again and once he was on the same side of the road as the bank he turned to the right. He proceeded down the sidewalk which was parallel to the road. He continued to move with a limp because he was careful and never knew who might be watching.

CHAPTER THIRTY

Randy Palino, a small man standing just over five feet tall, was leaning up against the side of the Wells Fargo Building. He held a cigarette between his index and middle finger. His other hand was shoved deep into his pocket and was grasping his cell phone. He tried to look casual. He wore a black-leather biker's jacket that had a large yellow dragon on the back of it. Along with the jacket he wore blue jeans and black tennis shoes. Randy Palino looked around the corner of the building searching for a certain someone.

Nothing.

He leaned back against the wall and placed the cigarette between his lips. He sucked in then blew out a big puff of smoke. That's when the phone in his left jacket pocket started to vibrate.

"Hello," he said into it.

"He's coming," the voice on the other end of the line said.

Palino peeked around the corner again. "Then where is he?"

There was an immediate answer. "Be patient, you dwarf! He's headed straight for the road and to where you're standing."

Palino took a quick peek around the corner again, and he shook his head. "I'm not seeing him."

A laugh came from the other end of the line and the voice said, "Doesn't surprise me, Randy. If it wasn't for me, you wouldn't ever get anything done!"

"Well, guess what?" Palino said. "All you ever do is give me a hard time! I still don't see him..."

"Easy, Randy," the voice said in between laughs. "He's across the road right now."

Randy peeked around the corner a fourth time then leaned against the wall again.

"I. Don't. See him!" Palino said annoyed.

The voice on the other end of the line broke into a hysterical laugh, then said, "Give him about ten, fifteen seconds, and he'll walk right down the sidewalk by the road directly in front of you."

Palino began to count in his head, and thirteen seconds later the only person he saw was a man dressed in blue. The man walked down the sidewalk with a limp. Palino let the man get about fifty to sixty yards away before he stepped away from the wall and lifted the phone back up to his ear.

"Really? You think that's him?" he whispered.

A groan echoed through Palino's phone. "Yes, you idiot, that is him! He's not stupid! All he did was change his appearance! Use your God-given brain, Randy!"

Palino walked swiftly over to the sidewalk.

"Do you know where the agents from the Bureau are?"

There was a pause then the voice answered, "Yup, they're still running around the Super-Mart looking for a tall, black-haired man wearing a gray hoodie. The punks aren't as smart as they think they are."

Palino nodded, still trailing the man covered in blue.

"He turned left, heading straight for the old Hotel, Hotel," he said.

Randy Palino kept himself about a hundred yards behind the man he was trailing, occasionally ducking behind garbage cans, sides of buildings, and cars. The man in blue was pulling open the hotel's front door when he spun around. In the nick of time, Palino dove behind a small, white car.

Palino stayed put behind the car for what seemed like ages before he dared to look around and expose himself. When he finally did, he didn't see the man anymore.

Palino lifted the phone back to his ear. "You still there?"

"Yup," the voice answered.

"He went into the hotel. The agents are coming out of the store now. They're headed for the road and straight for the ATM."

Palino stayed crouched behind the Honda.

"What do we do now?" he asked.

"Wait it out and make sure the FBI guys don't find out."

"Okay," Palino said.

The voice then said, "If you need me, call me. I'll be waiting in the car in the Super-Mart parking lot."

"Okay," Palino answered and hung up the phone.

He looked left and right then approached the hotel.

For the second time that day, Kyle and Kuron stepped into the Wells Fargo bank. They walked straight up to the desk.

Kyle, flashing his badge said, "Is there any viable way you can look up a man by the name of Ryan Turner and his recent withdrawals, and maybe purchases using his card?"

The blonde front desk man examined the two agents and began typing away at his computer.

"Here," he said, "it's all under the name of Ryan Turner."

He turned the computer screen to Kyle and Kuron and the agents moved closer to the screen. There was an extensive list of dates matching up with different purchases and withdrawals. After a little while of studying the list, Kyle turned to Kuron.

"Anything stand out to you?"

Kuron nodded and kept his focus on the screen.

"Yeah," he said. "Yesterday morning, ten dollars at Cold Stone. Today, withdrew a few thousand dollars from here, and…a couple of minutes pays for a room at Hotel, Hotel. He used his card after withdrawing cash, why?"

Kyle put one hand on each side of the screen.

He turned to the man and asked, "Where is Hotel, Hotel?"

Without hesitation the man replied, "A block or two to the west, then turn to the left, keep on going straight. It's fairly decent-sized for being an old hotel and for the most part, it's easy to find."

Kyle slapped Kuron on the back. "Let's go."

The two bolted out the door, headed down the sidewalk, turned left and after about two blocks turned to the left again running through thick crowds of people directly toward Hotel, Hotel.

CHAPTER THIRTY-ONE

"He's on the first floor; room 108. He went into his room just a few minutes ago."

Randy Palino sat cross-legged in the lobby of Hotel, Hotel as he held his cellphone up to his ear. The television on the wall in front of him was running the CNN channel.

"Good work," the voice on the other end of the line said. "The FBI agents are headed your way now. Be ready."

Palino glanced at the front door of the hotel. "I will be. Now, why again are we doing this? What is our objective?"

"Keep an eye on Turner and don't let him get caught. Don't ask why, because I don't have any idea. It's the boss man's orders. And whatever you do, try not to make too big of a scene."

"You got it," Palino said. "They're walking in now."

"Good luck," the voice on the other end of the line said.

Kuron and Kyle threw open the front doors to Hotel, Hotel, and ran up to the counter on their right.

"Has anyone recently checked in under the name of Ryan Turner?" Kyle asked the woman at the front desk.

The scraggly old woman at the counter immediately answered. "Yes, a very nice young man. Why are you asking?"

Kuron showed the woman his badge. "We are from the Bureau, ma'am. It's of immense importance that we find him."

"Oh, dear," the old woman said. "Let me look."

Kyle and Kuron exchanged glances, and patiently waited. The woman slowly maneuvered the cursor around on her computer screen. Five seconds passed by, then ten, then fifteen. Kyle anxiously tapped the top of the counter with his fingers. Finally, the elderly woman looked up from the computer screen.

She cleared her throat. "Ryan Turner checked into room 108. Oh, and that's right, a young lady was with him."

Confusion immediately spread across both agents' faces.

"A girl?" Kyle asked.

"That's right. We had very limited rooms, and he told her he'd get a room for her. I didn't hear some of the other things he told her."

"Room 108," Kyle said, "where is it?"

"Down the hallway to your left; it'll be the fourth door on your right."

Before the woman finished her sentence, the two agents were already running down the hallway.

Out of the corner of his eye, Randy Palino watched the agents converse with the woman at the front desk. After some brief discussion, the two began to run down a hallway behind Palino. He pulled himself up to his feet, and slowly made his way toward the two FBI agents. The agents were now in front of room 108. Palino casually strolled over to the men. He passed by room 102…104…106. He stopped and pretended to take a phone call. Just then, the bigger agent of the two threw himself into the hotel door causing it to break off its hinges. The now broken door flew open, and a piercing scream erupted from room 108. Palino shoved the phone into his pocket, and with his other hand whipped out a Desert Eagle pistol from inside of his leather jacket. In three strides, Palino was there at the opening of room 108. He stood feet shoulder-length apart, both hands grasping the pistol, pointing it inside the room. As he had expected, the agents stood side by side, guns drawn, yelling, "Freeze! Freeze!" into the room.

He also spotted one king-sized bed, a nightstand next to it, a door to the bathroom which was just to the left of the room's entrance, and a flat-screen television on a dresser across from the foot of the bed. The room was simple but nice. What Palino didn't expect to see was a young, petite black woman sitting upright on the bed, her eyes wild with fear. It caught Palino off guard; almost to the point where he didn't see the shorter FBI man turn around.

"Stay where you are!" Palino commanded. "And you too, big guy, or I'll shoot your buddy right here and now. Both of you, slowly place your guns on the floor. Now!"

The agents immediately did so.

What in the world is going on?

Kuron's mind was reeling as he and Kyle crouched down and set their firearms on the floor.

Who is this guy?

"Now, put your hands where I can see them," the little man in the slick leather jacket commanded.

Stunned and confused, Kyle and Kuron did as they were told. The short man backed up slowly.

"Now come out of the room. Nice and easy."

Hands in the air, the agents did so. Kuron looked the little man up and down. He had never seen him before in his life.

"Against the wall," the gunman instructed.

Reluctantly, Kyle and Kuron stepped to the side of the door and pressed their backs against the wall. In unison, the two agents took a deep breath. They had been on the other end of the gun in this situation before, but this was a first for them both.

Kuron and Kyle were both patted down by the short tough guy, then the man put the muzzle of his pistol to the back of Kyle's head.

"What are you two doing snooping around here?" the little man asked.

Instead of answering, Kyle began to ask the questions. "Who are you?"

The short man grabbed the barrel of his pistol and pistol-whipped Kyle in the side of the head. Kyle fell hard onto his knees. Kuron restrained himself from attacking the perpetrator. Kuron was furious. He kept his eyes low, staring down at the floor.

Who does this guy think he is?

Kuron's hands, which were pressed against the wall, balled up into fists. He knew he could kill the little man right then and there. One punch. That's all it would take. But he kept himself composed. He wouldn't let his anger take over the best of him. A crazy, unknown man was holding a gun to Kyle's head. One wrong move and the trigger might be pulled. He couldn't risk his friend's life. Kuron took a deep breath, and then another…in, then out. In, then out. He had to be patient. He had to wait for his opportunity. He had to wait for the perfect moment.

CHAPTER THIRTY-TWO

Palino's mind was racing. He probably looked cool and confident on the surface, but he was scared...terrified. This was out of his comfort zone. This wasn't supposed to be happening. In past situations like this, the two agents would already be dead. He wouldn't have thought twice about killing them both. But, that had been one thing he was instructed not to do. He noticed the rage beginning to spread across the black FBI agent's face. Palino shifted his eyes toward the massive agent.

"Don't try anything you're going to regret. I can see it...you want to kill me, don't you? Don't you?"

The agent said nothing. Aside from the killing, this was Palino's favorite part in his line of work: ticking people off.

"Malaya..." Palino said licking his lips, "do you know a beautiful woman by the name of Malaya Taylor?"

The big agent pursed his lips and clenched his fists even tighter.

"Maybe you don't," Palino continued, "but I sure do, and, man, is she a fine woman. I can't wait until I see her again. I'll tell you this much, as soon as I am done with you two, I'm catching the first flight I can out to New York City."

The black agent's lips now curled into a snarl. Randy Palino could feel his heart pounding hard against his chest.

"Well, since he won't talk," Palino said, "he might as well take a little nap."

Palino then hit the agent who was on his knees, hard across the back of the head. The agent fell to the ground, unconscious. The bigger agent lost his cool. He turned around with his fist back, but Palino already had his pistol's muzzle shoved against the agent's throat.

"You touch me, big guy, and I won't hesitate to pull the trigger. Don't even test me."

Kuron froze. This little guy meant business. He wasn't messing around.

"So, let me ask you, what are you two doing here?" the short man asked.

"I'm not telling you a thing," Kuron spat out.

"Oh, really? Well, if you know what's best for you, and what's best for your pretty little wife, you'll just answer the question."

Before Kuron could say a word, Kyle groaned loudly, and rolled over onto his side. Kuron saw his opportunity…the perfect moment. Kuron looked down at Kyle for a split second and so did the gunman. The gunman only took a quick glance, but it was just enough. As he looked down to his right at Kyle, the gun in his hand also shifted slightly to the right. Kuron seized his opportunity. He kneed the little man hard in the midsection. In almost the same motion, Kuron swung his right hand and knocked the pistol out of the attacker's hand. The pistol clattered across the floor. The little man doubled over. Kuron then slammed his knee into the attacker's face, knocking him down onto his back. With one hand, Kuron lifted the attacker off the floor by his throat, and violently shoved him against the wall.

"Who are you, huh? Who are you?" Kuron yelled into the little man's face.

I can't breathe, I can't breathe!

Blood poured out of both of Palino's nostrils, and out of his mouth. His midsection hurt badly, and his lower ribs felt as if they might be broken. His feet dangled in the air, and he kicked repeatedly at the FBI agent.

"Who are you!?" the agent screamed into Palino's face again.

Palino couldn't speak. He couldn't even breathe. The FBI agent's grip on Palino's neck was only getting tighter. All Palino could think about was trying to get a breath. He lashed out at the agent's face with his fingernails, but his short arms couldn't quite reach. Palino kicked and kicked; his feet connecting repeatedly with the big agent's shins and knees. This didn't even begin to faze the FBI agent. Out of the corner of his eye, he could see policemen bursting through the hotel lobby doors. Palino didn't care. His kicking legs slowed, his eyesight was blurred and getting worse, and his lungs felt as if they were going to explode. Randy Palino knew he was about to die.

CHAPTER THIRTY-THREE

Kuron kept his right hand wrapped tightly around the short guy's throat. He squeezed, not his hardest, but close. He watched as the man's eyes began to roll into the back of his head. He didn't want to kill this man, but he wanted the little man to think so. The man's white pupils began to show more and more, and his legs and his arms slowly stopped flailing.

He's had enough.

To his left, Kuron noticed LAPD officers running right at him. Kuron released his grip on the man's neck, and the little man fell to the floor. Lying on his side, the little guy let out a long, exasperated breath, his chest heaving in and out.

"Put your hands in the air and step away from that man!" boomed a voice to Kuron's left.

Kuron followed the voice's orders. Kuron looked over to see an old muscular policeman with a short scruffy beard. He was briskly approaching Kuron with a handgun held out in front of him.

BANG!

Kuron suddenly fell to his knees, and then down onto his side, rolling and writhing in pain. He yelled out and grabbed his left calf with both hands. He yelled out even louder when he looked down at it. His pant leg was covered in his own blood. The dark red blood quickly began to stream down Kuron's leg and onto the floor, turning the white carpet red. Every police officer froze, exchanging looks with one another. Kuron looked in the direction of the policemen and women. There was a second "bang" and Kuron's ears began to ring.

He then watched as the old, muscular policeman's chest practically blew apart. The scruffy policeman instantly fell onto his back, dead, with a gaping hole in his chest. The remaining officers started up in mass chaos and confusion as they ran for cover, leaping over couches, chairs, tables, and the front desk. Kuron tried to stand but couldn't. He rolled over simultaneously until he hit the wall opposite of Kyle and the small mystery man. He then pulled himself up into a sitting position with his back pressed flush against the wall. Across from him, Kuron could see Kyle still lying on the ground. Then, unbelievably, he started to lose sight of Kyle. Dense grayish-black smoke began to fill the entire hallway, causing Kuron to cough uncontrollably as he inhaled the dark smoke. Suddenly, he had forgotten about his injured leg as the smoke engulfed him, burning his eyes and his lungs.

This isn't helping my cause.

Palino laid on his stomach, shielding his face with his arms, doing everything he could to keep from inhaling the dense smoke.

What is going on?

Palino uncovered his face, and immediately broke into a coughing fit. He couldn't see a thing. The smoke was thick. He leaned his back against the wall and forced himself to stand. He needed to get out of there. Now. Unsteadily, he scrambled down the hallway, the opposite direction of the hotel lobby. He hadn't gone very far when he felt a fist crash into the side of his head. The blow caused him to spin in a full circle before falling hard to the ground. As he hit the floor, his eyes fluttered closed. His head was throbbing.

Severe pain shot through his head and down his neck. He then felt a pair of hands grab him and lift him up into the air. He felt his body get swung over a thick, broad shoulder. That was the last thing he remembered before fully losing consciousness. He didn't even hear the eerie voice speaking to him.

"You failed, Randy…and it's going to cost you."

CHAPTER THIRTY-FOUR

"Now, you have a great day, mon!"

Ryan handed a wad of cash to the cab driver behind the wheel of the taxi. Ryan pulled himself out of the cab, shut the door behind him, and tapped the top of the car twice with palm of his hand. The taxi drove off, and Ryan walked through the giant double doors in front of him. He kept moving on past the doors, then after a while, stopped and made his way over to the back of a line. Slowly, but surely, he was at the front of the line. Ryan leaned on the desk in front of him. Behind the desk, a woman stood wearing a nametag that read "Becky".

"Name, and date of birth?" she asked.

Ryan scratched the back of his head. "Ryan Turner. Six, four, eighty-five."

He hoped the FBI hadn't publicized his name and the incident back in New York City. He assumed that they didn't. Why? Reputation, national trust, self-image. The FBI wouldn't want the public to know about this dilemma. Still, he kept his fingers crossed.

"Let me see here," Becky said, scrolling and clicking with the mouse. "Turner…Turner…there you are!"

She glanced over her computer at Ryan. There was a whirring sound coming from the printer behind her. The sound ceased, and a boarding pass fell out of the printer. Becky scooped it up, handed it to Ryan, and grinned.

"Have a nice trip, Mr. Turner."

Ryan returned the smile. "Thank you very much, ma'am."

He turned his back to the woman, making his way to a nearby escalator. He stepped onto it, and it ascended him upward. As he reached the top, he broke into stride. He looked down at his boarding pass.

Rome, Italy, here I come.

CHAPTER THIRTY-FIVE

Palino's eyes fluttered open. His entire face burned and ached. There was a sharp pain in the side of his head. He attempted to sit up, but immediately became nauseous and lightheaded. Almost passing out, Palino laid back down and turned his head to the left to see the back of a car seat. Through his fuzzy vision, he could see a man sitting in the seat with his hands grasping the wheel. The man was tall and muscular, and wore dark-tinted Ray Ban sunglasses, and wore a charcoal colored suit from head to toe. Lying across his lap was a small semi-automatic rifle. Palino knew right away who the man was. He knew him well.

"I am so sorr…" Palino started to say.

"No, Randy, I am sorry for *you*," the man said, interrupting Palino, "because sorry doesn't cut it around here."

Randy Palino grimaced. He knew that he'd messed up bad. He realized that he could have blown the whole operation if he had ended up in the hands of law enforcement. Almost as bad, he had lost Turner. His one job, priority, objective, was to keep track of Ryan Turner, keep him alive, and keep him out of the FBI's hands. He didn't know what the ultimate plan was, but he knew that for now Turner was supposed to be kept alive. At a stoplight, the car came to a halt behind a dense line of traffic. The driver looked into the rear-view mirror through his sunglasses.

"If it wasn't for me, Randy, you know where you would be right now? Your sorry self would be in the hands of both the LAPD *and* the FBI."

The car remained stationary, and Palino clenched his jaw at a sudden rush of pain in his head.

When the pain slightly ceased, Palino said, "I know, I was in a tough spot, Z. I didn't know what to do…"

"You don't get it, do you?" the driver spat out. "You can beg, you can plead all you want, but you screwed up and you screwed up big time."

Palino pursed his lips and tried shifting his body into a more comfortable position on the back seats.

"Zarius, it-it could've been a lot worse! I'm…"

Zarius Zaloma slammed his fist on the dash. "Oh, really? Because I don't think that it could have gone much worse. For example, Randy…where is Ryan Turner?"

CHAPTER THIRTY-SIX

Kyle slowly stood to his feet. He felt weak and shaky, and leaned against the wall for balance. Kuron was directly across from him on the floor, leaning his back against the wall. Kyle kept himself propped up against the wall until his vision fully returned and his head stopped aching. He staggered over to Kuron, who was holding his lower leg and cursing.

"Kuron?" Kyle said, crouching down beside Kuron. "What happened, man?"

Kuron looked over at his friend.

"I got shot in the leg, Kyle. Don't know who did it. It all went down so fast. I don't know what is going on, man. I don't know what happened."

Kyle looked toward the lobby to find heads peering over couches, chairs, and tables. He knew in an instant that they were law enforcement.

"Are any of you going to do something?" Kyle yelled out at the men and women in the lobby.

About a half-dozen police officers snapped out of the trance they were in and, guns in hand, ran toward Kyle and Kuron. Three of the six, stopped next to the FBI agents, but said and did nothing. Kyle was fuming.

"Quit standing around! Help the man out!" Kyle said, gesturing toward Kuron.

Kuron nodded in agreement. The officers glanced around nervously then knelt next to Kuron. Kyle propped himself back up against the wall as a sudden surge of pain rushed through his skull. When the pain faded, Kyle began his search. He had to find out what was going on, and he had to fast. The first things he discovered were the grenade shells lying upon the hallway floor. There were two of them. Kyle lifted them off the floor, one in each hand, and examined them.

Smoke grenades.

He had seen many smoke grenades before but had only come across these style of smoke grenades twice. Both times, he was dealing with Cybris Caine.

Kyle stuffed the grenades into his jacket pockets and made his way for the lobby. Three police officers crouched down around a body. Kyle walked up behind the group of police.

"What happened here?"

All three officers stood and took a step back. Lying face down on the floor was a gray-haired policeman in a navy-blue uniform. Kyle bent down, and then rolled the dead officer onto his back.

"Wow," Kyle said under his breath.

The old policeman's chest was drenched in blood, and a gaping hole spread across his chest. Kyle shook his head from side to side. He looked each police officer in the eye.

"So, is someone going to tell me what happened here?"

A tall woman in a navy-blue police uniform spoke up.

"Yes, we got a call. The woman who called said there was a little man who was holding two other men at gunpoint. And she said she was here in the hotel, first floor. We were all at lunch together, just across the block. So, we arrived here, but it was the other way around; your friend was holding a little man by the throat and had him shoved up against the wall in that hallway. You, of course, were lying there on the floor. The chief yelled out at your friend, and then it was absolute chaos from there. The Chief's chest practically blew apart, and he died right there on the spot. We had no idea what to do. It caught all of us off guard. Before we could react, the hallway began to be filled with a thick, vile-smelling smoke. We all ran and took cover behind the closest object we could find. We couldn't see a thing down the hallway. The smoke finally cleared somewhat, and now here we are."

Kyle scratched his chin, trying to fully process the story.

"And you have no idea who the shooter was?"

All three officers shook their heads.

"What about the little guy that attacked us? Where is he?"

The woman, who had spoken up earlier, spoke again,

"We have no idea," she said. "Before the smoke, he was there on the floor. When the smoke started to clear, he was gone."

"I see," Kyle said. "Thanks, ma'am. Thank you all for coming, and I'm sorry for your loss."

Kyle crouched over the dead Chief of Police's body.

"He was obviously shot from the front," he mumbled to himself.

Kyle stood to his feet. He started to move out toward Kuron but stopped short. He had completely forgotten about the young woman who was in room 108. He turned around sharply.

"Guys?" he said calling out to the policemen he had just spoken with. Who was it that made the phone call earlier?"

This time a short, Hispanic male officer spoke up.

"It was a young woman," he said. "We don't know what her name was. She said she was staying here at the hotel."

Not saying a word, Kyle turned back to the hallway and broke into a trot. His sights were set on room 108. He reached the doorway to the room and had a queasy feeling in his stomach. He took a deep breath and stepped across the threshold.

Kyle's heart instantly dropped. The young woman, who had been alive and well just moments ago, was lying on top of the bed, her head resting on a pillow soaked in red blood. There was a bloody, gaping hole directly in the middle of her forehead. The woman's eyes stared blankly up at the ceiling. Kyle caught the lump in his throat and walked deeper into the room. He moved over to the bedside. The woman was beautiful. She had high cheek bones, a perfect little nose, and long jet-black hair. She was slender and had to have been in her early twenties. As he gazed down at the woman, he noticed a white iPhone lying next to her bloody head. He reached over and picked it up.

He pressed the home button, and to his surprise the phone didn't have a passcode. The cell phone's home screen appeared, showing various apps and icons. Kyle navigated his way to the phone's caller list. As he had expected, the most recent call was an outgoing call to 9-1-1. She was the reason the police showed up. Still, this did not answer any of the questions floating around inside of Kyle's head. He proceeded on to search through the phone's text messages. There was nothing out of the ordinary. There was no sort of communication with Ryan. He opened the most recent string of messages. The conversation was held with "Momma." He began to read through them.

"Have you gotten a room yet, baby?" –Momma
"Yes, I found one."
"Cheap?"-Momma
"Very! Ha-ha. A nice man purchased a room for me. He was a crazy looking Dodger's fan, but he was very sweet. (:"

"Aw, what a good man. That is awesome. Much love, Kendra. Be safe, baby."-Momma

"Love you Momma"

Kyle shook his head and tossed the cell phone back onto the bed. Ryan was slick; real slick. He always had been. Just like that, Ryan had given them the slip.

"Wow," Kyle said, rubbing the back of his neck.

He knew he had just gotten played like a drum. Ryan used his credit card, luring Kuron and Kyle in, and he gave his room to a random woman. Then, he left in a hurry. Clever. Simple, but clever. Kyle felt like an idiot. He should have known that Ryan was too smart to just nonchalantly use his credit card right now. Besides, why would he have done so after withdrawing such a large sum of cash? Kyle felt so gullible, so stupid. He should've known that Ryan wasn't going to be that easy to catch.

Kyle walked over to the large window in the room. He stepped on broken glass scattered across the floor and pulled back the curtains to conclude that the window was broken. He rubbed his head vigorously with his hand, as pain began to surge through his skull again. Usually he instantly recognized details like the broken glass, but he was off his game. The head injury wasn't helping his cause much. Kyle did have some assumptions in his head though. He assumed that whoever had killed this woman also killed the LAPD Police Chief. He guessed the shooter had broken through this window, and most likely had done so by shooting his way through it. He guessed it would only take a little bit of searching the room to find the bullets stuck in a wall or furniture. Cybris Caine had a major part to play in all of this. Kyle knew that for a fact. He also knew Ryan had slipped away, and that is what bothered him the most.

"This isn't going too good, is it?"

Kyle spun around to find Kuron standing in the doorway of the room.

"Yeah, not really," Kyle replied.

"The leg isn't as bad as it looks," Kuron said. "I wouldn't let them take me to the hospital. They are going to find me some crutches though."

Kyle nodded his head. "I hope not. If that's the case, as soon as you get your crutches let's go home. We are more than done here."

CHAPTER THIRTY-SEVEN

The flight's duration was 12 hours long, and with Rome being 9 hours ahead of Los Angeles, it was 5 p.m. when the plane finally landed gracefully onto the runway at the Fiumicino Airport in Rome, Italy. Having no luggage or personal belongings, Ryan was off the plane, out of the airport, and stepping into a white Italian cab in little to no time. He plopped himself into the backseat, and in his best Italian, told the driver to take him to the Rome Cavalieri Hotel.

"Cavalieri?" the driver asked.

Ryan nodded in reply. The car shifted into drive and rolled forward. It felt good, really good, to finally be on the ground in Rome after the non-stop, 6,347-mile-long flight. He knew he had given the FBI the slip…at least for now. But it felt great, even if the feeling was only going to be temporary. The flight gave him time to really think, and time to finally sleep. He replayed the past 44 hours countless times in his head. There were many questions, many holes, but there were some things he knew for sure: Kyle and Kuron had chased him down, the FBI would track him down again soon enough, and above all else, he knew that he had to find Cybris Commodus Caine.

He had the strong, indescribable feeling that if he found Caine, he would find some answers. So, he would take advantage of his time in Rome, and give himself a chance to think, work things out inside his head, and hopefully get a lead on Caine. Ryan had the feeling too that if he was patient enough, Cybris Caine just might find him. Rome was as good of a place as any to find Caine. It was where he and his

unidentified wife supposedly lived, and where the two owned
the world renowned La Pergola restaurant, which sits atop the
Rome Cavalieri, Waldorf Astoria Hotels & Resort. The taxi
came to a halt, and Ryan looked out his window to see the
front doors of the beautiful hotel. Ryan payed the driver in
cash, then shook his hand. He exited the little Ford car and
walked into the hotel. Standing behind the front desk was a
stocky young man. In a thick, but friendly-sounding voice,
the man said something in Italian.

"Parlo in ingles," Ryan said.

The man at the front desk nodded. Ryan noticed the
nametag on the man's chest read "Felicio."

"Felicio," Ryan said, shaking Felicio's hand, "one room,
please."

Ryan held up one finger. Felicio nodded, and then typed
away at his computer for a moment. Felicio shrugged.

"Only one room? Five-hundred dollars."

He had expected the high price, so he nodded, and
handed the man $1,000.

Ryan held up two fingers. "Two nights."

Felicio nodded, got Ryan's name which Ryan said was
Jamison Lloyd, then handed Ryan his hotel room card.

"Three-zero-two," Felicio said.

Ryan shook Felicio's hand. "Grazie."

Ryan entered the closest elevator and ascended upward
to the third floor. The doors slid open, and to his right was
room 302. Once inside, Ryan was in awe. Inside wasn't a
single room, but instead a beautiful suite. The floor was a
shiny white marble, and beautiful paintings hung on the
walls. The suite consisted of three rooms. The first was a
kitchen/hang-out area. As Ryan walked into the suite, to his
left was the kitchen section of the room. In the section were a

decent-sized refrigerator and freezer, a large sink, cabinets and drawers, an oven, a stove top, and a microwave. Directly across from him was a huge recliner that sat across from a large flat-screen television, and next to the recliner was a sofa. An entryway was located next to the television, and through the entry was a bedroom. The bedroom was fabulous. It consisted of a king-sized bed, covered with white silk pillows, sheets, and bed spread. To the right of the bed was a long window looking out over Rome. To the left of the bed was a nightstand with a gold lamp on top of it. To the left of that nightstand was a doorway leading into a bathroom that contained two sinks, a hot tub, a pearl white toilet, and a large walk-in shower.

"Wow," Ryan said aloud as he entered the bathroom.

After a long shower, Ryan freshened up, threw on his one pair of underwear, and jumped into the bed. Within minutes, Ryan was sound asleep.

CHAPTER THIRTY-EIGHT

Ryan slept hard throughout the night and didn't awake until six o'clock the ensuing morning. He washed his face, and then threw on his clothes. Once dressed, he made his way down to the first floor. Just outside his room, he passed by a young man who was conversing with someone on his cell phone. Ryan nodded to the man and made his way over to the elevator. Once the elevator stopped on the first floor, he went into the dining area where a free continental breakfast was being served. There were various choices of food, but Ryan decided on a Brioche bun and a cup of black coffee. A woman wearing an apron appeared next to Ryan and she filled a basket with Biscotti. His stomach rumbled at the site of the Biscotti. He grabbed two from the basket and smiled at the woman.

"Grazie," he said.

The woman nodded and smiled.

Ryan took a bite of the biscotti and made his way out of the hotel's front doors. What he didn't see was the apron-wearing woman behind him as she pulled out a cell phone. He didn't hear her, as in a hushed voice she spoke into the phone.

The woman spoke one single sentence in fluent Italian, saying, "Sta lasciando l'hotel."

She didn't wait for a reply and ended the phone call.

Ryan stepped out into the cool morning air and took a deep breath. He walked around the plaza, and no more than a minute later took a left and walked toward the D'Aloja Alessandra clothing store.

He also did not notice a man, who was trailing close behind him. The same man had just carried out a phone call with the apron-wearing woman inside of the Cavalieri Hotel. Everyone that knew him called him by the simple name of "X". X was a retired Russian military man. He had previously been a top Spetsnaz militant. He was above average height, standing just over six feet tall. He had broad shoulders and a wide chest. At 49 years old, he had salt and pepper colored hair and a few noticeable wrinkles upon his cheeks and forehead. X now wore a plain gray hoodie, matching sweats, and black tennis shoes. He had aimed to capture the look of a man taking an early morning walk. He kept his distance behind Ryan, trying to avoid looking suspicious. As Ryan made his way from the hotel and through the front doors of the clothing store, not once did he pay any attention to X.

CHAPTER THIRTY-NINE

There was a third individual that was paying extra close attention to Ryan. This individual was young, male, and did not have any sort of affiliation with X, nor the woman from the Cavalieri dining area. He had short, dark, messy-styled hair. He was a couple inches under six feet tall, and thin. Like X, he too was a military man, but had served the opposite side of the world. He was a decorated U.S. Army Ranger and resigned from the military due to personal reasons. He went by the name of John Drexel. Now, here he was, in the great city of Rome, trailing a rogue FBI agent by the name of Ryan Turner.

He too had purchased a room at the Cavalieri hotel. He demanded to have a room on the third floor and hoped to get one as close to Agent Turner's as possible. Room 310 was as close as he could get. Merely minutes ago, John had slipped his way into Ryan's room as Ryan opened his room's door and left. John stood next to Ryan's room, pretended to be speaking on the phone, and just as Ryan turned his back, John stuck his foot into the room, and stopped the door just before it closed shut. He continued in deep conversation with himself until Ryan entered the elevator. That is when he slipped into the room, and as fast as possible, installed a tiny device onto the smoke detector that was positioned on the ceiling just above the king-sized bed, and the same kind of device onto the smoke detector that hung in the living room type area. He had bugged and wire-tapped rooms before, so this process was easy for him. He was in and out of the room in a matter of minutes. The bug on the smoke detectors transmitted information straight to John's cell phone and would allow him to both see and hear the things going on in room 302.

The moment that he was done, he snuck out of the room, and sprinted down the stairwell to the lobby. As he busted through the stairwell door, he spotted Ryan Turner who was walking out through the hotel's front doors. John walked briskly out the lobby doors, and then kept his distance behind Ryan. He did not notice or give any thought to the man, who went by the name of X. X didn't pay any attention to him either. John casually strolled along behind Ryan until the agent entered the big clothing store. There was no need to follow him in, so John sat down on a bench outside the store's front doors. He pulled out his cell phone and pretended to dial a number.

"Hey!" he said into the phone. "Yes…yeah, I will wait here…can't wait to see you too…see you in a while…goodbye."

With that, John ended the fake call. Just as he slipped the phone back into his jeans' pocket, a man with broad shoulders and salt and pepper colored hair sat next to him on the bench. The two men exchanged glances, smiled at one another, and at the same time, each of them then grabbed a newspaper from the pocket of their hoodies and began to read. Surprised, they looked at one another again, laughed, and then continued with their reading; each man completely unaware that the other was also waiting for Ryan Turner.

CHAPTER FORTY

Ryan exited the D'Aloja Alessandra clothing store with four bags in hand. One bag contained a charcoal colored *Peter Millar Flynn* dress suit. Another bag held four pairs of underwear, and four pairs of black socks. The third bag contained two V-neck shirts that were solid black in color, a pair of khaki pants, and one pair of gray wool-sweats. Within the fourth bag was a pair of nice black sneakers, a deodorant stick, a cheap toothbrush, and a tube of toothpaste. Ryan walked casually back to the hotel, taking his time. He had always loved Italy, particularly Rome. He couldn't decide if he naturally felt drawn to Rome because he was born there, or because of his fascination with the Italian culture and the city of Rome as a whole. He had only visited Rome a few times, one of which was with Laura on their honeymoon. Ryan's mind wandered, and he thought of Laura. He thought of Kayleen. He thought of how perfect his life had become. He thought of how Laura had taken away all the pain and all the bad memories from his past that had forever haunted him. In that moment, he wished somehow, someway that he could snap his fingers, and everything would be back to the way it was before the dreadful day at J.J. Mauer's home.

Ryan approached the huge fountain at the front of the Cavalieri hotel and sat on the edge of it. He placed his bags next to his feet on the ground. It was almost as if he was back at home. He could feel Laura's touch, and hear Kayleen's laugh. He stared blankly at the hotel doors in front of him as his mind continued to wander. He could smell Laura's perfume, and see Kayleen playing in the backyard with a pink and white soccer ball. Ryan could picture himself now sitting in the living room, while watching an NFL football game. He could smell the scent of Laura's cooking coming from the kitchen in his home.

His mind travelled back to the last conversation he had with Laura, which took place before he left for his office to speak to J.J. Mauer:

Laura had just finished showering when he and Kayleen returned to the house. Her hair was damp and looked extra dark. She wore nothing but a towel. Not a touch of makeup appeared on her face. Her natural beauty was radiating. She was standing over the kitchen sink as she washed dirty dishes. She smiled her heart-warming smile as he and Kayleen walked in. Kayleen sprinted over to her mother. Squealing, she threw her arms around Laura's legs.

"Mommy! Mommy! We got a puppy. Look, look!"

Kayleen pointed at Ryan, who was holding the dog carrier containing the three-legged dachshund puppy.

Ryan smiled a sheepish smile and shrugged. "What can I say? You two girls have your way with me."

Kayleen ran back over to Ryan, as he closed the front door.

"Let him out," she said. "Let's show him to Mommy!"

Ryan set the carrier down and opened its door. The little dog hobbled out and immediately began licking Kayleen's legs. She squealed and bent over to scoop the dog up into her arms. Ryan could still vividly picture Kayleen in that moment. Her blue eyes shined bright. She smiled a huge, genuine smile as she carried the puppy over to Laura.

"Well, it's a mighty cute little dog, Kay," Laura said.

Proud as can be, Kayleen handed the puppy over to her mom. Laura smiled as she cradled the puppy.

"Well, Kay," she said, "do you have a name for him?"

Kayleen scratched her chin, and looked up at the ceiling, appearing to be in deep thought.

"I don't know," Kay said.

Ryan was standing next to Laura now. He kissed her on the cheek.

"Now, what about you, Daddy? Do you have a name for him?" Kayleen asked.

Ryan couldn't help but smirk.

"Yes, I actually do," he said. "I was thinking Tripod."

"Yes!" Kayleen exclaimed, unaware of what a tripod actually was.

"Tripod it is!" Laura proclaimed.

Unable to hold back her laughter, she handed the puppy back over to Kayleen. In a laughing fit, she covered her face with her hands.

"And what's wrong with you?" Ryan asked, throwing an arm around Laura's shoulders.

Laura playfully punched him in the chest. "You think you're so funny, don't you? You realize that name is going to stick now, right?"

Ryan chuckled. "I sure do! Hey," he said, changing the subject, "I have to go to the office and meet with Mauer really quick. Just drop Kay off at daycare if I don't get back before you leave to work. You can leave little Tripod here in the house. Just put him in the little carrier."

"Is everything okay?" Laura asked, looking into Ryan's eyes.

Staring down into the Cavailieri's beautiful fountain's waters, Ryan wished now that he had actually known that everything was going to be okay. Instead, looking back now, what he said ended up being a lie.

"Yes, everything's okay. I don't think there's any kind of emergency."

"There better not be," Laura said.

At that moment Ryan kissed Laura and walked to the front door. Just as he opened it Laura called after him.

"Ryan?" she said.

Ryan looked over his shoulder.

"I love you," Laura said.

"I love you too, Laura."

Ryan ran his fingers through the fountain's waters. Coins shimmered at the bottom of the fountain. He punched the water, and then stood to his feet. If only he could go back in time. If only things were back to normal. However, as of now, there was nothing he could do to make things go back to the way they were. There was no way to travel back in time. There was no way to erase what had happened. He snapped out of his trance and lifted his shopping bags off the ground. He had things to take care of. He didn't have time to reminisce and mourn. He had some work to do.

Ryan took his newly acquired clothes to his hotel room. He happily stripped off the clothes he had on, and threw on a new pair of underwear, the khaki pants, one of the new T-shirts, one pair of black socks, and the new dress shoes. It felt great to wear a fresh set of clothes. He tossed the old clothes in a garbage can and placed the rest of the newly purchased clothes in the room's large closet. Ryan sat down in the suite's nice recliner. He pulled a wad of cash out from his pocket. Three-thousand dollars he had drawn from the bank in Los Angeles. He counted out the bills in his hand. After the expenses of a plane ticket to Rome, a three-night stay at this hotel, and bags of expensive clothes, Ryan now had $1,150 left. He knew it would be plenty enough to cover the rest of his time here. Ryan could only imagine Laura's surprise and anger if she checked her bank account's status and saw a $3,000 withdraw. He and Laura made a decent amount of money, but Laura was smart, tight, and very conscientious of their savings.

Ryan immediately tried to refrain from thinking of Laura. He stood from his seat and made his way out the door. He had big plans for the day and decided he might as well start early. He needed to get a lead on Caine, and he needed a gun.

CHAPTER FORTY-ONE

Cindy C. Harrison sat at the foot of her bed with her
rose gold cell phone held up to her ear.

"I know," she said as she looked at her watch to find that
the time read 9:04 p.m. "I know, Laura. I am so sorry, girl... I
can't even imagine. I cannot begin to tell you how truly sorry
I am."

Cindy listened to the sobs coming from the other end of
the phoneline. She really was sorry. She could not imagine
being in Laura's shoes. Laura loved Ryan. Cindy had never
seen a person love someone like Laura loved Ryan. The love
they shared for each other, and the love they both showed for
little Kayleen was strong and real. Since the Turner's
marriage, Cindy and Laura had grown close.

"Yes," Cindy said. "Just remember that I am always here
for you... Always... You're welcome, girl. Laura, you are a
strong woman. You will get through this; I know you will...
Yes... Yes. Let's just get your mind off this for a sec, okay?"

Cindy grabbed her stomach and cringed, then grabbed a
pain pill from a container next to her side, popped the capsule
into her mouth and swallowed it without any assistance of
water.

"No, he isn't home yet. He and Kuron should be
returning here pretty soon."

Cindy looked out her window. As if on cue, she could
hear a car door shutting just outside the house. Cindy smiled.

"The appointment is tomorrow, right, Laura?" she asked.
"Oh, okay. I thought so. But my memory is not so good. I am
getting pretty old, you know?" Cindy chuckled. "And what
time should I meet you there tomorrow afternoon? Is 2:15, or

so, okay? Sounds good, dear. I'll probably take the subway. Are you excited?"

Cindy waited for a reply.

"You guess? Girl, come on now! What about Kayleen?"

Cindy winced as another wave of pain shot through her abdomen.

"Oh, I bet she is!" Cindy replied. "You two should come over for dinner tomorrow night, you know, after the appointment... Intruding? Girl, please. We love you! You are always welcomed here. I mean that."

On the other end of the phoneline, Laura thanked her. Kyle walked into the bedroom. He immediately grinned from ear to ear and posed up against the wall with his hand on his hip. Cindy pulled the phone away from her head as she giggled.

"Laura," Cindy said back into the cell phone, "I'll see you tomorrow. Stay strong. Love you, girl."

Cindy waited for Laura's reply then ended the call.

Kyle was still smiling. He was exhausted, mentally and physically, but Cindy could always brighten his day. She sparked life in him. They fueled each other's inner flames. They understand one another and jived the moment they met. Kyle looked at her now, and still saw the same woman he married just over a year ago. Cindy was African-American and stood at a stunning 5 feet and 11 inches tall. She had long, slender legs and could see eye to eye with Kyle. She was a beautiful woman. Kyle made his way over to the bed and Cindy stood to her feet. She threw her arms around her husband and squeezed him tight. After a moment, Cindy pulled away from the embrace. She placed her hands on Kyle's forearms.

"I missed you!"

Kyle kissed her on the cheek. "I sure missed you too."

Kyle reached behind Cindy's legs, wrapped an arm around the back of her knees, and used his other arm to wrap around her shoulders. Kyle lifted her up and set her softly back onto the bed. He leaned over her and kissed her softly. He gazed into his wife's dark brown eyes as he pulled away from her slightly.

"I'll never get over how lucky I was to have met you."

"Oh, please," Cindy said, "I was the lucky one. We've given each other the wonderful lives we now have. We have filled holes in each other's lives and made each other stronger. I'll always be grateful for that. My brother is just as thankful. But, aside from this mushy stuff, I mean, I know you haven't seen me in a while, but did you find him?"

"We knew he was in LA, but not once did we even see him. He gave us the slip. So, Kuron and I flew across the entire country for no reason."

Cindy laid her head on Kyle's shoulder. "It will be okay. You will find him. Don't you worry."

CHAPTER FORTY-TWO

The same words came out of Malaya Taylor's mouth as she and Kuron sat across from each other at the small coffee table in their dining room.

"It will be okay. You'll find him. Don't you worry." Malaya reached across the table to place a hand on top of Kuron's.

"Malaya?" Kuron said, pulling his hand out from under Malaya's.

"Yes?"

"It doesn't seem right."

"What doesn't?" Malaya asked.

Kuron rested his chin on his fists. "All of it. This whole situation with Ryan. Something is just really rubbing me wrong about it all."

Malaya nodded. "I know exactly what you mean, baby. I never want to get between you and your work, and I never want to question what you're doing at work, but I think you're wasting your time, Kuron. Something has been telling me that you are wasting your time going after Ryan."

Kuron stared down at the table. "Yeah, I don't know. The evidence is…"

"Kuron," Malaya said cutting off her husband, "we have been friends with Ryan for years. Eight years we've known Ryan. Do you really believe Ryan would kill Mr. Mauer? Do you really believe that?"

Kuron shook his head from side to side. "I don't. And if he did, there is more to the story. If he did do what the evidence says he did, then there must be a reason why. There must be someone behind what he did, who forced him to do this. I don't know. I really don't know. Even that wouldn't make much sense. I don't know what to think anymore...Kyle saw him there, Malaya. The bullet that killed Mauer came from Ryan's Glock. Plus, he ran. Why would he run? And the letter written to Laura, what was that about? Kyle got the forensic evidence reported back to him when we were on our way back home from Los Angeles. The only other fingerprints inside that house, aside from Mauer's, were Ryan's. Why though? Why kill Mauer? And then why kill the Shambles? How did they deserve that? The evidence in this case speaks volumes, but none of it makes sense to me."

Malaya looked Kuron in the eyes. She could see the true pain and confusion written all across his face.

"I know, baby. I know. It is hard to picture Ryan, a friend, as a cold-blooded killer. It just doesn't make sense. It's hard to swallow."

Kuron stood from his chair and wandered over to the kitchen sink. He placed his hands on the edge of the sink and stared out the window that was placed just above the sink. He stared blankly into the dark night. His mind was reeling. Malaya pursed her lips as she stood to her feet too. She walked over to Kuron and placed a hand on his left shoulder.

"So, I think what you and I both are feeling, and what we are both trying to say is…"

"Ryan was set up," Kuron said, finishing Malaya's sentence.

CHAPTER FORTY-THREE

Ryan's heart beat hard against his chest. It was hard for him to control his breathing, and refrain from being excited. He was positive that he had found a lead on Caine and found a gun all at once. It was just under an hour long walk to Vatican City from his hotel. He could've taken the trolley or called a cab, but he enjoyed walking. He wanted to put himself out there; he wanted to expose himself. He had hoped he would draw someone that worked under Caine. As he wandered through the Gardens of Vatican City, a certain man caught his eye. There was nothing too out of the ordinary about him; aside from the fact that it happened to be the fourth time Ryan saw the man that day. Ryan stood in front of the Fountain of the Sacrament with his hands clasped behind him. Out of the corner of his eye, Ryan could see him. The man. He wandered aimlessly behind Ryan, gazing at trees and bushes.

The man was older and had salt and pepper colored hair. He had broad shoulders and was in good physical shape. The first time Ryan saw him was when he went to the D'Aloja Alessandra clothing store early that morning. The man was right outside the Cavalieri Hotel, wandering around near the hotel's fountain. Then, even though he didn't pay much attention to it at the time, he noticed the same man sitting outside the clothing store. Then when he first got to the Vatican Gardens, he noticed the man trailing close behind him gazing at flowers while talking into a cell phone. This was the fourth time. There was no way these meetings were a coincidence. Still, Ryan pretended not to see the man. Instead, he had come up with a plan. He pulled some cash out of his left pants' pocket and wadded it up. He turned his body so that his right side was to the man who had been stalking him. He put the wad of cash up to his left ear and imitated a phone conversation.

Extra loud, and in a worried voice he said, "I will be right there!"

He hoped that the man fell for the act.

With that, Ryan returned the money to his pocket and broke into a sprint. He ran hard. He noticed a security guard standing on the path next to some bushes and veered in the guard's direction. Ryan pretended to stumble and fell into the officer.

"Sorry, sorry," Ryan said.

Ryan hugged the security guard, and smoothly grabbed the officer's badge that hung from the man's belt. He stuffed the badge in his right pocket, stepped back and told the officer to have a good day.

"My mother. Sick!" he said, and then continued to run toward the Sala Clementina museum.

He ran until he came to a split in the path just in front of the Sala Clementina. He chose to go down the left path. He slipped off the sidewalk and hid behind a tree, peering around the tree back toward the way he came. He caught a few looks from random tourists, but they continued on their way, paying no mind to Ryan. Ryan waited. Fifteen seconds went by…then 20…then 25… and there the man was, trotting down the sidewalk toward the Sala Clementina. Ryan held his breath as the man stopped in his tracks at the place where the path split. There were people everywhere. The man began to swim through the crowd and walk toward the world-renowned museum. Ryan crossed his fingers, hoping the man would come his way. He did. He chose the left path leading to the museum. At the fountain, Ryan had noticed the man was wearing a jacket. He guessed the man had a handgun, and he guessed it would be inside his jacket or in his waistband. As the mystery man got close, Ryan stepped out from behind the tree and bumped into the man head on.

Instead of apologizing, Ryan threw open the man's jacket with one hand, and quickly frisked the inside of the jacket with the other.

Nothing.

In a split second he reached around the man's waist and found a pistol stuffed into the waistband of his pants. Ryan removed the gun, grabbed the man by the wrist, and spun around the man until he was behind him. Ryan shoved the pistol into the man's back.

"Walk."

The man did what he was told. Ryan kept the gun pressed up high on the man's back, where if he had to fire a shot, the bullet would likely do some damage to the guy's heart and ultimately kill him.

"You're making a bad mistake," the man muttered as they approached the museum.

Ryan said nothing.

"Go left," Ryan ordered as they got close to the steps of the museum.

The man turned left. Ryan kept the gun's muzzle pressed against the guy's back. Ryan's luck continued to show itself. Just then a cab pulled up to the curb next to the museum.

"Hey! Hey!" Ryan yelled as a short red-headed man and blonde woman, who were holding hands, started to enter the cab.

The couple turned around.

"Polizia!" Ryan cried out.

The couple froze. Just then, the man that Ryan was escorting spun on his heels and swung at Ryan's face. He almost connected. The man was quick, but Ryan was quicker. Ryan ducked, avoiding the punch. He popped back up and swung the butt of the handgun, connecting it with the man's jaw. The man dropped to the ground immediately. He was out; unconscious. He fell hard onto his back and Ryan bent down over him.

"Polizia!" he yelled back at the couple by the cab.

The two exchanged glances. Ryan motioned the couple over, showing them the badge that he had stolen. The couple trotted over. Ryan lifted the unconscious man up by his shoulders and motioned to the couple for them to help. The man with the woman grabbed the unconscious man by the legs, and Ryan then motioned with his head over to the cab. Reluctantly, the red-headed man assisted Ryan in carrying the unresponsive individual over to the cab. They slid the mystery man's limp body into the backseat of the cab and the cab driver turned around in surprise. The driver was a woman, and her eyes were as large as saucers. Ryan flashed the security guard badge at her. She sighed. Ryan threw the back door of the cab closed. He nodded at the couple who had helped him and handed the red-headed man two one-hundred-dollar bills. The red-head looked surprised but smiled a warm smile and showed the money to the blonde woman who was with him. Ryan opened the cab's right back door and slid in next to the unconscious man. He laid the man's legs on his lap.

"Cavalieri Hotel," Ryan said. "Veloce. Polizia!"

The car shifted into gear and the cab sped away.

CHAPTER FORTY-FOUR

In 15 minutes, the cab arrived at the Cavalieri Hotel. Somehow, the man had only regained consciousness once. About halfway through the ride, he began to wake up, but Ryan immediately pistol-whipped him across the side of the head and knocked him out cold again. Now was the tricky part: finding a way to get the man up to room 302 without anyone seeing and becoming suspicious. Ryan stepped out of the cab, and then walked to the other side of it. He opened the door and grabbed the unconscious man by his arms. Ryan started to drag the man out of the car when he heard a voice behind him.

"Need some help there?"

Ryan glanced over his shoulder to see a young dark-haired man smoking a cigarette. Saying Ryan was surprised is an understatement.

The man smoking a cigarette spoke up again, saying, "I know how it goes having friends who like to have a good time. They get pretty trashed sometimes."

Ryan was thrown off guard and began to stutter. "Y-yea-yeah!" he said. "Thank you. I appreciate it."

"No problem," the man said, as he tossed his cigarette on the ground and stomped on it. "My name is John."

With John's help, Ryan got the salt and pepper haired man out of the cab. John removed his sunglasses that he wore on his face.

"He might need these so that we don't get too much grief from the hotel employees."

John then placed the glasses on the unconscious man's face.

"Good thinking, man," Ryan said.

Ryan stood on the unconscious man's right, John stood on the left, as they both held the man up in a standing position. Ryan slung the man's right arm over his shoulders, and John swung the man's left arm over his shoulders. The two then drug the guy through the hotel lobby, into the elevator, and into room 302. John helped Ryan lay the unconscious man onto the couch in the room.

"Is there anything else I can do for you, buddy?"

Ryan shook his head as he gazed down at the man on his couch.

"No," Ryan said. "Thanks again. And the name is Ryan; Ryan Turner."

"Good to meet you, Mr. Turner," John said, as the two shook hands.

"Are you staying here at the hotel?" Ryan asked.

"Yeah, I'm here for a few nights," John replied.

Ryan nodded. "Well, hey, if you want, I'll buy you dinner tomorrow night upstairs."

"At the La Pergola?" John asked. "How could I pass that up?"

Ryan chuckled. "Yeah, it's a pretty fancy place. I'll make the reservation for tomorrow night at 7."

"Sounds good, man. Thank you! I am here on a business trip, so that will be a nice change of pace for me."

"No," Ryan said. "Thank you, John. You don't realize how much of a help you really were."

John nodded, then left the room.

Ryan gazed down at the unconscious man.

Who is this guy?

Ryan retrieved a sharp steak knife from a drawer within the room's kitchen space, went into the bathroom and got a

towel. He cut the towel into two long strips. He returned to
the living room area and tied the mystery man's ankles
together with one towel strip, and then tied the man's wrists
together behind the man's back with the other strip. Ryan
grabbed the man and sat him up in a sitting position. He
returned to the kitchen area, retrieved a glass bowl, and filled
it with cold water. He walked back over to the couch and
threw the water on the man's face and slapped his cheeks.
The man's body jerked violently. His eyes darted open. He
began to moan and thrash around.

"Good morning, sunshine," Ryan said.

The man said nothing.

"Tell me, why were you following me and who are
you?"

The man smirked. "They call me X. You know who I
am."

The name immediately rang a bell. Ryan remembered
who he was. He was one of Cybris Caine's top men, and
Ryan now had him in his grasp.

"Oh, yeah, the retired Russian military man. You work
for Caine. Yeah, I do know you. You're a piece of work."

X smirked again but said nothing.

"Why were you following me? Where is Caine?"

X shrugged. "I don't have to tell you anything. I would
die first."

"Don't tempt me into making that happen," Ryan
growled.

X laughed uncontrollably.

"Talk!" Ryan said, grabbing X by the throat.

X then spit into Ryan's face. Ryan was fuming now. He
reared back and with his right hand punched X hard across
the face.

"You know, I am going to give you one more chance. Where is Caine?"

X chuckled to himself. "He is in Rome. I'll tell you that much. And I will tell you, you made a mistake doing this to me. Mr. Caine won't spare you now. And there is no way you're ever going to be able to find him. He will send men after you, and it will get ugly fast. Seriously, you are in *his* hotel, in the same building as *his* restaurant. What is your end game here? And just saying, Turner, I have got dibs on your pretty little wife. Her and I are going to have some fun. And I have some friends of mine that will buy your little daughter for a pretty penny for sure. It'll be great, I'll tell you that."

That pushed Ryan past the point. He had had enough with this scumbag.

"Honestly?" Ryan said. "I was giving you a chance to live. I was giving you a chance to work with me. I really was. But, it looks like that isn't going to happen, is it?"

X smirked but didn't say a word. Ryan pulled a cell phone out from his pocket.

"Because, you see, X, I have got everything I need right here in the palm of my hand."

X cursed under his breath. "You have no idea what you are doing."

"No, I know *exactly* what I am doing. I'm going to send Caine a little message, and maybe he'll realize I mean business."

"Oh yeah? And how are you…"

Before X could finish his sentence, Ryan quickly grabbed X by his head and with one smooth, hard movement, snapped the man's neck. Just like that, the man by the name of X was dead. Ryan used the phone to snap a picture of the limp body lying upon the couch and sent the photo to the number under the contact "Mr. Caine."

Under the picture Ryan typed, *"It's your move, Caine. We need to talk."*

CHAPTER FORTY-FIVE

About 40 miles away, Cybris Caine wasn't worried about receiving any sort of text message. He was busy. Caine stood in a giant basement somewhere beneath the city of Rome.

"If you want something done right, do it yourself, right? It is a very old and somewhat annoying statement, but, oh is there a lot of truth to it. Isn't that right, Randy?"

Cybris Caine leisurely paced around a wooden chair that Randy Palino was tied to. The chair sat in the middle of the basement, where there were no windows, and just a simple lightbulb hanging from the ceiling above the chair. A string hung from the bulb and dangled just above Palino's head. Palino's eyes were large as saucers and bloodshot. He squirmed in his chair, murmuring under the tape over his mouth.

"What? What is that you say?" Caine said, rubbing the barrel of a pistol up and down Palino's neck.

Palino mumbled again under the tape over his mouth.

"Oh," Caine said, "you're trying to say that I am right. Well, of course I am. When am I not right, my friend?"

Randy Palino flinched at the touch of the handgun. He tried to turn his head at the sound of a door opening and slamming behind him.

"Oh, what do we have here?" Caine said. "Mr. Zarius Zaloma, what a pleasant surprise! Nice of you to join us again."

"My pleasure," said Zaloma as he entered the room.

"Have you heard anything of Ryan's whereabouts?" Caine asked as Zarius Zaloma strolled toward him.

"Nope. Nothing."

"Hmm," Caine said, "I'll contact X here in a little bit…now, let me ask you, Zarius, what should we do with our little friend here?"

Zarius Zaloma stepped in front of Palino and stood shoulder to shoulder with Caine. He looked Randy in the eyes. Fear was written all over Randy Palino's face.

"What should we do?" Zaloma said, restating the question. "Well, Ryan was smooth. I wasn't expecting that either. He played it off well. He's smart. I think Randy should get a second shot. He's a great asset in what we have going on, sir. He's a good guy to work alongside. Plus, we are back on Turner's trail. We have him where we want him again."

Caine smirked. "You are right about a few things; Ryan did play it smooth, he did give you two the slip…but, Randy, there is a reason I pay you the big bucks to do things like this. I have lofty expectations of you. You failed me. That's all there is to it."

Caine walked up directly behind Palino and ran his fingers through the little man's hair.

"Yes, Ryan is where we want him, to a certain degree. He came to Rome of all places, which is lucky for us. But, I am not so sure about the whole 'second shot' deal."

Caine began to walk back toward Zaloma, then stopped in his tracks. He stared Zaloma in the eye. With his back to Palino, Caine whipped his Desert Eagle pistol out and fired a shot behind him, hitting Palino square in the chest. Palino jerked forward and let out a muffled scream from behind the tape over his mouth. Cybris Caine smiled at Zaloma. He moved closer to Zaloma, until their faces were inches away from one another.

"You know," Caine said, "now that I think about it, I do believe our good friend here deserves a second shot."

No sooner did the words leave Caine's mouth did he turn around and fire a second shot at Randy Palino, hitting him directly between the eyes. Caine smiled from ear to ear and felt his cell phone vibrate inside of his pocket. He removed the phone, and his heart stopped. His blood began to boil.

On the phone screen was a single picture with a text message beneath it.

'It's your move Caine. We need to talk.'

Cybris Caine clinched his left fist and yelled out. His scream echoed throughout the basement. Beads of sweat appeared upon his forehead. Caine yelled out again. He aimed his handgun at Palino and emptied the gun's clip into the dead man's head and chest. **'Click, click'.** Once the clip had been emptied, Caine stood over the dead man, panting. Sweat now ran down his cheeks and dripped off his chin.

"Zarius?" Caine spat out, staring down at the ground.

"Yes, sir?" Zaloma said, taking a step forward.

"We have a change of plans. Call Shaka."

"Will do, sir…and tell him what?"

Caine took a deep breath and turned to look at Zaloma. "Tell him to gather some of our men. Tell him to lead a raid on the Cavalieri Hotel. Ryan Turner dies tonight. He does *not* leave that hotel alive."

CHAPTER FORTY-SIX

It was 7 p.m., Rome, Italy time. Ryan sat there on his hotel bed, as comfortable as can be. He sat watching a rerun of a professional tennis tournament playing on the television across from the foot of the bed. He wore the shorts he had previously purchased that day, and one of the V-neck shirts. It had taken him awhile to decide what to do with X's body. In the end, he only had one good choice. He decided upon stuffing the body underneath the bed. It was disturbing and morbid, yes, but he didn't have too many options. For hours now, Ryan sat there constantly checking X's cell phone, hoping to receive a call or text message of some sort, but he received nothing. He was becoming restless. Repeatedly, he questioned himself and his actions.

Did I screw up? Did I really expect Caine to text back?

Ryan had murdered one of Caine's right-hand men. Caine couldn't have taken it well. Ryan was becoming *very* uneasy. Ryan tapped on the glass in his hand that contained ice water.

Why didn't I just call Caine; try to negotiate X's life.

That was the thing though, Caine wasn't one to negotiate. Ever. He was his own man; he ran on his own terms. Trying to negotiate might have only put Ryan's life more so at risk. At the same time, he still hadn't received a text or call back from Caine. He had the feeling that he had let his anger take over him; that he had snapped and acted out of rage. He had the uneasy feeling that he had really messed up.

On X's body, Ryan had found a switchblade, one full clip to X's 9mm Smith & Wesson handgun, and a small, fully-loaded, classic revolver that was tucked away in a holster located on X's right calf. The old revolver was fascinating to Ryan. He applauded X's taste in weaponry. The small handgun from X's calf was a classic Colt Detective Special .38 Revolver. Ryan reached over now and picked the revolver up from off the floor. He looked over it. The gun had been first developed in 1927 as a shortened version of the Police Positive Special handgun. It was designed to be easy to carry and conceal. The revolver had a short 2-inch barrel, along with a 6-shot cylinder. Ryan loved the little gun.

The Smith & Wesson was nice too. It was a Smith & Wesson SD9 VE, Semi-Automatic, 9mm, 4-inch barreled gun. Ryan used to carry one exactly like it when he first entered the Bureau. Between the six bullets in the Colt, the full 11-shot clip in the Smith & Wesson and the extra clip; Ryan had 28 bullets at his disposal. He just didn't realize how soon he'd end up having to make use of them.

Ryan yawned and looked at the time on the cell phone on his lap: 7:17 p.m. Ryan was totally oblivious; unaware. He didn't have the slightest idea regarding what was about to happen. He was completely and utterly blind to the fact that at that very moment, a dozen armed men had just arrived at the hotel.

They had pulled into the hotel parking lot; all crammed together in one van, and each of them with the same goal in mind: to kill Ryan Turner.

CHAPTER FORTY-SEVEN

Shaka Nukawa was 20 years old and built like an
ox. He stood at exactly 6'6" tall and weighed around 240
pounds. Just like the 11 men with him, Shaka had a skull
tattoo on the side of his left calf. He stepped out of a big
white van, stretched his legs, and breathed in the cool night
air. He wore black slacks, a gray long-sleeved shirt, and a
black topcoat. In his right hand he casually held a Glock 19.
Shaka whistled a tune as he walked toward the entry of the
Cavalieri, Waldorf Astoria Hotel. Trailing behind him were
11 armed men, who were all under his command. The group
walked through the front doors of the hotel and into the
lobby. Shaka grinned as he gazed at the small group of people
that occupied the lobby area. Every one of them stood
completely still, as if they had all suddenly turned to stone.
Their jaws hung to the ground. Shaka gave a big, friendly
wave as he continued to stroll through the lobby.

He glanced over at the front desk where the receptionist
stood behind. The receptionist wore a nametag reading:
"Felicio". Shaka gave him a wink as he passed by. Shaka
stopped abruptly in front of the elevators. A thought had
suddenly popped into his mind. He turned around to face the
group of men behind him.

"Wait right here," he said in a thick African accent.

Shaka briskly made his way over to the front desk, and
smiled at Felicio, who stood wide-eyed behind the desk.

"Hey-y-y there, Felico. I need a key."

As if he was playing a game of charades, Shaka acted
out putting a key into a door.

"Room 302," he said.

The young receptionist quickly shook his head. Shaka lifted his Glock and pointed it at Felicio's wide chest. The gesture was enough to sway Felicio. He quickly scrambled around, and then handed Shaka a keycard. Beads of sweat covered the young receptionist's forehead and nose. Shaka gladly jerked the keycard from Felicio's hand. He then reached over the counter before him, and patted Felicio on the shoulder. The young, nervous man flinched at Shaka's touch.

"Grazie," Shaka said, before making his way back over to the elevator where his men were waiting for him.

"Here, Vail."

Shaka handed the room key over to a man by the name of Vail.

"He is in room 302. We go in, and we take him out. It is that plain and simple. Vail, you and your group will go up first. I highly doubt we need all twelve of us barging in. That just gives a higher chance for collateral damage, and more likelihood of him connecting a bullet with some of us. I and my group will wait down here. The walkie-talkie I gave to you earlier? Use it to communicate with me if you need to. We'll be waiting right here by the elevator; and please, don't kill anyone other than Turner, unless it is completely necessary. Remember, Turner is smart, and deadly. Don't believe he will go down easy. He could be asleep and all it takes is one of you putting a single bullet in his head, but don't plan on it being that simple. Expect the worst. Be prepared. Stay together. Get the job done."

The elevator doors opened behind Shaka, and a woman and her child stood inside. They each had bewildered looks on their faces as they stiffly exited the elevator. Shaka nodded to Vail.

"Let's go!" Vail said.

He and five other men entered the large elevator. Inside, Vail pressed the button indicating the third floor. With that, the elevator doors closed, and the six men started their ascent to the third floor of the Cavalieri hotel.

CHAPTER FORTY-EIGHT

Ryan felt very uneasy. The feeling was sudden. It was unexpected. He wanted to ignore it but couldn't shake the undeniable feeling that was now tearing at him. He picked up the Smith and Wesson. Something didn't feel right. His sixth sense was kicking in; the thing that he had always been known for, and that had made him an exceptional agent in the FBI. His mind was racing. Random theories of why he was feeling uneasy bounced around his brain. Caine never texted back, never called; nothing. Ryan had angered the most dangerous man in the world. He knew that much. Caine was going to get him back, he just didn't know how…he hoped he wouldn't take his anger out on Laura and Kayleen back at home. It was a possibility, but not a very strong one. At least Ryan convinced himself it wasn't.

Then what? Ryan was in Rome. He knew the great city of Rome was a prominent place to Caine and his operations. Even more specifically, he knew that the very hotel he was in had close ties to Cybris Caine. Someone was coming for him. Ryan was sure of it. He was in the heat of the moment when he killed X and sent a picture of the man's dead body to Caine. He acted on anger and an impulse. He had a feeling that Caine had done the same when seeing the picture of X. Ryan powered down the television, bringing the suite to absolute silence. Ryan stood from his bed and walked into the living room area. He stared at the room's door, listening intently. Then he heard it. Someone moving around outside his room…no, not *someone*, but multiple people. Then he heard an object fall to the floor, landing with a hard thud. Following the thud was a whisper: a man's voice.

He couldn't make out what words were being said, but the tone was sharp, angry. Ryan wasn't sure what to do, so he just crouched down where he stood. Both hands on the Smith and Wesson, he extended his arms out, pointing the gun at the door that lead into his room from the hallway. Whoever was behind the door, he was ready for them. Then he heard a click: the sound informing him that his door had just been unlocked. Ryan's right pointer-finger tightened on the trigger.

Very slowly, the door swung open. Ryan kept his breathing controlled. He kept his eyes locked on the door. The barrel of a small rifle peeked into the room. Then the rest of the gun found its way into the room. Then came a pair of hands grasping the firearm, and just above the hands was the head of a man that began to come into view. Ryan watched as the man's eyes started to shift in his direction, and Ryan fired one single shot, hitting the gunman directly between the eyes. The man fell to the floor, dead as a doornail.

Ryan dove backwards into the bedroom area and crouched against the wall parallel to the doorway separating the bedroom area and the living room area. His ears were then filled with the sound of multiple gunshots. However, none of the shots were being fired into his hotel room, but instead the shots sounded as if they were being fired outside in the hallway. Confused, Ryan peeked around the wall he was using for cover. The bottom of the door to the suite was now pressed against the dead man's body. More surprising though, was the fact that another gunman was inside the room, standing against the door, bracing himself against it. He paid no attention to Ryan.

Ryan immediately pulled his gun upward and fired two shots, hitting the armed man in the chest. The man didn't notice Ryan until it was far too late. He never stood a chance.

The bullets struck the man's heart, killing him almost instantly. His knees buckled, and he fell flat onto his face. Two more shots erupted outside in the hall. Ryan stayed where he was, waiting for more gunshots to fire. He heard nothing though. Stealthily, Ryan moved to the door and pushed it open, ramming it into the lifeless body of the second gunman. Holding the handgun out in front of him, he stepped out into the hallway. Directly in front of his door laid four bodies. Ryan immediately inferred that each man on the floor was dead, until the body farthest to the right began to move. The man attempted to lift a gun in Ryan's direction. Ryan whipped his pistol around and fired one single shot into the man's head. Ryan kept his gun ready as he surveyed the hallway but saw no one aside from the six dead men.

Who did this?

Ryan stepped over the bodies scattered across the floor. As he did, he heard a deep, muffled voice. It was coming from one of the bodies. Ryan shifted his gun to aim at the body.

The voice continued.

"Vail?" it said. "Vail, do you read me?"

Ryan knelt next to the body of a short, skinny man. Clipped onto the waistband of the scrawny man's pants was a walkie-talkie. Ryan grabbed it and put it up to his ear.

"Vail. What's going on?" the deep voice from the device asked.

Ryan pressed a button on the side of the walkie-talkie and spoke into it.

"Vail is dead. Who are you?"

There was no answer right away. A few seconds passed by, then the voice chuckled. "I must say, I'm impressed. I'm not at all surprised, but impressed, yes."

The voice belonged to what Ryan could guess was a male, who had some sort of African accent.

"Well," Ryan said, "I am really happy I am able to impress you, but who are you and where are you? Why did these men come here?"

The man on the other end of the line chuckled again. "So many questions, Mr. Turner. I am Shaka. There you go. Those men you killed? They work under me. I work for Cybris Caine. We came to this wonderful hotel here to kill you. Those men there with you though? God rest their souls, but they were the…how do I say this…they were the 'B' team. They were the 'reserves'."

"Send whatever you want at me. I want to talk to Caine, and I'm not going to let myself get killed off before that happens. So, I recommend that you and whoever else is here to leave now. Leave and tell Cybris Caine that we need to talk. No one else has to die tonight."

Shaka laughed. "You see, Turner, that's where you are wrong. Someone else does have to die tonight. You do, Turner. You and I both know I can't leave here until that happens."

"Good luck with that," Ryan said.

There was no reply. Ryan didn't expect one. There was movement to Ryan's left, and he turned his body quickly in that direction. It was John Drexel exiting his hotel room.

"John!" Ryan cried out. "Get back into your room. Now!"

John stopped and stared at the bloodied bodies strung out across the hallway. He still didn't move a muscle.

"I heard all the gunshots. What is happening?"

"John! There are men here. Dangerous men! You need to get back in your room now! You're not safe."

John snapped back into reality, gazed confusedly at Ryan, and slowly backed up into his room.

I highly doubt he's real thrilled about me buying him dinner now.

Ryan stepped back into his room. He dragged the two bodies that were in his room, over to the kitchen area and tossed them both in a heap. He then slammed the room's door closed.

Now what?

Ryan wasn't sure what to expect next. He made his way into the bedroom area. He pressed his back up against the wall that separated the bedroom and the living room area. Then he waited. The walkie-talkie that was now clipped to his waist began to come to life.

"I have an offer, Turner," Shaka said.

Ryan pressed and held down a button on the side of the walkie-talkie. "I'm listening."

"You want Caine, right? Well, I can give you Caine. Turn yourself over to us, nice and quietly. It will be easy. We will take you to Mr. Caine, and instead of us having to kill you, we will allow Mr. Caine to kill you himself. I am sure he'd be more than happy to do so."

"Not going to happen," Ryan said sternly.

Ryan listened as Shaka took a deep breath into his walkie-talkie.

"Don't say I didn't offer."

The moment Shaka finished his sentence there was a huge **BANG** followed by a **CRASH** directly behind Ryan. Ryan could instantly smell smoke.

The door...

Ryan held his breath and counted to himself: one...two...three...and then dove out from behind the wall.

CHAPTER FORTY-NINE

He landed on his stomach. He held his gun out in front of him and fired wildly toward the suite's doorway, where a door once stood. The door had been blown off its hinges and knocked to the floor. Amid the thin film of smoke were two men. They were both tall and light-skinned. Ryan fired five shots before they could react. The first two shots missed the men completely, hitting the wall behind them. The third shot hit one of the men in the thigh, and the fourth bullet hit him the throat, causing him to drop his rifle and grab his throat with both hands. Blood seeped between his fingers and ran down his chest. The last bullet sailed into the side of the other man's skull. His whole body twitched violently as he fell dead to the floor. Ryan rolled quickly back to his right as bullets sprayed in his direction.

Two down, but how many more left to go?

Ryan glanced down at the Smith and Wesson in his hand. He only had three more shots left in this clip. There was a pause in the fire in his direction, and Ryan took the cue to glance around the corner of the wall he was pressed up against. Crouched down on his haunches, he saw two men who were both crouched down in the doorway of the room. They fired mercilessly in Ryan's direction the split second he looked around the wall. Ryan felt two bullets zip just in front of his face as he pulled back into cover behind the wall. Ryan waited until there was another pause in shots being fired. Once there was a momentary cease in fire, he stuck the 9mm out from behind the wall and fired three shots into the direction of the two men he had just seen. He heard one man cry out in pain but didn't look to see the damage he had made.

Ryan tossed the 9mm to the floor and pulled the revolver from his waistband. He cursed to himself, wishing he had another 9mm clip handy. Ryan then listened to another barrage of bullets being fired, but these shots weren't coming from inside his room. He took this as his chance. He dove out from behind the wall and slid across the floor, firing four shots from the revolver. It felt as if he travelled across the floor in slow motion. Time seemed to almost stop. In the matter of a single second, Ryan saw the men. One was hunched over holding his side; his hands looked as if they had been painted red. He was stout and had a belly that hung over his belt. He wore blue jeans and a white tank top. His head was shaved bald, and he had a short, scruffy beard. The other man held a handgun in his left hand, wore white tennis shoes, khaki pants, and a white T-shirt with some sort of big symbol across the front of it. The man had long brown hair that was tangled and hung down to his shoulders. Ryan fired two shots before he even hit the ground. Each bullet found its target.

The first one fired hit the long-haired man in the abdomen, and the ensuing shot hit him in the chest. As Ryan hit the floor, he fired two more shots. They both zipped through the middle of the other guy's forehead. The bald man dropped to the floor, and landed flat on his face in a heap, with his rear-end sticking straight up in the air. The shaggy-haired man didn't die instantly. Staggering around, he managed to lift his left arm and fire two shots in Ryan's direction, both bullets flying just to the side of Ryan. Fearlessly, Ryan jumped to his feet and fired one bullet that flew through the staggering man's skull. Ryan kept the revolver extended out in front of him as he made his way toward the door. There was no sign of anyone else in the hallway, aside from a new lifeless body that had fallen atop another dead gunman. Ryan quickly did some simple math in his head. He had killed six men; seven including X. However, there were eleven bodies strung out between the hallway and room 302; twelve including X. Someone else, aside from Ryan, had taken out five of them. Ryan was thankful. He didn't care too much about who had helped him yet. Ryan examined the various bodies spread along the floor of the hallway.

Which one of you is Shaka?

Ryan hadn't been able to take a deep breath and really take things in until now, and the scene around him was horrific. Brain matter and blood were splattered on the white walls of the hallway. The white carpet now had dark red patterns infused within it. The scene was bad, but Ryan had seen worse, and none of these men were innocent. He had no love lost for what had happened here. Ryan looked over each body individually. Every dead man was Caucasian, and none of them fit the picture of Shaka that Ryan had painted in his mind.

Coward.

Ryan pulled the walkie-talkie from his waistband and spoke into it. "Shaka, where are you?"

There was never a reply.

"Shaka," Ryan said again, "where are you?"

Again, no one answered. Maybe one of the dead men was Shaka…but deep-down Ryan didn't think so.

"Polizia! Polizia!"

Ryan turned to see a large group of police officers charging at him from down the hallway. Instantly, Ryan dropped his revolver, clasped his hands behind his head, and

slowly dropped to the ground onto both knees. The policemen
swarmed him, and one grabbed him and immediately cuffed
him. Officers pulled Ryan up to his feet and sat him down
against the wall across from room 302. An officer knelt in
front of Ryan and sputtered something off in Italian.

Ryan shook his head, and replied, "Parlo in inglese."

The officer shook his head, looking frustrated. He then
turned and conversed with a black-haired policewoman. The
woman nodded then approached Ryan. She knelt in front of
him.

"My name is Martina. I work for the police department
here in Rome."

Ryan nodded.

"What is your name? What happened here?" she asked.

Ryan shrugged. "I am Jamison Lloyd...and I don't
know; I really don't. These men busted into my room and
tried to kill me. I spoke to one of them using a walkie-talkie
that I found on one of the dead bodies. The man I spoke to
went by the name of Shaka. He said they were here for one
reason, and that was to kill me. He told me he wouldn't leave
here until that happened."

Martina was shocked. "That is crazy. Why would they
do this? And what kind of skills possessed you to take down
all these men by yourself?"

Ryan shrugged. "Again, I really don't know. I did
stumble across a street transaction earlier today that looked
like it involved drugs. Maybe I saw something and someone I
wasn't supposed to? I don't know...I was hanging out here in
the hotel and was attacked by one man that called himself
'X'. Scared out of my mind, I found a way to kill him. But, I
was worried I would have no evidence of what happened, so I
didn't tell anyone. Not very long after, all these men showed

up. So, really, I have no idea what exactly is going on. I saw a tattoo of a skull on a few of the men's legs too, what does that mean?"

Martina pursed her lips. "If the tattoo is what I think it is, then you are dealing with Cybris Caine."

Ryan slammed himself up against the wall and enlarged his eyes.

"No," Ryan said. "No, y-you can't be serious?"

"I am afraid so, sir."

"Why do you have me handcuffed? What if more people come for me? Ma'am, please let me go."

Martina placed a hand on Ryan's shoulder. "Please, please calm down, Mr. Lloyd. Everything will be okay. We are here now, and you have nothing to worry about. Besides, after what the man at the front desk said, what some of the people downstairs told us, and the man who called told us, you are going to be free to go. Caine terrorizes this city day in and day out. And especially after speaking with you, you are at no fault here."

"Thank the Lord," Ryan said. "Please can I round up my stuff and go? Please?"

The woman stood to her feet and ushered over a fellow police officer. They conversed then Martina turned back to Ryan.

She bit the inside of her lip. "You killed all these people...how?"

Ryan bit the inside of his cheek. "Well...I guess I must be honest with you. I used to work for the CIA back in America. Before I entered the Agency, I was a Navy Seal. I have seen a lot, and I know a lot. I don't think these men were expecting the pushback and response that they got. But ma'am, I came here to visit an old dying friend, please, can I go free? I know I probably should be taken in for questioning and all that, but please can you let me go? I need to see my friend, Gregory, and leave here as soon as I can. I have been here and gone through far enough."

Martina looked to be in deep contemplation for a second.

"Okay," she said bending over and removing Ryan's handcuffs. "You are free to go. Get your belongings and leave as soon as you can. You can probably imagine, we far too often have to deal with this sort of antic from Caine."

Ryan nodded in thanks and trotted into his death-filled suite. He instantly approached the bed. He reached underneath the bed and pulled X's body out. He left the dead body lying out in the middle of the floor. Ryan gathered up some of his random belongings including the two handguns and the ammunition to them. He quickly scurried out of the hotel room, stepping on and over deceased bodies.

He made his way down the elevator, stepped into the lobby, and walked outside through the front doors of the hotel. Just as he took his first step outside, the phone in his pocket vibrated. Ryan stopped abruptly. He removed the cell phone from his pocket and stared down at the screen. On the screen was a text message. The contact's name that had sent the message was Mr. Caine. It read:

Maybe we do need to talk. Tonight. Just you and me. The pigs' investigation inside the Cavalieri should be done with quick. Dinner at La Pergola. 10 o'clock sharp. You have my attention.

Ryan grinned. He didn't know why exactly, but he did. Then that small grin grew into a smile that in turn started up a fit of laughter. Ryan had been pushed over the edge. He was exhausted; mentally and physically. He didn't know what Caine's end game was for tonight, but he knew one thing for

sure: he was prepared to kill Cybris Caine. Ryan didn't want
to talk; he didn't care at all about what Cybris Caine would
have to say if he did want to talk. Ryan checked the time on
the cell phone in his palm. *8:17 p.m.* He had an hour and
forty-three minutes. Ryan made his way over to the large
fountain in front of the hotel. He sat on the ledge of it, facing
the hotel entrance. Then he waited. It was about to be the
longest hour and forty-three minutes of his life. Time
couldn't pass by fast enough for Ryan Turner.

CHAPTER FIFTY

Back in New York City it was 2:17 p.m. Laura Turner sat in an Ultrasound room next to Cindy Harrison; anticipating the moment Dr. Trayton Fremont would give the big news.

"Gut feeling?" Cindy asked, putting a hand on Laura's shoulder.

"I don't even know," Laura said solemnly.

Cindy squeezed Laura's arm. "Laura, look me in the eye."

Laura slowly turned her head away from the screen displaying the inside of her womb and looked into her friend's eyes.

"Don't let the situation you're dealing with right now change your outlook on this little baby. This is _your_ baby. _Your_ blood. Nothing can change that. If anything, this baby can bring you happiness; happiness that you're missing and need right now."

Laura shook her head from side to side as she returned her gaze back to the monitor.

"So, Mrs. Turner," Dr. Fremont spoke up, "your friend here is having a baby boy. Now, you? It looks to me, that you are going to have double the work that Mrs. Harrison is going to have."

Laura raised her eyebrows. "Double the work…so you're saying it's a girl?"

Fremont chuckled. "That would be a great assumption based on my statement but think harder. Think _twice_ as hard."

Laura looked to be in deep thought, and then her mouth fell open.

"Wait," she said. "No. But...there is no way! I can't possibly be having twins. There is a mistake...h-how didn't I know..."

"Laura?" Fremont said.

"How am I just-just finding this out now? The last ultrasound..."

"Laura?"

"Showed me with just one baby. One! Or did it? How didn't I..."

"Laura!" Dr. Fremont exclaimed.

Laura finally took a deep breath and looked up at the doctor.

"Laura, you are having a baby boy. *One* baby boy."

Laura placed a palm on her forehead. "Sir, why did you have to do that? You know I'm gullible, right?"

Fremont smiled. "Doctors can have some fun too, you know."

Cindy threw her arms around Laura and gave her a long hug.

"Congratulations, Ms. Laura," she said.

Laura managed a slight smile. "Thank you, Cindy, thank you."

The two women thanked Dr. Fremont, and soon enough they were walking out of the hospital and heading for their cars.

"Laura?" Cindy said as they reached their vehicles that were parked side-by-side.

"Yes, Cindy?"

"Sit down in my car, let's talk."

"I'm okay, Cindy..."

"No, you're not, sugar," Cindy said, as she opened up her car's passenger side door, motioning for Laura to get in.

Laura stepped inside while Cindy went around the car and got into the driver's seat.

"What is on your mind? Let it all out," Cindy said.

Laura stared blankly ahead. "Nothing."

Cindy reached over and placed a hand on Laura's left knee.

"Talk to me. I'm here. Let it all out."

"There is a lot running through my mind…a lot," Laura muttered.

"I have all day," Cindy said, folding her arms across her chest.

Laura took a deep breath, and for the next hour she did exactly as Cindy said. She said what was on her mind. She let it out…she let it *all* out.

Cindy C. Harrison took the long route home. When driving, every route in New York City was a "long" route, but she made sure to take extra time to get home. She genuinely felt terrible for Laura. She couldn't even begin to fathom what Laura was going through. She couldn't imagine the pain Laura was feeling. Over-and-over again, she replayed the conversation with Laura in her head. Laura had wanted a baby boy for so long. When Laura first got the news that she was pregnant, she and Ryan already had baby names in mind: Aria if the baby was a girl; Ryan if it was a boy. Ryan Jr.; named after his father. But now, Laura didn't know. She didn't want to name her son after a killer, which brought Laura into expanding on another subject. Ryan.

She explained her feelings about the whole situation with Ryan. She was incredibly angered, but still in denial.

She could not wrap her head around what Ryan had allegedly done. She explained how it made no sense to her, yet that at the same time it seemed to be true. She told of the different theories Kyle had given to her regarding what had happened with Ryan, and why he did what he did. Laura explained that she had a sickening feeling Cybris Caine was involved. She had no idea why. She didn't even know much about Caine, but the feeling was there. Laura's heart was broken; shattered.

Her life-long friends, Gerald and Shirley Shamble, were dead. Kayleen cries herself asleep every night asking if her dad will ever come back home and asking what happened to the Shambles. The baby inside of her was the son of a wanted murderer, and that is what tore her up inside the most. Laura kept saying how this was the second time something like this had happened. She stated that it was the second time the man of her life had disappeared; the second time she had been left with a fatherless child. When Laura got on this subject, she really broke down into tears. She bawled, and for the first time ever, she opened up about Kayleen's father to Cindy. She told all about the man, and who he had been. Like wildfire, anger spread across Laura's face as she spoke about the man. Cindy had told Laura to let it all out, and she did that and more.

After the hour of conversing, Cindy had many questions floating around her head, and felt much sorrow for her dear friend, Laura Turner.

CHAPTER FIFTY-ONE

Inside the 'La Pergola' restaurant, Ryan was seated by a hostess at a table set for two. Ryan was dressed in his newly purchased suit. Already, he was sweating.

"Your waiter and Mr. C will both be here shortly," the hostess said with a smile.

Ryan nodded as the woman left the table. Ryan checked the time on his cell phone. *9:58 p.m.* Two minutes. Ryan surveyed the room, and saw nothing out of the ordinary, but he reminded himself to stay prepared for anything. Midway through his second scan of the restaurant, a waiter stepped up to the table.

"You speak English, no?"

Ryan was startled and looked over at the waiter. "Yes, I speak English. How are you?"

"Very well, sir. I am Eugene. I will be your waiter tonight. May I start you off with a drink? We have the finest selection of wines. I recommend the Sassicaia wine. It is quite good, I do say."

Ryan raised an eyebrow. "Yeah...sounds good."

"I'll be right back with two of them, sir."

With that, Eugene swiftly walked away. Ryan checked the time again. *10:00 p.m.*

Where is Caine?

Ryan scanned the restaurant another time. Once again, there was nothing out of the ordinary. The waiter quickly returned to Ryan's table with two glasses of wine in hand.

"Thank you," Ryan said.

"My pleasure," said Eugene. "I see your friend hasn't arrived yet...I'll return in a bit to take your order."

Ryan waited, and waited. It was 10:08, and there was still no sign of Caine. Ryan fidgeted with his wine glass, and almost took a drink of the Sassicaia wine, but he decided against it. He didn't think Caine would be one to poison him, but he didn't want to take his chances. Instead, he swapped the glass in front of him with the glass at the other end of the table. He guzzled down the entire glass of wine. It quenched his thirst momentarily. Beads of sweat covered his face and he wiped them off with the back of his hand. Ryan checked the time on the phone again. The moment he did, it buzzed in his hand. A text message appeared on the screen. The message was from Mr. Caine. It read:

How do you like my wine?

Ryan's heart began to race. His hands shook. A shiver travelled down his spine. Ryan pulled his small revolver from out of his waistband and placed it on his lap. Ryan replied to the text:

Where are you?

A minute later, there was an answer.

I said how do you like my wine?

Ryan gazed around the restaurant again, searching intently for Caine.

I'm not going to play your games. Where are you?

Ryan could almost picture Cybris Caine laughing.

How. Do you like. My wine?

Ryan took a deep breath, stuffed his handgun back into his waistband, stood to his feet, and typed:

It was good.

He surveyed the room again. He spotted out various people typing away on their cell phones, but none of them appeared to be Caine. Ryan placed the phone inside his right suit jacket pocket and made his way toward a nearby restroom. Just as he entered the men's restroom, the cell phone vibrated in his pocket. Ryan pulled it out and looked down at the phone screen.

You going to drain the tank I see?

Ryan nodded at an elderly man who was washing his hands, and then leaned against the side of the nearest stall. He typed:

Where are you?

Almost immediately, Ryan received another text. But he didn't check right away to see what it said. His vision had suddenly become blurred. Splotchy black spots fogged his vision. Ryan closed his eyes and shook his head. He then stared down at the cell phone screen, and typed, only to be interrupted by an incoming message:

Feeling drowsy yet agent?

Ryan's fingers began to tingle; his arms and legs felt weak. Again, he typed:

Where are you?

Ryan's legs were becoming wobbly; his vision was worsening.

What is wrong with me? he thought

Another message came in:

Come and get me.

Ryan quickly walked back to the door of the restroom but fell to one knee just as he reached the door. A man leaned down over him and asked a question in Italian. Ryan's head was throbbing, and he paid the man no mind. Ryan stood back up to his feet. He pushed open the door and stepped back into the noisy atmosphere of the restaurant's dining area. The moment he stepped out of the restroom, even with his blurred vision, he saw Caine. He sat at the table Ryan had been at only moments before. Cybris Caine lifted a glass of wine into the air and took a sip. He smiled a smile full of pearly white teeth.

Ryan's heart pounded hard against the inside of his chest. He started to run in Caine's direction, and attempted to pull the revolver out from his waistband; however, he was unable to. He stumbled left to right as he approached Caine. Ryan now saw Caine as if he was at the end of a long, dark tunnel. Caine looked to be the size of a mere speck. Ryan's legs buckled underneath him. He stumbled and fell against a table. Food and drink splattered all over his face and clothes. Ryan didn't even notice though. He also didn't hear the numerous people yelling at him. He fell to his knees and couldn't stand up. The last thing he saw was Cybris Caine walking to him, and the last thing he heard before blacking out was a deep, bone-chilling voice.

"Let me ask you again. Feeling drowsy yet, Agent?"

CHAPTER FIFTY-TWO

He awoke feeling the cold concrete ground beneath him. He could now make out the dark, ominous walls surrounding him. He realized where he was. Prison. Jail. The pen. He knew the prison that he was in too. He immediately recognized that he was in a cell located in the Ryker's Island facilities. Ryan was in one of the most dangerous prisons in the world, and it was in his home city of New York. He already hoped he'd get transferred to a state facility sooner rather than later. Ryan had put numerous criminals in the prison he was in now, but never did he imagine finding himself in the confinement of a cold, dark, Ryker's Island cell.

He pushed himself up into a sitting position and slid his butt across the floor until his back was pressed up against the wall straight across from the cell door. His head was throbbing.

"How in the world did I get here?" he said aloud.

Questions circulated through Ryan's mind.

What happened? Where is Caine? Why didn't he just kill me? Why am I still alive?

All the questions and confusion didn't help with Ryan's massive headache. Nothing made sense to him anymore. His thoughts trailed back to Rome…he had been so close to Caine…Ryan's memory of his encounter with Caine was foggy at best, but he couldn't recall anyone being surprised or taking any notice to Cybris Caine.

Why was all of that so? How could the most wanted man in the world just waltz around in the restaurant, and no one act at all surprised?

As much as Ryan hated it, he knew the answer. Caine was powerful. Lots of people respected him. Many people throughout the world sided with Caine, and the rest of the world was deathly afraid of him. Nobody wanted on his bad side. Everyone knew who he was and knew what he was capable of. The truth was, Cybris Commodus Caine had the world in the palm of his hand.

Ryan put his face into the palms of his hands. He cried. Ryan felt exhausted; defeated. The crying caused his head to throb even harder, but he didn't care. He let the wet, burning tears stream slowly down his face.

CHAPTER FIFTY-THREE

Ryan suddenly awoke, having not realized that he had fallen asleep so suddenly. His eyes burned, his head ached. He stood up from the cold concrete floor and staggered across the tiny prison cell. He plopped himself down onto a wooden bed with a single pillow upon it. Lying there, he felt emotionally, mentally, and physically drained. His entire body ached. If there was one positive to be found, his injured arm no longer hurt, and as he gazed down at it, he realized that the wound had been properly treated and stitched.

How long was I out of it...and why didn't Caine just kill me?

Ryan turned his head toward the prison cell door at the sound of it opening. The metal door swung slowly inward, and Ryan watched as Kuron Taylor stepped into the dark prison cell. Kuron held a pair of handcuffs in his right hand.

"Get up," he stated.

Ryan did as he was told, avoiding eye contact with Kuron. Kuron grabbed Ryan harshly, and cuffed his wrists behind his back. He then nudged Ryan hard in the back. Ryan began to walk toward the door but felt Kuron grab him by the back of his shirt, just as he reached the doorway.

"Why, Ryan? Why?" Kuron whispered.

Ryan kept his head down, ignoring the big man behind him. Instead, he continued to walk. Kuron shook his head and nudged Ryan in the back.

"We'll turn left and keep going straight until we hit the end of the hallway."

Ryan did exactly so. Once to the door, Kuron reached around Ryan and knocked on the door. Within seconds, the door swung open. Ryan instantly recognized the man inside who had opened the door. His name was Phillip Gutierrez. Before working as a guard at the prison, Phillip worked in the FBI as a forensic accountant. Standing at 5'8" tall and weighing 210 pounds, Phillip was an Iraq veteran and a Medal of Honor recipient. He lost his left arm at war. Two years ago, his wife died giving birth to twins. Neither of the babies made it. His life had been far from easy, but Ryan was sure that he didn't know a more stellar, classy man. Phillip was one of the best men Ryan had ever met. Ryan nodded at Phillip as he passed by, and Phillip nodded in return. Then to Ryan's surprise, Phillip patted Ryan on the back.

With his knee, Kuron nudged Ryan in the back, knocking him forward a step. In the middle of the room Ryan stood in was a table with one chair on each end of it. Ryan walked over to the table, and Kuron pulled out the chair closest to the door.

"Sit," he said firmly.

Ryan flopped down into the chair. He gazed around the room. Phillip had closed the door behind them, and the veteran now stood in front of the door, facing the back of Ryan's chair. There were no windows; not two-sided or even one-sided windows. Zero windows, and only one table, two chairs, himself, Kuron, and Phillip. Ryan shifted his body in his chair, leaning back and looking up at the ceiling.

"Ryan?" Kuron said in a faint voice, as he sat down in the other chair.

Ryan kept his eyes locked on the ceiling above him. He said nothing.

"Ryan, talk to me."

Ryan said nothing.

"ARE YOU KIDDING ME, RYAN?" Kuron exclaimed, slamming his fists on the tabletop. "LOOK at me!"

Although Ryan still didn't speak a word, he sat up straight and looked Kuron Taylor in the eyes. He could see the true pain in Kuron's eyes. Kuron took a deep breath and leaned forward.

"You and me, Ryan, let's talk."

Ryan kept his eyes locked on Kuron.

"Just talk to me, man," Kuron said. "It's just you, me, and Phillip. This isn't being recorded, this isn't being monitored; nothing like that. We just need to talk."

Ryan bowed his head and broke into a coughing fit. Once the fit ceased, he lifted his head back up and looked back at Kuron, but still said nothing.

Kuron let out a deep breath. "Ryan, you have to talk to me, man. Just start throwing things out there. Just let it all out."

Ryan glanced over his shoulder at Phillip, and then at a slight crack in the ceiling above him. He rested his eyes on Kuron. He still said nothing.

Kuron's face was turning a bright red. "You fool! You are a sorry…"

Kuron caught himself just before his fists slammed the tabletop again.

For what seemed like ages, the room was completely silent. After the silence, Kuron leaned forward in his chair. He clasped his hands together on the table.

"I can help you, Ryan. I can help you. Now you just need to let me. Help me to help you."

Ryan raised his eyebrows but said nothing. Another minute of silence passed by. After what seemed like eternity, Ryan finally spoke.

"What is it that you want to talk about?"

Kuron fought the urge to roll his eyes. "Did you…who killed J.J. Mauer and the Shambles?"

Ryan froze. "What did you just say?"

"I asked you, who killed Mr. Mauer and the Shambles?"

"What happened to Gerald and Shirley?" Ryan asked coldly.

"Ryan, answer my question."

"No!" Ryan spat out. "What happened to the Shambles?"

Kuron was surprised by Ryan's sudden change of tone.

"They are dead," he answered. "And a note was left at their home. The note was written to Laura and signed by you."

Ryan's mind was reeling. His head throbbed even harder now. His heart ached. However, he knew he had to keep his cool.

After an awkward moment of silence, Kuron spoke up again.

"Who. Killed. J.J. Mauer?"

Ryan pursed his lips. "Okay, I'm going to make it short and sweet for you. Mauer is dead. Someone shot him in cold blood. Someone was in his home, came up behind him, and shot him in the back of the head. It could've been me, it could've been anyone. Evidence suggests that it was clearly me. I ran. I ran and never looked back. I flew to LA and you and Kyle followed closely behind. Once there, I threw you and Caine's men a curveball… yes, I knew I was being trailed by two men other than you and Kyle. I knew that. Their names are Randy Palino and Zarius Zaloma. I recognized them the moment I saw them. I had seen and dealt with them before. Zaloma was sitting in a car in the Super-

Mart parking lot. Palino was leaning against the side of the Wells Fargo bank with a cigarette in his mouth.

"I checked into the hotel under a false name, gave my room to a young woman who was in line behind me, and I then caught a cab to the airport. I got myself a plane ticket to Rome, Italy. Once I was there, I purchased a hotel room, got myself a couple guns, a cell phone, and even managed to make a friend. At my hotel, a dozen men tracked me down and tried to kill me. That's the condensed version of my time in Italy. I don't need to go into detail.

"After the excitement at the hotel, I was supposed to rendezvous with Cybris Caine at the La Pergola restaurant. We were supposed to iron some things out, man to man. However, that of course didn't happen. I saw him though. And he was the last thing I saw before I blacked out in the middle of the restaurant. Now here I am, Agent Taylor. But none of what I just said, or what I didn't say is going to change your opinion on this whole situation. You already have in mind what you believe, what you really think happened. I could've came in here and begged and pleaded with you about how I am not guilty, whether it be true or not. Even given what I did tell you, you don't know whether it is all true or not. You have no way of knowing if I told the truth.

"Even if I came in here and admitted to being guilty of killing Mauer, how would you possibly know if what I said is true? You wouldn't. In your mind, you've decided what you're going to believe. You have always been one to go with your gut feeling. I don't see how this situation can be any different. Go with your gut and find the truth."

With that, Ryan stood up from his seat, moved toward the door and stopped in front of it. Phillip stayed put.

"We are done here," Ryan said.

Phillip looked at Kuron, who had his face pressed into his left palm.

"Take him back to his cell," Kuron said.

Phillip opened the door and led Ryan back to his cell. Once there, Phillip removed Ryan's cuffs, and closed the cell behind him. Ryan laid his head down on the pillow at the head of the cell bed, and within seconds, he was sound asleep.

CHAPTER FIFTY-FOUR

Kuron remained seated in the room. He watched intently as Ryan was escorted to his cell. As Kuron assumed, Ryan didn't try anything funny, but instead walked himself back into his cell with no problem whatsoever. Kuron didn't know a more intelligent man than Ryan. He was always straight and to the point, and his knowledge and wits were incredible. He was right too. Kuron did have his mind set on what he believed was true of Ryan's situation. His mind was made up. He and his wife already had an in-depth conversation about the whole matter. His gut feeling told him that Ryan was innocent, even though at first glance the case looked to be perfect.

Per evidence, Ryan was guilty without the shadow of a doubt. But Kuron knew there was something missing. Something didn't fit. Something about the whole situation didn't feel right.

Yet, what about Ryan's gun? His fingerprints? And why would he run? Why wouldn't he try harder to defend himself? Also, what was the deal with Caine's signature tattoo on Ryan's ankle; why hadn't anyone ever taken notice of it before? The letter written to Laura? What was that all about? What was Cybris Caine's part to play in all of this?

The numerous questions flooded Kuron's thoughts.

"He didn't do it, did he?"

Kuron was surprised at the sound of Phillip's voice breaking the silence.

Kuron looked up at Philip. "I'm glad that I'm not the only one who feels that way, Phillip."

Kuron then watched as Kyle Harrison entered the room, dressed in a casual T-shirt and light khaki shorts.

"Phillip," Kyle said, nodding to the veteran prison guard.

He sat down and gazed across the table at his fellow FBI agent.

"Kyle," Kuron said, as he nodded at his friend.

Behind Kyle, Phillip pushed the room door closed.

"Well," Kyle said, "here I am. Now let's talk."

"Kyle," Kuron said, "Ryan didn't kill Mr. Mauer."

Kyle placed his hands behind his head and leaned back in his chair, exhaling a big breath.

"Oh really? Who gave you that idea? Wait, wait...let me guess...Ryan?"

Kuron glared at Kyle. "As a matter of fact, no, no he didn't. What is your problem, Kyle? I've known Ryan for years now. So have you! I have gone over the whole situation repeatedly in my mind. Something isn't adding up. There is a detail we are missing, or a lead we haven't latched onto. There is something we have failed to see or consider. Above all else, what would possibly drive Ryan Turner to kill J.J. Mauer? And his neighbors, the Shambles?"

Kyle lifted an eyebrow. "I presented a handful of possible theories to Laura. Every one of them is plausible in its own way. Ryan was just as good of a friend to me as he was to you. So, don't you dare think for a minute that I don't feel just as bad, if not worse than you about this whole deal. And I don't have a problem...I am doing my job. Simple as that."

Kyle's face was red. Perspiration covered his brows.

"Okay," Kuron said. "What are those theories? And I can imagine how bad you feel too. I am by no means saying that you don't feel horrible about all of this. I'm just frustrated. I feel you might be acting a little heard-headed and blind…I mean, this is our friend, Ryan, that we are talking about. We should, in a way, be giving him the benefit of the doubt. Am I wrong in saying this?"

Kyle leaned forward in his chair, staring at Kuron with disgust.

"Hard-headed and blind?" Kyle asked. "I'm going to pretend like those words didn't just come out of your mouth. Do you not know a single thing about evidence, Kuron? Do you not understand how the law works? How this Bureau works? I'm pretty sure you're not a rookie. I would be a fool not to believe that Ryan is guilty. Until we prove differently, Ryan Turner is guilty for the murder of J.J. Mauer, and Gerald and Shirley Shamble. Plus, I was there. I saw him in Mauer's house, Kuron. He ran! Then, almost immediately afterward, the Shambles were killed.

"I've been at the head of this investigation and have worked alongside the forensics team that is on this case. *All* the evidence is against Ryan. It is a homerun case; the cases you and I have always loved to have. There is no way around evidence until it is proven false, or until more evidence is found to illegitimatize the previous evidence and case. Just because he's a friend, and a colleague, we won't go against evidence and our better judgement. I never would have guessed Ryan would do something like this. NEVER! But, this is my job; this is our job as agents. With Mauer gone, and Ryan behind bars, the Bureau needs us now more than ever. Okay, enough of my rant…the theories I have?

"One, someone, possibly Caine, forced Ryan to do what he did. I mean, we found those grenades that belonged to his organization. He is obviously in some way involved.

Somebody could have threatened him in some way; possibly threatened to hurt his family.

"Two, he did it for his own financial benefit. Ryan really wasn't getting paid much for everything he did. Now with a family, he felt a lot of pressure to care for them. With Mauer dead, Ryan would have most likely assumed his position, which would've led to a much heftier paycheck and it would take him out of the field, which significantly lessens his chance of death and amount of stress.

"Those are the two main theories I've developed. No, they're not perfect or polished by any means, but it's what I have so far. As much as it hurts me to say this, from what we know right now, Ryan is a killer. He has innocent blood on his hands, and until proven otherwise, he is overwhelmingly guilty."

Kuron shook his head, keeping his eyes down. He had wanted to have a heart-to-heart conversation with Kyle about Ryan. He had hoped Kyle was having some of the same feelings and doubts, but that didn't look to be the case. There was no point in carrying on this conversation. Kuron was frustrated, but Kyle had made several fair points. In so many ways Kyle was right. Kyle was stuck on the belief that Ryan was guilty and talking to him was only going to anger Kuron more.

"Honestly," Kyle chirped in again, "I don't even know why you brought me here. It has been a complete waste of time for us both. So, you come up with this off the limb meeting between us for what? I was expecting something important; something worthwhile. But, no, you drag me in here to waste my time when I could instead be spending time with my pregnant wife at home. Sometimes I don't know about you, Kuron. Seriously. Now do you actually have something we need to talk about, and can discuss, or, no?"

Kuron's blood was boiling now. He clenched his fists and slammed one on the table.

He stood to his feet. "Screw you, Kyle. Screw you. You and your ego. You're so full of yourself. You always have been. If you won't help me find answers and you won't help Ryan, I will. I don't need you anyway."

With that, Kuron stomped past Phillip, and threw open the door.

"You are suspended," Kyle said, calling after Kuron. "Two weeks! I don't even want to see your face around. I'll talk to Director Felix about it immediately. I can't let your personal feelings get in the middle of an investigation. I'm only doing what is right. I am sorry, Kuron."

Kuron didn't even bother to respond. He continued marching out the door and threw Kyle the middle finger.

CHAPTER FIFTY-FIVE

The killer was making his way over to his Harley
Davidson when his cell phone rang. It vibrated
simultaneously in his pocket. He pulled the phone from his
pocket to see who was calling. He glanced down at the name.
Not here.

He placed the phone back into his pocket and hopped
onto his bike. He was one of the few people in the world who
had the ability to call that number back, and he would put that
benefit to use. He started up the Harley and grinned at the
purr of its engine. He loved speeding through the New York
City traffic on this bike. It made life easier; not always safer,
but easier. He crossed a bridge and drove until he spotted a
McDonalds.

He squeezed his bike between two cars across the street
from the McDonalds and used a crosswalk to get to the other
side. The killer made his way inside the fast food restaurant.
He stood in line for ten minutes before making his order of
one Big-Mac, an apple pie, and a large Sprite. The restaurant
was jam-packed. He looked over toward the Play Palace, and
saw a large family exiting the play area. Once he received his
food, he decided an open table in the play area would work.
He chose a table at the far end of the Play Palace. He began to
watch a young family directly in front of him. The husband
and wife sat by one another, holding each other close. They
watched and laughed as their giggling daughter slid down the
windy slide.

The killer didn't start eating right away but continued to
closely watch the little family. He missed it. He missed the
moments like the one that young family was having. He

missed the feeling of true happiness that came along with a family. Watching the three took him back in time, reminding him of the love and happiness he once had. Things weren't at all bad right now for the killer; really, life was good. In many ways, life was going better than it ever had before. He watched as the little girl slid down the slide a second time and fell off once she hit the bottom of it, landing on her butt, hitting the ground with a thud. On impact, she broke into a laughing fit. The killer smiled and dug into his food. He wolfed it all down and slurped up his entire drink in little to no time. Just as he finished off his Sprite, he pulled his cell phone out of his pocket, and dialed the number that had called him before. He lifted the phone to his ear.

"Bic Mac and an apple pie, huh? That's my favorite. Certainly, can't go wrong with that."

The killer immediately began to survey the restaurant around him. He swallowed, despite there being no food or drink in his mouth.

"Yes, it's my favorite too, sir. Where are you?"

"As a matter of fact," the deep, eerie voice said, "I was just at McDonald's myself."

The man in the Play Palace stood up from his seat to survey the restaurant a second time. He still couldn't spot out the individual who spoke on the other end of the phoneline.

"You're in New York City?" the killer asked.

There was a laugh on the other end of the line. "Of course, I am, I just love this marvelous city. I was practically standing behind you, my friend. Remember, I am a man of many looks and disguises."

The killer quickly thought back to when he was waiting in line to order his food.

"The old man. You wore blue jeans, a ratty white shirt, and a fedora on your head."

"Bingo," the voice said. "Now this is why I love having you around."

Before the killer could respond, the voice on the other end of the line continued.

"Now, I have a change of plan. Before, you know, I thought having Laura killed would be icing on the cake, but I'm not so sure about that now. Our plans have continued to change throughout all of this. We have Ryan behind bars now where he is no longer a factor in any of this. There is no point in killing Laura. It would hurt Ryan, but it would only make people start to question things. We could set it up to look like a suicide, but again, that just leads to more investigating, which leads to more room for error. So, I've got a new plan, and it is a fabulous one, if I do say so myself. First things first, I want you to take the little girl. Kidnap Kayleen and bring her to me. You know where I'll be."

The killer nodded. "Yes, sir. When?"

"Tonight," the voice said. "I want her in my possession by sunrise."

"Will do," the killer replied as he threw away his trash.

He then found the nearest exit and trotted across the street toward his motorcycle.

"We have had a few setbacks, but things are falling into place now," the voice said. "The end of all of this is close."

The killer leaned himself up against his Harley Davidson. "Or the beginning."

"Yes," the cold, deep voice said, "or the beginning."

With that, the phoneline went dead.

CHAPTER FIFTY-SIX

It was 5:45 p.m. when Kyle Harrison arrived back at Ryker's Island. He made his way inside the infamous prison, went past the security check points, and was escorted by a prison guard past rows of occupied cells until he came to Ryan Turner's cell. Part of Kyle didn't want to come back, but he felt he owed it to Ryan. He wanted to get an idea of what was going on in Ryan's head. Inside the cell, Ryan was lying down atop his bed. He was sound asleep. The prison guard who escorted Kyle unlocked the jail cell and ushered Kyle inside.

Kyle looked down at his friend and felt a surge of pity and hurt for him; the same pity and hurt that had caused him to return to the prison. He knew he was being harsh with Kuron, but Kuron was an emotional person and he could let his feelings and emotions get the better of him. He didn't want Kuron's personal feelings getting in the way of a very touchy investigation. Kyle approached Ryan's bedside. He wanted desperately to hear what Ryan had to say for himself. Ryan's eyes fluttered open at the sound of the cell door closing behind Kyle.

"Good morning, sunshine," Kyle said.

Ryan glanced in Kyle's direction, and then closed his eyes.

"Ryan, come on, really?"

Ryan said nothing.

Kyle shook his head as he sat down upon the seat of the toilet inside the cell. "Ryan?"

Keeping his eyes shut, Ryan turned his head slightly toward Kyle, and then moved his head back to where his face was parallel with the ceiling. Kyle decided to let the silence linger on. It was a good five minutes before Ryan finally spoke.

"Why are you even here?" he said.

"I am here as your friend, Ryan. I am here to talk."

Ryan still didn't feel like talking, and all he could think about was getting rest…and his family too, of course. He missed them; he missed them badly. However, as much as he wanted to, he wasn't going to ignore Kyle. Ever since Ryan entered the FBI, Kyle had been the brother he never had. He wasn't going to just ignore someone who was family.

"Well alright," Ryan said, sitting up in his bed, "what do you want to talk about?"

"I think you know exactly what it is that I want to talk about."

Ryan shrugged. "About how bad the Yankees sucked this year, and how miserably they choked? Yeah, I don't even know why they are still allowed to have a team."

Kyle smirked, trying not to laugh. "That is no lie, it's sad, but true. Still, you know that isn't what I mean."

"I know," Ryan said.

He hated being in this position. He hated looking this way in front of his friends, colleagues, and family.

"Well, break it down. Ask me a question that I can answer," Ryan said, lifting his arms above his head to stretch.

He watched as Kyle racked his brain, searching for the right question to ask first.

"Hmm," Kyle began, "why did you run when I saw you at Mauer's?"

Ryan thought about the question for a moment before answering, "What else would I have done? If I didn't run, I'd have been in the same position I am in now."

Kyle looked to be somewhat baffled by Ryan's answer. "Really, Ryan? You can't be serious. You should've done anything else *BUT* run. How about turn yourself in? Play dumb? We could've helped you. And why go to LA? And why go to Rome?"

"Whoa, whoa," Ryan said, putting his hands up in the air. "Take it easy. One question at a time. And how about I ask some? Like, why would you shoot me, Kyle? Who does that?"

Ryan watched as Kyle's face became red, but then saw him try to hold back a smile for he realized the humor in Ryan's voice.

"The surprise and heat of the moment, I guess. But, hey, if you were able to shoot a man that day, why couldn't I have shot at one?"

Ryan ignored the last comment at first. "Why I ran? I had no choice. LA? That was just a matter of chance, really. Now, Rome? I have my reasons. And who says I shot anyone that day?"

Kyle had a perplexed look on his face. "Wait, so let me get this straight…you are telling me that you, in fact, *didn't* kill J.J. Mauer?"

"I didn't say that," Ryan replied.

"Then what are you saying?" Kyle asked as he stood to his feet and leaned his back up against the wall.

"I'm just asking a question."

"Well," Kyle said, "everyone I know aside from Kuron. Yes, even Laura."

Ryan's heart sank.

Kyle took a deep breath. "Even I have come to accept that you're guilty. It is one of those slam dunk cases. The evidence against you is overwhelming, I mean, there is a whole list of evidence against you. But, why? Why did you do it, Ryan?"

Kyle was dead serious now. There would be no more joking around.

Ryan studied the floor beneath him. "I am going to tell you the same thing that I told Kuron. Someone killed J.J. Mauer. That is a fact. It could have been me; it could have been anyone, really. Evidence suggests that it was me. Someone murdered the Shambles…" Ryan swallowed, then continued. "Evidence suggests it was me. I ran, Kyle. I went to Los Angeles, and you trailed closely behind me. I rigged up a disguise and gave you and Kuron the slip. I then caught a flight to Rome, Italy where I had quite the trip.

"I wanted to take care of a few things there. I saw Cybris Caine at the La Pergola restaurant, and he was the last thing I saw before blacking out. Now I am here. No matter what I say, it isn't going to change your opinion on all of this. You came in here with an outlook on this whole situation. I could sit here and plead my innocence to you, sure. But how could you know whether that is really the truth or not? In this field, very rarely does evidence lie. You are going to believe what you are going to believe."

Kyle nodded his head slowly, while gazing around the cold cell. He then reached out a hand toward Ryan. Ryan grasped his friend's hand, and to his surprise Kyle pulled him to his feet into a hug.

"I'm going to do everything I can to find answers. Hopefully those answers get you out of here. I love you, brother."

With that, Kyle pulled away from the hug and exited the cell. Shocked, Ryan was left standing there as the jail cell swung closed. He wasn't necessarily surprised at what Kyle said, but what he did. Tears were streaming out of Kyle Harrison's eyes. It was the first time Ryan had ever seen Kyle cry.

CHAPTER FIFTY-SEVEN

After his short meeting with Kyle, Kuron Taylor left
Ryker's Island and dialed his wife's phone number. He told
her that he had some things to take care of, so he would be
home late. Minutes after ending the conversation with
Malaya, Kuron arrived at J.J. Mauer's house. If Kuron was
being honest with himself, it was rage that brought him to
Mauer's home. It was rage and anger toward Kyle, and the
desire to prove him wrong. It was the first time in a few days
that the house didn't have investigators, crime scene tape, or
policemen swarming around and inside of it. Kuron pulled
his car into Mauer's driveway, squeezing in directly behind
J.J. Mauer's white Mercedes Benz. It was the first time Kuron
had been there since the homicide occurred.

He immediately noticed the house's shattered window.
He walked up to the front door, but found it was locked. He
shook his head and decided to enter the house through the
broken window. It was far from easy for Kuron to enter the
house by squeezing through the window, but in time, he was
inside. Once inside, he noticed that aside from Mauer's body
and Ryan's gun, the crime scene had pretty much been left as
is. The scene was practically untouched. He saw a spilled
coffee mug lying upon the floor. Coffee stains covered the
once white carpet. He strolled across the living room,
carefully examining the bloodied recliner, which he presumed
was where Mauer was shot.

He remembered Kyle saying that the former Head of the
Bureau was shot in the back of the head. Even with Mauer's
body gone, Kuron could see that this was in fact true. He
based this on the blood stains that appeared on the headrest

and backrest of the chair, along with the dried blood along the carpet in front of the chair and on the wall and television across from the recliner. Kuron wandered around the living room, kitchen, bathroom, and bedroom within the house looking for anything out of the ordinary or any kind of clue. He found nothing. He found himself back in the living room, standing behind the bloody recliner, staring blankly down at the chair. He stood there listening to the sound of the New York City traffic outside and the sound of his own breathing.

"What am I missing?" he asked himself out loud.

Kuron strolled over to the recliner that hadn't been occupied by Mauer when he was shot. He knelt next to the recliner and closely examined the chair. His eyes were drawn to a greasy streak along the arm of the chair. It looked to be coffee, as if someone had gotten coffee on their finger and rubbed it on the chair. He also noticed that the footrest hadn't been pushed all the way back under the down into the chair.

Someone had been here. Someone who was comfortable with Mauer.

Thinking back to a conversation he had with Kyle, Kuron remembered that the only fingerprints so far recorded from the crime scene were taken from the front door knob, the back of Mauer's recliner, and Ryan's Glock. Kuron thought about how the homicide may have occurred. So, based on the fingerprints, Ryan could've let himself in the house, sat down, had a cup of coffee, then went up behind Mauer and shot him dead. This seemed like the most plausible theory; however, the more Kuron thought about it, the more convinced he was that Ryan was innocent.

He tried to imagine Ryan wanting to kill Mauer. Kuron believed that Ryan would've chose one of two ways to go about killing J.J. Mauer. One: he would've knocked and waited for Mauer to let him in, made himself at home, found a reason to go up behind Mauer, and then would shoot him dead. Two: Ryan would let himself in, and immediately killed Mauer; getting in and out as fast as possible. Based on the evidence and what Kuron had observed so far, he didn't believe either of those processes were probable. Ryan's fingerprints had been found on the handle of the front door, which cancelled out the idea that Mauer had let Ryan in.

From Kuron's examination, someone had sat down in this recliner and wiped coffee on the chair's left arm. Above all else, Ryan was one of the most intelligent men Kuron knew. Kuron was positive that Ryan wouldn't have made the simple mistake of leaving fingerprints on the doorknob. If Ryan wanted to murder someone, he would've done it much more efficiently, and he wouldn't leave so much obvious evidence against himself. Ryan was innocent; Kuron was sure of it.

Kuron took a second look at the streak of dried coffee across the left arm of the recliner.

There must be fingerprints here.

The investigation had practically been closed already due to Kyle being an eyewitness of Ryan standing over Mauer's body, Ryan running from the scene and from the law, Ryan's gun being found on the murder scene and being declared as the murder weapon, and Ryan's fingerprints on the door knob, the gun, and Mauer's recliner. There was plenty of evidence against Ryan. Plenty. Kuron recognized that no one had even considered, or maybe even seen the small, faint streak of coffee on the side of the one recliner's arm. Kuron removed his cell phone from his pocket. He dialed a number and put the phone up to his ear.

After four rings, a voice answered, "Gary Richards."

"G-man!" Kuron answered back. "I need your help."

Gary Richards, A.K.A "G-Man", was one of the most valuable individuals within the FBI. He was always a huge help to Ryan, Kuron, and Kyle whenever they were out in the field. Countless times he acted as their eagle eye and watched over them. He didn't exactly have a job title. He was the "techy guy"; "the geek". Gary could break into any sort of computer or electronical system. He was a master when it came to forensics and evidence.

The G-Man was more technologically advanced than anyone else in the entire bureau. He had a mind like no other and was as loyal as can be. Whenever Kuron was in a bind, or needed something, G-Man would always be more than willing to help. Along with Kyle and Ryan, G-Man was a dear friend to Kuron, and was part of the tight-knit group of friends that Kuron, Ryan, and Kyle made up. Gary Richards was like a swiss army knife, although he had never killed a person, and could never hurt a fly.

"So, tell me, have you been involved in the recent case concerning Mr. Mauer's death?" Kuron asked.

"Yeah," G-Man said. "The whole deal with Ryan? Sucks, huh?"

"Yup, it really does," Kuron said. "Now, don't tell Kyle that I talked to you. He put me on a B.S. suspension, so I'm not even supposed to be here, but I am at J.J. Mauer's house right now. What all did you and your team run tests on?"

"There was a respectable number of things we tested. I ran tests for various fingerprints, which in turn all ended up being Ryan's. I discovered that the bullet that ended dear Mr. Mauer's life came from Ryan's Glock."

"So, all the evidence you tested pointed to Ryan?"

G-Man snorted. "Yes, sir, everything. It is quite the predicament that our dear friend Ryan has found himself in."

"No joke," Kuron replied. "Did you run any tests of prints on the recliner that Mauer wasn't killed in?"

"Umm...no, no, not to my knowledge. I may be incorrect, but I do not believe we did."

Kuron nodded as he gazed down at the coffee stain on the arm of the recliner.

"Can you do me a huge favor, G-Man?"

"Depends on what it is, and how splendid my reward will be."

"Well, I have found a streak of coffee along the side of the left arm of this chair. I think there may be prints."

"And?" G-Man asked.

"And what?"

"You managed to leave out the reward part. I'm a tad bit curious as to what I will get in return."

Kuron rolled his eyes and began to reply, but was cut off by G-Man.

"No, I am kidding, compadre. Mr. Gary Fraze Richards here at your service, Agent Taylor. I will be there in just a little bit. I just finished my daily dose of video games, so I don't have anything better to do."

Kuron smirked. "I will be here. Thanks, man, I owe you."

Kuron then ended the phone call. He fidgeted with the phone in his hand and asked himself the same question he had asked earlier.

"What am I missing?"

CHAPTER FIFTY-EIGHT

Inside J.J. Mauer's bedroom is where Kuron found the answer to his question. Under the king-sized bed, he found exactly what he was looking for. A clue. Something he was missing. He discovered a small stack of papers, officially typed and marked. Among the papers were resignation and promotion documents. The top document was a letter written by J.J. Mauer to the Bureau. It was written in the form of an address/speech speaking to those within the FBI. Kuron sat down on the bed and read the letter. The date read November 13th, 2017: a day after Mauer's death. It read:

Good afternoon, everyone,
It is a pleasure to stand before you today. You are my family; every single one of you are my brothers and sisters. I have grown to love and respect you all. My career at the FBI has been a blessing, and the best time of my life. I couldn't have been blessed with better men and women to work with. I am not good with words, as you all may know. So, to cut straight to the point of why I stand here today. Very few of you know, but I have been diagnosed with stage 4 colon cancer. I want to inform you that, because of my health and other things, I am retiring. My days at the FBI are over...

CHAPTER FIFTY-NINE

The killer was nervous. Very rarely did nerves ever get the best of him; however, in this very moment they did. Everything needed to go smoothly. There was little room for error. From head to toe he was dressed in black, blending in with the pitch-dark night. He was crouched down on his haunches next to a window that looked into the living room of a cozy little house. The house was located on 158th Avenue in Jamaica, New York, just to the west of Crossbay Boulevard and Shellbank Basin.

The killer peeked into the window to see two women sitting down next to one another. The killer recognized the women the second he laid his eyes upon them. Laura Turner and Cindy Harrison both stood to their feet. They hugged each other, and then Cindy headed toward the front door of the house. It looked as if she was leaving. As Cindy exited the house, Laura sat back down on the sofa and began to read a book.

The killer took this as his cue. He slunk around to the back of the house where he came upon a back porch. He went up onto the porch and stopped in front of the door leading into the house. He turned the doorknob to find that the door was unlocked. The killer smiled underneath his ski mask.

How careless can a person be?

He slowly opened the door. He peered inside the house. His eyes gazed down a long hallway that had doors along each wall.

Clear.

He knew the house like the back of his hand; he came prepared. He knew the first room on his left was little Kayleen's bedroom. The bedroom door was open.

Perfect.

The man snuck quietly into the bedroom and found exactly what he was looking for. On the bed, curled up under the covers, was Kayleen. In the completely dark room, he could make out the shape of her little body underneath the covers. He carefully closed the door behind him and started to approach the bed.

Tiptoeing, he continued to make his way to the sleeping little girl. He could hear nothing but his and Kayleen's breathing.

SQUEAK!

The man stopped dead in his tracks.

"Kayleen?" Laura called from the living room. "Kayleen, are you okay?"

Kayleen tossed and turned, and mumbled some incoherent words, but then fell back asleep. The killer breathed a sigh of relief, and then his heart stopped.

Footsteps.

Avoiding the obnoxious squeaky toy that he had just stepped on, the killer threw himself onto the floor, and in the same motion slid underneath the bed. Things were no longer going so perfect.

"Kayleen?" Laura whispered, as she stepped into the dark bedroom.

She flipped on the light switch next to the door, which brightly illuminated the entire room.

As he laid curled up under the bed, the killer held his breath. He didn't know whether Laura had seen him or not. He didn't think she did. He hoped that she didn't, at least. His chest and head throbbed from having to hold his breath. He listened as Laura whispered softly to her daughter. He couldn't hold his breath much longer. He was sick and tired of the delaying. He had a job to finish.

He then pulled his automatic pistol out from his waistband with amazing precision. The gun's safety was already off, and it was fully loaded, although he knew it would only take one bullet to kill Laura, if need be. He locked his eyes on Laura's long, slender legs.

Gosh she is perfect.

It was partly why he hated her, and why part of him in that moment wanted to kill her; right then and there. Yet he couldn't…he didn't think that he ever could. It was a relief to him when his objective had changed from killing Laura to abducting Kayleen.

The room went dark, and the moment he heard the door click shut, he let out a long-exasperated breath and carefully rolled out from underneath the bed. He stood to his feet, this time avoiding the annoying, noisy little toy. As he stood over the sleeping girl, he revealed a small syringe out from a pocket inside his jacket. He then slowly pulled back the covers, revealing the little girl. She tried to grab for the covers and mumbled some words.

The man then clasped a hand over the little girl's mouth and with his other hand shoved the syringe's needle into the girl's neck. Kayleen jolted violently at the contact of the cold needle and screamed; however, no sound escaped past the man's strong hand. One scream was all she could muster before the syringe's contents kicked in, taking effect on her little body, and causing her to go limp. The man stuffed the syringe back into his jacket and lifted the girl tenderly into his arms. With that, he approached and opened the bedroom window, and escaped into the dark night.

CHAPTER SIXTY

Mr. Mauer was planning on retiring...*and had spoken to Director Trey Felix about Ryan taking the position as Head of the NYC Bureau. Why would Ryan kill Mauer if he was to take his place?*

Kuron sat down on the edge of the bed, placing the stack of papers next to him. He gazed at the television that was positioned on the wall straight across from the foot of the bed. As he did so, a memory flashed through his mind. The memory was from a little over a year ago:

He had sat in the exact same spot on the same bed he sat upon now. Kuron had decided to visit J.J. Mauer that day. Mauer's wife had just passed away, and he had come down with a bad intestinal infection, which little did anyone know that it was leading up to colon cancer. Kuron had been worried about his emotional and physical health, and frequently visited Mauer throughout the span of about a month.

"Thank you for coming, Kuron. Means a lot," J.J. Mauer had said while lying on his bed, flipping through television channels.

Kuron was on his feet now, preparing to leave. He reached out a hand to Mauer, and Mauer ceased from changing TV channels to shake Kuron's hand.

"My wife is making her famous spaghetti and meatballs tonight, sir, if you'd like, you are welcome to come over, or I can bring you a plate?"

"Thank you for the kind gesture, Agent Taylor, but maybe another night. I don't have too much of an appetite tonight."

Kuron nodded and glanced up at the TV. Kuron went to turn his eyes away from the screen, but then took a second and third glance at the television. Kuron stared at the flat-screen in awe. He waved his hand in the air and watched on the screen as it portrayed him performing the action. It wasn't a reflection, but live footage of the bedroom Kuron and Mauer were in. J.J. Mauer jumped, realizing the channel he was on, and bobbled the TV remote in his hand before quickly changing the channel. He then sighed and returned to the channel that had taken he and Kuron by surprise. The screen displayed an overhead view of the bedroom.

"You are probably curious as to what exactly this is," Mauer simply stated.

Kuron waited for Mauer to continue.

"Secret, hidden, untraceable cameras. They are located throughout the house."

Kuron looked closely at the television, and then up at the ceiling where he presumed the camera was.

"The cameras are very, very small. They are hidden within the ceiling, and like I said, are impossible to trace."

Kuron folded his arms across his chest. "That is incredible. You're the man, Mr. Mauer."

A rare smile spread across Mauer's face. He pressed a few buttons on the remote and a whole new picture appeared on the screen. This time, Kuron found himself looking at an overhead view of the living room.

"Like I stated before," Mauer said, as he changed the channel to show a view of the kitchen, then the bathroom, "I have a camera in every room, and even outside in the front

and back of the house. I have this place monitored 24 hours a day, 7 days a week, 365 days a year. You are the only one who knows of this. I trust you, Taylor."

Hearing Mauer's last sentence, Kuron's heart filled with pride.

Kuron snapped out of his daydream. He scrambled to find the television remote.

CHAPTER SIXTY-ONE

Laura screamed at the sight of her daughter's vacant bed and fell to her knees. She no longer had any feeling in her arms or legs. The bedroom felt as if it was spinning around her. She opened and closed her eyes, hoping she would wake up from the nightmare she had just found herself in.

"No, no, no!" she sobbed.

Tears flowed down her flushed cheeks. She crawled to the side of the bed and threw her face into a pillow.

The cool night air flowed into the room through the open bedroom window. Laura stood to her weak, staggering legs, and furiously ruffled through the bedspread and tossed around the pillows that covered the bed. Her entire body violently trembled. Her teeth chattered uncontrollably. She wept like a child. Sobbing, Laura slammed her fists on the bed.

"Kayleen!" she wept.

With hazed-over eyes, she looked out into the night through the open bedroom window. All she could think about now was a two-syllable name. The same name that had racked her brain and engulfed her thoughts for the past few days.

Ryan.

She staggered out of the bedroom, entered the garage, and stumbled into her car. It would take a while to reach her destination in her car, but it would give her time to think. Minutes later, she was driving through the New York City streets, tears obstructing her vision, still hoping she would wake up from this nightmare.

CHAPTER SIXTY-TWO

Kuron eagerly punched in the "zero" key ten times, and the television screen before him came to life, displaying a list of dates. Kuron's mind wandered back to the memory of his and Mauer's discussion about the surveillance system. He could almost hear J.J. Mauer's voice now:

"Push in the zero key ten times, and you can watch any surveillance footage from now to a year from today. The dates are listed in chronological order from the most recent to the oldest feed."

Kuron took a deep breath.
This is it...I can finally find the truth.
Kuron was frustrated with himself for forgetting about Mauer's system. He felt like a fool, but it was better late than never. Kuron found the date he was looking for: November 12th, 2017. On the screen, video footage began to play. At the top right corner of the screen read "12:01 a.m." Although the house was completely dark, all twelve boxes of film located on the big television screen were perfectly clear. The twelve smaller screens within the big screen were each different camera views throughout the various parts of the house.
"Wow," Kuron said out loud. "Night vision cameras...Mauer was really something."
Kuron held down the fast-forward button and the time on the screen began to rapidly progress.
He fast-forwarded until the time read 5:40 p.m. His heartrate started to soar. In one frame, J.J. Mauer was in the kitchen making coffee. *5:46 p.m.* Kuron stared at the frame

that displayed footage of the living room and the front of the house. He waited patiently for someone to appear.

A man began to walk up to the front door of the house. Kuron leaned closer to the screen. The man wore a hood. Kuron was unable to recognize the person's face.

"Who are you?" Kuron said out loud.

That is when a second voice filled the bedroom. "Stand up. Now!"

Kuron froze. His eyes still focused on the screen.

"What is this?" the voice said.

Suddenly the sound of gun fire filled the bedroom, and the television was blown to pieces.

Kuron stood up and turned slowly toward the bedroom door. He was astonished when he saw who the voice belonged to.

"Agent…Agent Castillo? What are you doing?"

"That is the same question I was about to ask you," Castillo barked. "Place your hands behind your head, nice and easy like. You know the drill."

Castillo pointed his handgun in Kuron's direction.

Kuron looked down at Castillo and shook his head. "What do you think you're doing, Aaron?"

Aaron was young and new to the Bureau. From what Kuron had known of the young man, he was real laid back, level-headed, and respectful. The last minute or so, more than proved otherwise. Aaron Castillo was short in stature, had black slicked-back hair, a Roman nose, and was always dressed to impress.

Castillo smirked. "I'm aiming a gun at your big head, what does it look like I'm doing?"

Kuron didn't answer. He didn't know what to do or say.

With his gun, Castillo motioned toward the shattered TV. "I enjoyed watching that with you there for a second. It was very interesting; real exciting. Mauer was a weird fool, wasn't he? He was smart though. Hidden cameras…huh, isn't that something? Kuron, you almost had something going for you there, didn't you? You were so-o-o close, so close. Man, to stick your neck out there for Ryan, that is really something. He is…*was* lucky to have a friend like you." Castillo's eyes lit up. "You have guts, I'll give you that, but I've never been able to stand you, so killing you will be a pleasure."

"Please," Kuron said as Castillo finished his last sentence. "Please, tell me who killed J.J. Mauer. Just so I have the peace of mind before I die. Who did it?"

Castillo chuckled. "You're pathetic," he spat out. "How about you tell me?"

"You did," Kuron said quietly.

Castillo smiled. "Maybe, maybe not. And you will never know. There is a storm coming, Agent Taylor." Castillo rolled out his neck. "It is just a shame that you won't be here to watch it take its course."

Kuron closed his eyes, and the split second before the bullet met its target, he heard the deafening, but all too familiar, sound of a gunshot.

CHAPTER SIXTY-THREE

It took a little while, but soon enough, Laura had
arrived at Ryker's Island. On her way to the prison, she made
a phone call to Kyle describing what had happened. He was
almost as upset as Laura. She explained that she was on the
way to the prison to see Ryan, and Kyle stated he would
make sure the prison was expecting her and would set Laura
up with a visit. After the phone call with Kyle that was full of
tears, parking her car, and going through various security
checkpoints and a police escort, Laura was now seated in a
small cubicle. In front of her was a large plate of glass, and
on the other side of the glass was a single chair.

She had no idea how she was going to react to seeing
Ryan. She wasn't prepared, whatsoever. But she needed
answers, and she needed them now. She had finally ceased
her crying. She had an almost unbearable headache. Blood
pumped behind her ears. She took a deep breath as she waited
for Ryan to appear. She knew she had to be strong…for
Kayleen.

There was a loud **'clang'** on the other side of the glass,
and behind the chair on that side, a door swung open.
Through the door stepped in a prison guard, followed by a
man wearing cuffs on his wrists and ankles. Following the
cuffed man was another prison guard. Laura locked eyes with
the prisoner. She bit her lip.

Don't you cry Laura. Don't do it.

However, as her unshaven, blue-eyed husband sat down
across from her, tears streamed down her face in a flurry.

Ryan wanted to do the same. He really did. Laura meant everything to him. In the end, nothing else in the world mattered to him. Her and Kayleen were everything.

But what is she doing here now? Why so late in the night?

After an uncomfortable silence, Laura finally spoke. "Ryan…" she said, keeping her eyes down.

"Yes, Laura?" Ryan said. "What's wrong?"

Ryan clenched his teeth the second the sentence left his mouth.

What's wrong? Really, Ryan? What ISN'T wrong?

It was a bad question, and he knew it. Laura lifted her head up and Ryan locked eyes with her once again. Her eyes were red and puffy, her face was pale; she looked exhausted and drained. Something had happened.

Ryan now leaned forward with pleading, loving eyes. "Laura? I know you probably hate me right now, and I don't blame you. You have all the reason to hate me. What happened though? Why did you come here, Laura? What happened?"

Laura's eyes suddenly changed. Her eyes turned cold. She started to yell something but caught herself. A minute passed by…then two…then three. Finally, Laura's expression changed; her whole demeanor did.

She began to shake, and her lip quivered. "Kayleen is gone, Ryan. Ryan, she's gone."

Laura broke down into tears again. Ryan absolutely hated seeing her like this. It broke his heart, and it took everything he had to not break down too. His mind was reeling now…

What does she mean that Kayleen is gone?

Ryan cleared his throat. "What do you mean she is gone? Honey, you have to tell me what happened."

Laura slammed a fist into the glass before her. "Don't call me that! Don't you dare call me that! Screw you, Ryan." Laura bit her lip. "My daughter is gone. I know what you did, and I know about all the evidence, and the nice tattoo on your ankle. I know about it all, but I didn't come here to talk about you. I couldn't care less about you, Ryan. But what happened is that my daughter is gone. Someone took my Kayleen from me. Someone took her."

Sobbing, Laura cupped her face in her hands. Ryan felt his eyes glaze over. A single tear ran down his left cheek. His heart had shattered at the sound of Laura's harsh words, but again, he really couldn't blame her.

Laura's head came up out of her hands. Her eyes had a new look to them. She was heartbroken and defeated.

"I'm... I'm sorry..." Laura whispered. "I'm sorry. I just..."

"Don't you ever apologize to me, Laura. You have nothing to apologize for. Never have you done anything where you've needed to apologize to me. Now me on the other hand..." Ryan moved his eyes away from Laura for a few seconds, then continued on. "What happened to Kayleen? Laura, you've got to talk to me."

Laura went to open her mouth, but no words came out.

She blew out a breath. "Cindy was at the house. We were having our regular get-together. We were watching a movie, eating some snacks. Cindy left, and I decided to sit in the living room and read a book. I then went to the kitchen to grab a cup of milk, and thought I heard something in Kayleen's room. I knew she had already fallen asleep, so I was curious as to what the noise was. So, I went to check on her. The light in her room was off and she was sound asleep. Everything seemed fine, but…I should've woken her up, Ryan! I should have stayed with her. Something! I should've…"

"Laura, stop," Ryan said firmly, cutting off his wife. He leaned his face closer to the glass. "Go on. What happened after that?"

"I left her room and went back to the kitchen," Laura said, sniffling. "I got a glass of milk and sat back down to read my book. Then, out of the blue, I had the sickest, most indescribable feeling in my gut that something was wrong. As much as I tried, I couldn't shake the feeling. I returned to Kayleen's room. She was gone. The window in her room was open, and she was nowhere to be found. I searched around the room, the bathroom, the rest of the house, the yard, the street…nothing. I returned to her room and bawled like a baby. Someone took my baby girl, Ryan. She is gone."

Ryan felt weak to his stomach. His head was spinning, his face burned.

"Who has my little girl? Who took her, Ryan? Huh, who took her?" Laura cried.

Ryan stared blankly down at his feet. "Laura?" he said. He felt Laura's gaze lock onto him.

"Get me Kuron. Tell him I need him," he said.

"Are you kidding me? Are you even listening to me?"

"Get. Me. Kuron."

Laura's eyebrows scrunched up, and she shook her head and bit her lip. "What is the matter with you, Ryan? Listen to me! Kayleen is gone! I know you must know something about this! I know it. Someone…"

"Laura!" Ryan exclaimed, cutting off Laura's sentence. "I don't know, okay? I don't know who did this, but I do know one thing. You need to get Kuron, okay? You must. I beg of you."

Ryan called over the guards and stated that he was ready to go. He stood to his feet and turned to leave but turned back around toward Laura. He looked her in the eyes.

"I love you," he said, before turning back around and heading to his cell, hoping with all his heart that he would see Kuron Taylor before the night was over.

CHAPTER SIXTY-FOUR

Kuron Taylor opened his eyes and looked down at the blood splatter on his torso. He blinked twice, grabbed at his chest and abdomen, and then stared down at the floor below him. His eyes locked on a dead body lying in the doorway of the bedroom. It was Castillo. Above the body stood a quivering man, wearing large prescription glasses. He was short, scrawny, had brown hair that was thin and unruly, and wore jeans with holes in the knees and a navy-blue hoodie. Never in his life had Kuron been so happy to see Gary Richards. Kuron grabbed at his bloodied shirt again, realizing the blood he was covered in was, in fact, Aaron Castillo's.

"God bless you, G-Man," Kuron said as he kicked Castillo's body over onto its back.

G-Man remained standing in the doorway, with a star-struck look on his face.

He snapped out of the trance he was in and shoved his Glock into the holster on his waist. "I have never, ever shot a man, much less killed a man. It is quite the crazy feeling, I'll have to say."

"Well," Kuron said, looking over Castillo's dead body, "there is a first time for everything, especially in this business, my friend. I'm just glad that today was the day you decided to pull the trigger."

G-Man shook his head from side to side. "It is a weird feeling…I can't describe it. I'm just glad I arrived in time."

Kuron dug into Castillo's pants' pockets and retrieved a cell phone from them.

"Yeah," Kuron said, "I'm glad too. You definitely couldn't have come at a better time."

Kuron powered on Castillo's cell phone. A picture displayed as the phone's lock screen. It was a photograph of Castillo and his fiancée.

"Crazy…" Kuron said.

"I always thought Aaron was a good dude," G-Man said, walking over to Kuron and looking over his shoulder at the cell phone.

Kuron attempted to unlock the phone, but found it was protected by a password.

Seeing the picture on the phone, G-Man spoke up again. "I only met her once, but she seemed like a good woman too. It's a shame. What was Aaron doing anyway? What all did he say to you?"

"I don't know, G, but I have the feeling that he could've been behind all of this insanity with Ryan and Mauer. I don't think he is the main piece in all of it though. I don't get that impression. I guarantee there is someone higher up; the headmaster, the person at the top of the totem pole. Someone else is directing traffic and pulling the strings. He told me that 'A storm is coming'." Kuron handed the cell phone to G-Man. "Is there any chance that you can unlock this for me? I want to know who this guy has been in contact with."

Gary Richards nodded. "For sure." He grabbed the phone from Kuron. "I got you covered. I'll head back to headquarters from here and take care of all of this. I'll look over the prints off the recliner too. I was looking them over when I came in, and then I heard the ruckus going on back here. But, Kuron? You're saying Aaron Castillo may have killed Mauer? And the Shambles? And that is pretty trippy…he said a storm is coming?"

Kuron shrugged. "Yeah, crazy, huh? I really don't know if he killed Mauer or not. I really don't. It is obvious that he is in some way involved. When he came in and was going to kill me, I was watching footage of the night Mauer was killed. Mr. Mauer has a surveillance system all throughout his house that is on 24/7. I had forgotten all about it until being in this room sparked the memory of when he showed me the system. I'm the only one who knows about it. However, Castillo came in knowing I was here. I think someone else is monitoring this house. Mauer's cameras aren't the only ones here...there is something brewing, and something twisted going on, and I don't like it one bit, especially if my hunch is correct about who is the brains of this whole operation."

G-Man pushed his glasses higher up onto his nose. "That is incredible," he said. "Basically, a security system with one heck of a memory. I would guess the hard drive is hooked up to the television...or what used to be a television, in here. I bet you that I can recover the hard drive, Kuron. I'm pretty sure I'd be able to do that."

Kuron's eyes lit up. "That would be awesome, my man. That video is huge. It's the key to finally finding the truth behind what happened the night of November 12th."

G-Man strolled over to the broken television. He pulled and jerked on what was left of the tv, until the entire thing fell off the wall. He fidgeted around with various cords and pulled apart various parts of the television.

"Aha!" he exclaimed, as he excitingly grabbed a cord that was hanging from the wall down to the television. He followed the cord from the wall all the way down to the broken television.

After a few seconds of banging around and tugging on television parts, G-Man came up with what looked like a little memory card.

"Got it," G-Man said. "If my guess is right, this thing will be hard to break into. It'll be protected like crazy. It'll take a lot of time, but I bet you I can break into it."

"Perfect," Kuron said.

G-Man scratched his chin. "You said that you might have an idea as to who oversees this whole operation. Who exactly do you think that is?"

"Well," Kuron started, "I hope I'm wrong, I really do, but when I visited Ryan at the prison, he talked to me a little bit about a certain someone. He tried to take him out in Rome. Me, him, and Kyle had tried to bring him down quite a few times in the past."

"Wait, wait, hold up," G-Man said, putting his hands up in the air. "You're not saying that *THE…*"

"Yup," Kuron said. "Cybris Commodus Caine. I hope I'm wrong, but if my hunch is correct, who knows what is going on here. If I'm correct, then Castillo was right, G-Man. A storm is coming."

Just then, Kuron's cell phone vibrated in his pocket, causing him to jump. After four rings, he had it out and up to his ear.

"Laura?" he answered. "It's late…what is going on?"

On the other end of the line, Laura took deep breaths before answering.

"Kuron, Ryan needs you. He wants to talk to you. He told me to get you."

Laura's voice was very shaky.

"Okay?" Kuron said, somewhat confused. "I just spoke with him today. Is everything okay?"

Kuron left the bedroom and started to pace back and forth. There was a long pause before Laura spoke again.

"Please. Just, please, go see him. I beg…" her voice cracked.

Kuron waited for her to finish. Something was amiss.

"Just go visit him," she said.

"Laura, what's wrong? I need some more substance than just the fact that Ryan needs to talk to me. What's going on?"

Laura's voice sounded lifeless and cold this time. "Kayleen is gone. She was taken. Someone took my daughter."

Kuron's eyes went wide. He stopped pacing.

Someone took Kayleen? How does this fit into everything else, or does it?

"Laura, you've got to tell me everything. What do you mean? What happened? You need to tell me all that you can."

Laura ignored the questions. "Go see Ryan. He told me to get you…and Kuron?"

Kuron Taylor blew out a breath.

"Yes?" he said.

"Find my little girl…please."

Kuron nodded. "I promise you, I won't rest until she is back home and safe. I promise."

His cell phone beeped twice, informing him that the conversation had just been ended.

"Sounds like you've got to adios," G-Man said, peeping his head out from the bedroom.

"I guess so," Kuron said. "Keep in touch with me about what you find. If you need to go home and get some sleep, do it. It's past midnight, I wouldn't blame you. You can investigate this stuff in the morning. I have even more on my plate now."

G-Man scrunched up his face. "Sleep? What in the world is that? I'm a video game and coffee addict, I have no idea what sleep is. This forensics stuff and electronic crap? This is what I live for, man. I'm not about to go to sleep. I'll be in touch with you, my friend. I should have some results and answers for you by early morning."

"I owe you one," Kuron said.

"Nah, man," G-Man said, placing a hand on Kuron's shoulder. "You actually owe me two now."

Kuron smirked as he patted G-Man on the back. "You are a real one, G. We'll be in touch. Be careful. Always be watching your back, and I'd try to get out of here as soon as possible. If someone is monitoring this place, they'll be coming for us. So, we need to get out as soon as we can."

"Definitely. Be safe," G-Man replied.

Kuron exited the house and walked outside into the brisk November night.

CHAPTER SIXTY-FIVE

Ryan's cell door swung open and in stepped 6'7" tall Kuron Taylor.

"Leave us be," Kuron said to the prison guard who had just escorted him. "I'll close it all up when we are done."

Sitting on the awfully uncomfortable bed, Ryan sat and watched as the pudgy prison guard pushed the door to a near close and left. Kuron didn't bother taking a seat anywhere.

"Kayleen is missing, Ryan."

Ryan stretched, nodding his head slowly. "Yeah, I'm aware of that. Laura was here not too long ago."

"Wow," Kuron scoffed. "She actually came to see your sorry self."

Kuron seemed to say it jokingly, but Ryan wasn't in the mood.

He stared coldly at Kuron. "Now isn't the time. Listen, I don't care at all about myself. I don't care if my life is at risk or falling apart, but I sure do when my family is in danger. That's when things aren't okay. That is when I lose my cool."

Kuron nodded solemnly. "I understand, Ryan. You shouldn't be cooped up in here, especially now that your daughter is missing, and that your wife is at home distraught and alone. I know you are innocent…G-Man is helping me prove so, and we are on the brink of a break through. I know you had nothing to do with Mauer's death."

Ryan pounced to his feet. "I'm innocent?" he asked. "Am I really? Then who else would've killed him, huh? What breakthrough evidence did you find to prove me not guilty? What makes you *SO* sure that I didn't have anything to do with Mauer and the Shambles' deaths? Huh, Kuron?"

Ryan could see Kuron's surprise at his sudden outrage.

Ryan tried to settle himself down. He felt Kuron place a hand on his shoulder.

"I have found evidence. I've found proof that you are innocent, man. I got you. Like I said, as we speak, G-Man is working on some things to prove so. It's not a matter of *if* you walk, it's a matter of *when.* Ryan, Aaron Castillo is dead. Right before I came here, he tried to kill me. I was lucky enough that G-Man arrived in time to save my life. He's the one that put a bullet in Castillo's head."

"Hold up," Ryan said, shrugging Kuron's hand off him. "Aaron? Aaron Castillo? He tried to kill you?"

Kuron nodded his head. "Yup. I think Castillo was responsible for Mauer's death, but I don't think he was working alone."

Ryan nodded. He said nothing.

"The two men you said you knew in LA? We came across one of them in the hotel and got into a scuffle. In the middle of it, the hallway we were in filled up with smoke. Gunshots were fired, and a bullet struck my leg. Lucky enough, I have a good doctor here, and the bullet didn't do too much damage; just hurt like crazy."

"Yeah, I've noticed you walking with a bit of a limp," Ryan chimed in.

Kuron continued. "When the smoke cleared, we found out that the smoke originated from a couple smoke grenades that had Cybris Caine's 'CCC' engraved on them. We then found a woman dead in the hotel room that had been purchased under your name."

Ryan's heart sunk at the sound of that news. He felt sick to his stomach. He had never wanted that to happen.

"Long story short, you already knew it, but Cybris Caine's men were tracking you. You said you met up with Caine in Rome. So, I know he is involved in this, even though I don't exactly know how. I also have no idea why you've been drawn into something like this...now the evidence? We found fingerprints that look to belong to someone other than Mauer. I found footage of the night Mauer was killed, and I found papers that stated Mauer was retiring from the FBI and wanted you to take his place. I also got ahold of Castillo's phone. G-Man is working on uncovering everything right now. You are innocent, Ryan. It is only a matter of time until you are legally free to go, but your family needs you right now. Your wife, your little girl, the baby, they need you."

Ryan stuck his tongue into the inside of his cheek. "He'll kill my family, Kuron. If I am out there running around free, he will kill them. You just don't get it. I'm in this cell to protect my family. That is why I am here, and that is why I have been willing to stay in here."

Kuron grabbed Ryan by both shoulders. "Listen to me. Little Kayleen is gone. She is NOT safe, and you need to find her; not me, not Kyle, but you do. With that said, I do promise you, man, that I will do everything in my power to find that little girl. I'll do everything in my power to bring down Caine too. I will do everything I can to make that happen. He has been slinking around for far too long."

Kuron looked up at the single camera positioned on the ceiling above him. He was thankful that they didn't pick up sound.

"Knock me out," Kuron said.

Ryan lifted his brows. "What?"

"Knock me out, Ryan. Hit me. Right now. Just one blow to my head, and you get out of here as fast as you can."

"Kuron," Ryan said, putting his hands up in the air, "there is no way I can knock you out. Even if I could, I wouldn't."

Kuron glanced behind him, then up at the camera again, and back at Ryan. "Well then, my friend, you sure better make it look like you can."

CHAPTER SIXTY-SIX

Ryan walked out of his cell and threw the door closed behind him. He pulled up his saggy pants and made his way by rows and rows of cells. This was one of the few times that he cursed Kuron for being so huge. He placed Kuron's black-rimmed Ray Ban sunglasses on his head and came to a stop in front of an elevator door. There was an identification scanner next to the doors. Ryan placed his hand up against the scanner. He was relieved when the scanner's screen turned green and the doors slid open. Ryan smiled. His ID was still in the prison's security system. With a sly smirk on his face, Ryan entered the elevator and started his decent to the parking garage. After passing a few security check points, Ryan was free. He drove Kuron's car across the bridge leading from Ryker's Island to New York City. He was free at last. He rolled down a window to let the cool air flow through the car. As he did so, prison sirens erupted behind him. For the first time in days, he felt alive. Ryan Turner was free.

CHAPTER SIXTY-SEVEN

"And Goo-o-o-d morning, beautiful New York City. Looks like we are in for a lovely day today. We are looking at a low of forty-four degrees, and a high of fifty-six. There is a high chance of rain later today. Now, to other news, moving on to the opposite end of the news spectrum…"

Tim Mathers, anchor of the Fox 5 News station at six in the morning, flipped some papers around, and began to speak up again.

"It is stories like this that make my job hard. Last night, five-year-old, Kayleen Turner…my mistake, Kayleen Johnson, was abducted from her home. There are currently no leads on who kidnapped the young girl. The incident occurred at approximately 10:30 last night. If you have any information on this matter, please don't hesitate to call the following numbers."

The news anchor was silent for some time as two phone numbers appeared on the television screen underneath a picture of Kayleen.

The anchor appeared on the screen again and cleared his throat.

"And now on to more not so good news. At about two a.m. this morning, havoc broke loose at the Ryker's Island Prison. Ryan Turner, former FBI agent and step-father of Kayleen Johnson, escaped from the prison facilities. Nobody has seen any sign of him. Turner was imprisoned and awaiting trial for the murder of four individuals, one of which was the Head of the NYC Bureau, J.J. Mauer. This is the first that our news station has been informed of Turner's crimes and of Mr. Mauer's death, but Turner is on the loose and we need your help to find him."

A mugshot of Ryan Turner appeared on the screen.

"So, please, if you see this man or know of his whereabouts, contact local law enforcement immediately. Ryan Turner may be armed and is very dangerous."

Cybris Caine sat sprawled out on a sofa. He smirked at the sight of Ryan Turner's face filling the screen.

"Your help and cooperation are definitely needed to bring this man in. Once again, please, if you have any information on Turner, do not hesitate to inform law enforcement. Now onto our next story: a dog saves a young boy's life. Yesterday afternoon…"

Cybris Caine powered off the television and shook his head. He took a long drag from the cigar in his mouth, and then typed a phone number into his cell phone.

"Hello?" a voice answered.

Caine didn't even bother greeting the person on the other end of the line. "It seems our dear friend, Ryan, is on the loose. I knew it was a possibility that Kayleen's disappearance might lead to that. And as you know, Castillo is dead. Things are changing at quite the pace. I need you to do me a favor." Caine stroked Kayleen's hair. She was lying down next to his thigh, sound asleep. "I think this little girl here needs to be reunited with her mother."

"And what do you mean by that, sir?"

Caine looked down at Kayleen. "Bring her to me. I want Laura Turner in my possession. Things are finally getting interesting."

"And when do you want this done?"

"Now," Caine said sternly before hanging up his phone.

CHAPTER SIXTY-EIGHT

Feeling guilty and knowing law enforcement would be searching for Kuron's car, Ryan had dropped the car off at Kuron's house and was on foot now, with a single dollar in his pocket. With the knife he had retrieved from Kuron, Ryan had cut his pants at the knee. He used the knife to make an extra hole in the belt he got from Kuron too, so that the huge pants wouldn't fall off. He unbuttoned his shirt halfway, and covered his face, bare feet, and shirt with dirt and grime. It was gross, but it was a dire part of the "disguise." On his back, he wore a large brown backpack which he had stolen from a homeless man after a small scuffle. With his unshaven face, ratty clothes, dirty self, and the large backpack, Ryan looked like the typical New York City hobo. The only difference being that most homeless men don't carry around a Glock 21 and a large dagger in their possession.

He walked down 23rd street, keeping close to the packed sidewalk. He had been wandering the New York City streets for about an hour now, not sure what to do or where to go. He didn't know if Laura would be home and didn't know how she would react if she saw him. He knew he would have to go home at some point though. The only thing he was sure of was that he needed to get a lead on Kayleen. He had it decided in his mind that someway he was going to find out who took her that night. However, for the first time in his life he didn't know where to start. Aside from Kuron, he didn't have anyone on his side, and even Kuron was limited in what he could do right now. Ryan walked over the crosswalk to the other side of the street.

He had decided on what his first move was going to be. He knew a guy by the name of Tay Wang. Wang was originally from Hong Kong and moved to the states a little over a decade ago. He was a sketchy figure, to say the least. For about a year now, the FBI had been closely monitoring Wang and his actions. Awhile back, the Bureau got a tip that Wang was involved in distributing illegal weapons to the inner-city gangs in New York City, particularly to those involved with Caine. After some investigation, the FBI found that substantial amounts of illegal weapons were being exported out of New York City to various parts of the United States. The original investigation into Wang is what led to the bust at Mongolie's Restaurant; however, even with small busts, like Mongolie's, the Bureau hadn't been able to find enough proof and evidence to link Wang to any illegal activity. All along, Ryan knew Wang was involved, yet the FBI couldn't legally arrest him, for they had no true evidence against him. Wang was smart and covered his tracks well.

CHAPTER SIXTY-NINE

Ryan came to a halt in the middle of the sidewalk
where people bumped into him, cursed him, and acted as if he
didn't exist. He tried to think of where to go next. He knew
where Tay Wang lived, but wasn't sure what the fastest route
would be. He hoped and prayed Wang would be at his
residence.

Wang lived in a high price apartment within the Whitney
Condos building. Whitney was located on 33rd East, 74th
Street, between Madison Avenue and Park Avenue. It was a
beautiful building and was about an hour's walk from where
Ryan stood now.

Ryan didn't want to waste time by having to walk, but
he didn't have much of a choice; however, an idea came to
mind. He decided to put his homeless look to beneficial use.
He removed the bag from his back, sat down against a wall,
and begged and pleaded every passerby for money. Due to
the friendliness and selflessness of a few people, Ryan had
received $25.61 in the matter of five to ten minutes. Some
people's thoughtfulness never ceased to impress Ryan. In a
world with so much darkness, there were still many good
people.

Ryan caught a cab and fifteen minutes later he had
arrived at Whitney. He thanked the taxi cab driver and gave
him all $25.61. He had arrived, but now the tricky part was
actually getting inside the apartment complex. Individuals got
into the building by either getting buzzed in by someone at
the front desk or using a key card to enter. Ryan didn't have a
key card, and there was no way the front desk would ring
Ryan in. So, he decided to wait at the back of the building

next to the backside door. Ten minutes passed by, then twenty…and finally, a young woman exited out the door.

"Good morning. Have a wonderful day," Ryan said to her.

The young, blonde girl ignored him completely, which was fine by Ryan, who stuck his foot in the door the second she turned her back to him. The swinging door closed on Ryan's foot. As quickly as he could, he slipped into the building. Ryan removed his backpack and threw it down on the floor. He wouldn't need it. He ascended the staircase next to him and stopped on the third floor. He stepped out of the door to the stairway and stared down a long hallway.

What now?

Ryan's answer came almost immediately. At the far end of the hallway from him, Ryan watched a pizza delivery man knock on an apartment door. An idea clicked in his mind. He swiftly walked toward the man. The delivery guy handed a box of pizza into the room he stood before, received a wad of cash, and turned to leave, his back to Ryan. Ryan looked all around the hallway to find that he and the pizza delivery man were the only two people in the hallway.

"Hey!" Ryan yelled out.

The man turned around to look at Ryan with a disgusted look on his face.

"Yes?" he said.

Ryan trotted over to the man and reached out a hand. The man awkwardly shook it.

"This may sound crazy, especially the way I look right now, but I need your help," Ryan said.

The pizza deliverer took a couple steps back. "Bro, I don't know you, but I have to get back to work."

He turned to leave, but Ryan firmly grabbed him by the arm. He looked the man in the eye.

"Buddy," Ryan said, "if you help me with this one thing, I will give you anything you want…I mean, to an extent."

The deliverer shrugged off Ryan's hand. "You?" he said, chuckling. "You will give me anything? What could *you* possibly give *me*?"

Ryan looked himself up and down and motioned to his clothing. "Yeah, I don't look like much right now, but, I am a wealthy man and my wife is a nurse. We do just fine. Right now, our daughter is missing. Someone took her last night. I beg of you. I need your help."

The delivery man folded his arms across his chest. "If that is true, bro, you have my attention. Now, what could a young, broke, delivery man do to help you find your missing daughter? I mean, if you're some hobo asking for money, and using this story to get money out of me, nah, bro. I can't do that."

Ryan nodded, deciding to tell the young man the full truth.

"I work in law enforcement, and I am currently under-cover. Therefore, I look like this. There are some bad people messing with those I love. One of them is in this building, and I need to find him. My wife and I are desperate, and yeah, I know this is a lot, and is probably hard to believe, but I need help."

The man let everything Ryan said sink in. "If everything you are saying is true, how exactly are you wanting me to help?"

Ryan tried to think of how to answer that question but decided there was only one way to do so.

"Umm, I need your hat, that bag you are holding, and your shirt."

The delivery man laughed. "What are you smoking, man? You're crazy."

The man turned again to leave.

"Wait, wait!" Ryan said. "Two-thousand dollars. Cash. All you have to do is give me your stuff. You can tell your boss that you were mugged by a hobo. I'm serious."

The delivery man stopped, keeping his back to Ryan. "Two-thousand, huh?"

"Make it three," Ryan said.

The delivery guy jerked the cap off his head, tossed it to Ryan, and then threw his shirt off and tossed it to Ryan.

"I swear if you're lying to me, I'll find you and beat you down."

Ryan chuckled. "I'm not. Serafina Fabulous Pizza is just down the road, right? Where Madison and 79th street meet?"

"Yes, sir," the man said, now hatless and wearing a white V-neck undershirt.

Ryan threw the shirt over the grimy shirt he had on now and placed the cap atop his head.

"I'll find you," Ryan said. "I'll get the money to you as soon as possible. You have my word."

The delivery guy stuck out a hand to Ryan and Ryan shook it.

"Zane Linton," the man said.

"Ryan."

Zane smiled and left, pressing the down-arrow button on the nearby elevator. He stepped inside and descended. Ryan walked past the elevator and to the very end of the hallway. He stopped in front of the very last door on the left. He knocked on it twice and held his breath.

CHAPTER SEVENTY

He listened closely and could hear multiple voices inside the apartment. Ryan knocked twice more, this time much harder.

Footsteps.

The steps were getting louder.

"Yes?" a voice said from behind the door.

It was Wang.

"Yes, sir, Mr. Wang?"

"This is him."

Perfect.

Ryan cleared his throat. "I have your order here from the one and only Serafina Fabulous Pizza. No one does pizza better than Serafina."

Ryan smiled a fake, cheesy smile.

"I didn't order anything. Get out of here."

Ryan could picture Tay Wang looking Ryan up and down through the peephole on the door. Ryan kept his body close to the door, so that Wang couldn't see that Ryan wore cut-off pants and no shoes. He wore the cap pulled down over his face to keep Wang from recognizing him.

"Well, someone ordered pizza to room 201 at Whitney. Now here I am. No one does pizza better than Serafina."

"Yeah, yeah," Wang said. "You can stop saying that. Hey! Did either of you order anything from some pizza place?"

Ryan listened as two indistinct voices replied.

"Okay, listen. No one here ordered anything from you. Get lost."

Ryan listened as Wang walked away from the door.

Ryan knocked three more times. "I have your order from Serafina Fabulous Pizza. No one does pizza better than Serafina."

The footsteps inside stopped, and then started up again, getting closer to the door.

"Do you not speak English, punk?" Wang yelled. "Get lost!"

Ryan knocked twice more with his left hand, threw his bag down, and with his right hand, drew the Glock out from his waistband.

Just as he guessed would happen, the door opened inward, and Tay Wang stepped toward Ryan, only to be met with the muzzle of a gun pointed at his face.

Wang froze.

"Now maybe you'll want to listen. The only thing is, I'm not here to deliver a nasty pizza. Now turn around and walk."

CHAPTER SEVENTY-ONE

Wang did as he was told.

"Go left."

Wang did so, turning into a large living room area that held a huge sofa complex and a super-sized flat-screen tv on a wall.

Along the walls hung exotic paintings and statues. Sitting on the sofa were two young women wearing nothing but their underwear. Ryan rolled his eyes.

"Now, find somewhere comfortable and sit down." Ryan then glared at the two women. "And you two remain where you are, or I'll put a bullet in all three of you."

"Tay, baby," one of the women said, "what is going on? Help us, baby!"

"Shut up!" Ryan yelled out, shoving Tay Wang into the couch, and momentarily aiming his Glock in the direction of the women.

They both screamed and hugged one another.

"I better not hear another word from either one of you," Ryan said. "Don't test me."

The women looked petrified. Ryan assumed they got the point. He returned his focus to Wang, who calmly sat upon the couch, his hands in his lap.

"Mr. Tay Wang, it's been awhile."

Wang smiled. "It certainly has been. I'm honestly not surprised to see you here."

Ryan shrugged one shoulder and cut straight to the chase. "Where is my daughter?"

Wang shrugged. "How would I know? You're asking the wrong guy, dude. But, hey, if you want one of these girls, I can do that for you? That is about all I have to offer at the moment."

Ryan took a step toward Wang and punched him hard across the face. Ryan's hand stung from the impact. Wang laughed as he lifted himself back up into a sitting position. A stream of blood spilt out of the corner of his mouth, and he used the back of his hand to wipe it away.

"Let's try this again," Ryan said. "Where is my daughter?"

"You know," Wang said, "I really love the outfit. What are you, a homeless pizza delivery guy? It is definitely original."

Ryan's rage was only growing now. He wound up and hit Wang hard across the face, this time with the butt end of the Glock. Wang broke into a laughing fit.

"Do you realize I can sue you for everything you're doing right now?" Wang said in between laughing fits.

"Where is my daughter?" Ryan barked.

Wang shook his head. "Even if I knew where your daughter, or whatever, is, why would I tell you? Huh?"

"Because I know you," Ryan said. "You will do anything to save your own skin. And I will torture you and then I will kill you. I'll make it slow. I'll enjoy every single minute of it. As things stand right now, it would not hurt my feelings to do the same to these fine ladies over here, I'll do it in front of you, I don't care."

Wang stared at Ryan cross-eyed.

"Tay, please! Just tell him whatever it is he is asking to know. Please, Tay, please!" one of the women pleaded.

"SHUT UP!" Wang yelled.

The girls hugged each other again and started wailing.

Wang shook his head. "I don't know where your daughter is, okay? There. I have no idea. *NO* idea."

"You know what?" Ryan asked. "I'm guessing that you don't think I am serious. I think you're calling my bluff."

Wang smirked but said nothing as he crossed his arms over his chest. With incredible quickness, Ryan pounced onto Wang, and shoved his knife into the man's side.

Wang screamed out in pain.

"I am *NOT* bluffing, Wang." Ryan jerked the blade back and forth in Wang's side.

"Stop, stop! Please!" Wang played hard-headed and tough before, but Ryan knew he wasn't.

"Talk," Ryan said, one hand holding the Glock that was pointed between Wang's legs, and the other holding the knife into Wang's side.

"I give you my word," Ryan said, "I know you had dealings with Caine, and I know what you've been doing here in my city. I know about it all, but if you tell me where I can find my little girl, I will drop all of it. I promise you that, Wang. You will be able to live your luxurious life with your money, clothes, and whores without the FBI breathing down your neck. I will find Caine, and I will kill him, so he can't come after you either. I can promise you that too."

Wang grinned and looked away from Ryan. "You have no idea what you're doing. Besides, I'm my own man. Honestly, I couldn't give two cents about Caine. Sure, I respect the guy, but I don't bow down to him. He knows that too."

Ryan shoved the blade farther into Wang's side. The little man grimaced in pain.

"I know *exactly* what I am doing," Ryan stated.

Tay Wang stared Ryan directly in the eyes. "I won't tell you where your little girl is, because I don't know. I repeat. I do not know where she is! I will tell you something else though. Word on the streets has it that Caine's got plans for your wife. If you don't get home soon she is going to be gone, and depending on what Mr. Caine's next step is, you may never see her alive again."

Ryan jerked the knife out of Wang's side and stepped away. He couldn't decide if Wang was telling the truth or not.

"You're lying…you're lying!" Ryan exclaimed.

"Cross my heart, hope to die," said Wang. "That is all I know. Plus, Caine has big plans, Turner. Big plans. You have no idea what he is doing, and what he has been planning. You have no idea, and there is no way you can stop it."

Ryan started to think, his mind reeling. He didn't want to believe Wang, but he had to. If there was even a slight chance that Laura was in danger, Ryan had to respect it. He had to act.

"I believe you," Ryan said. "What do you know about Laura? How is she in danger?"

One hand holding his side, Wang shook his head back and forth. "I don't know what all Mr. Caine is planning. I just get all the hearsay. I do know that in one way or form, he is planning on taking your wife, and it doesn't sound like a good thing for her."

Ryan was stunned. "Wang, I need fifty bucks."

Tay Wang reached into his pocket and came up with a wad of cash in which he threw at Ryan.

"That's probably plenty," Wang spat out of his blood-filled mouth.

"You won't ever see me again," Ryan said. "I promise you that. And ladies, I'm sorry. I'm a father, whose daughter has been kidnapped. It's nothing personal. Now if word gets out about this, Wang, I will kill you. Plain and simple."

Wang chuckled and waved at Ryan. "Goodbye, Turner, and good luck."

Tay Wang wore an evil smile upon his face and Ryan didn't like it, but he scooped the bills off the floor beneath him and backed out of the apartment. Once in the hallway, he broke into a dead sprint toward the direction in which he had entered the building. His heart pounded as he waited for a taxi cab to pass by. Constantly looking over his shoulder, he impatiently waited for one. Finally, a taxi pulled over to the curb for him.

"8815, 158th Avenue, Jamaica, New York. A-S-A-P," Ryan said, handing the cab driver his newly acquired sum of cash.

The driver, who looked to be middle eastern, froze as he stared at the large sum of money. His eyes widened, and the car peeled out as he stepped hard on the accelerator.

CHAPTER SEVENTY-TWO

The cab pulled up in front of the place Ryan called home. Ryan leapt out of the back of the cab before the yellow car even came to a complete stop. In a dead sprint, Ryan ran to the front door of his house. He busted through the front door, Glock in hand.

"Laura!" he screamed out.

He stopped directly inside the door, waiting for an answer. There was no response. He felt sick to his stomach. In his heart, he prayed that he wasn't too late. He scanned the living room, two hands on his gun.

Clear.

Swiftly, but carefully, Ryan made his way into the kitchen.

Clear.

The master bedroom.

Clear.

Kayleen's bedroom…the hallway closet…the bathroom.

Clear, clear, clear.

The house was unnervingly quiet. All Ryan could hear was the sound of his own breathing, the house furnace working, and the humming of electricity flowing through the walls. Then the silence was broken by the ringing of the house's landline phone. Ryan considered ignoring it; however, he ultimately decided to find the phone.

He walked into the master bedroom and grabbed the phone off the nightstand next to the bed. Phone in hand, Ryan looked down at the caller ID, to find that there wasn't one. The screen was blank.

He answered the phone. "Hello, who is this?"

"The house looks great, don't you think?" the deep, bone-chilling voice said. "It's real nice and tidy-like. I don't know, maybe the tidiness is attributed to your absence the past few days, but it really does look good. Props to your wife. I really love how the bed is made, it has quite the unique bedspread. And your wife's lingerie that she has stuffed in that one drawer? Just wow. I mean, you have some great taste."

"Caine! I swear! I swear…"

"Easy, Ryan! Easy! We don't need to be swearing any. Where are your manners? Besides, there are women around, and speaking of, there is one beautiful woman who will be here in a bit, and I know she will just be *dying* to talk to you."

Ryan threw himself onto the master bed. "I swear, Cybris, if you touch her, if you hurt her, I will tear your throat out."

"My goodness, Ryan. Such anger," Caine said. "You really need to learn to contain it, to control it. Seriously, why so violent? You, my friend, should be undeniably ecstatic! Things are just starting to get interesting. I mean, finally! Now is the fun part. Now is the part we have all been waiting for. The fireworks, the grand finale."

Ryan stood to his feet and punched the wall above the nightstand.

"I don't know what you are doing," Ryan said. "I don't know your big master plan, or what the point of all this is. I don't know what you are trying to get at with me but leave my family out of this! If you want me, here I am! Punish me, torture me, kill me, do whatever you want with me, but leave them out of this. They have nothing to do with anything between you and me."

Caine laughed. "Tsk-tsk-tsk...is that not what I am doing here, Agent Turner? I am punishing you, I am hurting you, I am torturing you, and yes, I am slowly killing you. By hurting your family, *I hurt you*. Period. They have *everything* to do with what is between you and me. I could've killed you so long ago. You know that. Honestly, I should've put an end to you twenty some odd years ago, but let me ask you, where is the fun in that?"

CHAPTER SEVENTY-THREE

Sitting in a packed coffee shop, Kuron Taylor
fidgeted with the cell phone in his hand. After minutes of
doing so, while pondering and second-guessing, Kuron
finally decided to dial a particular number. After four rings,
there was an answer.

"Yes?"

"Kyle," Kuron said, "how's it going?"

"Well," Kyle began, "it's going pretty great. I'm just
sitting here having a nice breakfast with my wife. May I ask
you what day it is?"

"It's the eighteenth, I believe."

"No, Kuron, it is Sunday, and it is eight in the freakin'
morning. Now, tell me, what does that mean?"

Kuron rolled his eyes. "That it is your day off, you're
spending a nice, relaxing morning with Cindy, and I'm
interrupting."

Kyle laughed. "Ding, ding, ding! Bingo, my man. You
of all people have lots of days off right now, so please take
advantage of it. I'm serious though."

"Kyle," Kuron said, "listen to me, this is important. I got
a lead…"

"Kuron?" Kyle said, cutting Kuron's sentence short.
"I'm not even going to ask what you have been doing, but
you need to stop this. Do you hear me? You are suspended. I
wish it didn't have to be the case, but it is. This is a tough
deal we are in right now. It's hurting me just as much as it is
hurting you. I know that for a fact. Ryan is a brother to me,
yet you and I both must do what's right. You have way too
much emotion, too many personal feelings, and bias in this

deal. Kuron, you are going to end up putting yourself in danger, along with me and everyone else involved in this investigation. I don't know why Ryan did what he did, and I don't know who he worked with to do so, but I have a sick feeling that we're dealing with something big and very twisted.

"I have to protect you too, man, and that's why you need to keep your nose out of things. We have a great set of agents working to find what truly happened. This week, we are going to go hard into this case, and end it once and for all. Get some rest, spend some time with Malaya. I've got this under control. It'll all be over soon, I promise."

"Ryan is innocent," Kuron said. "Aaron Castillo…he tried to kill me, bro. He would've too, if G-Man hadn't shown up when he did. I was at Mauer's…"

"Kuron! You see what happens when you just go and do your own thing?"

"JUST LOOKING AROUND," Kuron continued, "for something, anything to prove Ryan's innocence. I found something too. I found something that is going to bring this case to an end faster than any of us could've imagined. There is a secret, hidden security system throughout Mauer's home. The system's history trails back a year and can be found on the television in Mauer's bedroom. I was getting there too, I was so close to finding the truth when Castillo came in. He pulled a gun on me, shot the television up, and told me that 'A storm is coming'. I don't know how he ties in, I don't know whether he killed Mauer or not, but I know that he is involved. There is a bigger picture."

"Aaron?" Kyle asked, sounding surprised.

"Yes, I never would have guessed him to be a rat," Kuron said.

There was a pause in the conversation before Kyle asked, "When was this?"

"Last night," Kuron answered. "It was before I received word that Kayleen Turner was missing."

"I heard about that. I feel so horrible for Laura. I can't imagine...why didn't you report Castillo's death?"

"Why? Because I was awake all night. I visited Ryan because Laura wanted me to. Ryan took me out and escaped, and I take responsibility for that. I forget how smart and tough the guy is. I spent the entire night searching for Ryan and especially Kayleen. I was at the scene and so was G-Man. We witnessed what happened, and there was no need to rile everyone up over Castillo, with everything else going on. Besides, G-Man is working on a few things, like recovering the video from the night Mauer was murdered, so the idea that Castillo was involved in Mauer's death is pointless too. G-Man will have what we need in no time."

"That's all true," Kyle said. "This is definitely a break through. Screw having the day off. Can you meet me at Mauer's?"

"On my way," Kuron replied as he ended the call.

Just as he shoved the cell phone into the right pocket of his black slacks, the phone rang. Kuron looked at the caller identification, and quickly answered.

"G-Man!" he said excitedly. "Any news?"

"For better, or worse, yes."

CHAPTER SEVENTY-FOUR

"Well?" Kuron said. "Let me hear it."

"First off, the security tape? I am on the threshold, looking in, right now. I've been working on it the moment I left Mauer's, thus, I am on the edge of a breakthrough with it. The dang thing was hard to crack into; it was protected like crazy. Although it has been stubborn with me, I am very close. I will have the film up and running at any second now. The fingerprints off the coffee stain? Those were quick and easy. It was hard to tell when they were from and if they are in any way associated with what happened to Mauer, so I look at the prints as our third most, per se, useful, important, or accurate piece of evidence."

"And?" Kuron said, urging G-Man to continue.

Kuron took a sip of his coffee, and almost spit it out as G-Man simply stated a two-syllable name. Kuron was surprised, but as he took a second thought to it, like G-Man said, the prints really didn't mean anything.

"Ah, I see," Kuron said finally.

"The phone. The last call was an outgoing call to one very familiar looking number, so of course, I opened up my own personal cell, and there the number was in my list of contacts."

"Who was it?" Kuron asked, finishing off his last drop of coffee.

G-Man gave him the same two-syllable answer.

"Let's just say, it will be very interesting to see who Mr. Mauer let into his home that night," G-Man said, before Kuron could make a remark.

"Yes, it will," Kuron said. "Any other recent calls that stood out to you?"

"Why, I thought you would never ask! There were a few numbers I didn't take any recognition toward; however, one did catch my eye. It came after the other call; probably fifteen or twenty minutes before your confrontation with Castillo. It was an incoming call that he received…now, Kuron, how about a quick quiz? Who do we know of that left over a week ago to go to his brother's funeral in Montana?"

Kuron stood from his chair and made his way for the shop's exit, tossing his coffee cup into the garbage disposal on his way out. He immediately knew the answer to G-Man's question.

"J.R., why?"

"Bingo. Jayren Raymond, my fellow tech geek. Now, answer this, why in the world would J.R.'s house phone call Castillo? I highly doubt it was the ugly little bulldog of his."

As he stepped into his car, Kuron thought about what G-Man said. "His brother? What did you find on him?"

"You are on a roll, Kuron! We've known each other for too long. Well, I used one of my trusty search applications that I developed and used it to look up the 'deceased' Jack Raymond, brother of Jayren Raymond. Instantly, a Facebook profile came up. With some snooping around, I was able to hack into his account, Facebook accounts are the easiest to do so, and I found him using 'Facebook messenger' to message a young lady, who didn't look to have the highest moral standards for herself. After a few flirtatious messages back-and-forth, the two exchanged numbers. Score! I had a way to contact the ghost himself. So, even though it was in the middle of the night, I gave Jack Raymond a call, and the son of a gun answered. Not only was he awake into the early hours of the morning, but he was high on something, and sounded like he was in some sort of club. Aside from all the details though, he is alive, Kuron. Jack Raymond is alive."

Kuron didn't know what to say. He threw himself into his car, and started the ignition; however, he didn't start to drive. "So, the funeral deal was just a bunch of…"

"B.S.? Yes. There never was a funeral."

Kuron shook his head. "It might be a good idea for me to give J.R. a visit."

"I agree," G-Man chipped in.

Kuron rolled out his neck. "I'll head there now."

"Sounds like a plan, Dan," G-Man said. "Keep your phone close, my friend. I am minutes away from getting this footage compatible with my computer."

"I will," Kuron said.

"Kuron?" G-Man stated, in an almost hushed voice.

"Yeah?" Kuron replied in question, bringing his car to a halt at a stoplight.

"Be careful," G-Man said.

"You too, G-Man, you too."

CHAPTER SEVENTY-FIVE

"Where are you?" Ryan said coldly into the phone.

"You'll find that out soon enough. Don't you worry about that yet. There is a cell phone in the drawer of your nightstand. I want you to grab it for me."

Reluctantly, Ryan opened the drawer, and there inside was a cheap cell phone. The phone he held to his ear went dead, and seconds later, the cell phone began to vibrate. So badly, Ryan didn't want to answer the device, but went with his better judgement. Caine had him pinned in a corner with his back against the wall, and Ryan knew the only thing he could do was play Caine's game. He flipped open the phone and placed the speaker up to his ear. He said nothing.

"Hello? Hello? Is anybody home?" Caine said in a sly, sarcastic voice.

"Yup," Ryan answered.

"Perfect!" Caine said enthusiastically. "Now, if you wouldn't mind, hop into your wife's cute little Prius, okay? Your beautiful lady so kindly left the keys in there for you. Once you get in, I want you to do exactly as I say."

Ryan walked out of his bedroom, and soon enough was in the garage, sitting behind the wheel of the white and black Prius. "Now what?"

"I believe you are forgetting something," Caine said.

Ryan was confused. "And what is that?"

"I applaud you for the valiant effort," Caine said. "However, I strongly recommend that you leave your gun at home. There will be no need for it."

Ryan pursed his lips and stepped out of the car. He walked over to the washer and dryer that were positioned against the wall. He set Kuron's Glock on top of the washer, and began to move back to the car, but reconsidered. He walked back to the washing machine, grabbed the gun, stuffed it back into his waistband, and returned to the car.

"Done," Ryan said, as he closed the driver's door behind him.

"Good try," Caine said. His voice didn't sound so playful this time. "Tests are fun, especially when I pass them. Don't play me for a fool, Ryan."

The hair on Ryan's arms stood up. He exited the car a second time and tossed the Glock onto the washing machine. He then returned to the Prius.

"Very good," Caine said. "Now, with the handy remote connected to the keychain in which your car key is on, open the garage door and leave. The black cars that you will see parked at the Shambles' home will lead the way. They will lead you right on 147th street, right on Riversdale Drive, and I guarantee you've been to little Harrison, New York before, right?"

Ryan, in fact, had. It was a small town with several farms. He guessed Caine was at one of the farms. He could picture Caine now, sitting in a large farmhouse or barn. Harrison. Somewhere that Caine could hide. Somewhere he could do anything and everything to Ryan and his family that he wanted to do. Ryan pulled the Prius out of the garage and turned to the right to follow one of the black cars that Caine had mentioned. The other car pulled behind him.

"Yes, I've been there," Ryan answered.

"Just look at her. Incredible…guess who just arrived, Agent Turner? Wow, you picked a good one."

Ryan pursed his lips. "Caine…I swear…"

Another voice spoke to Ryan through the phone now. "Ry-Ryan…"

A lump formed in Ryan's throat. "Oh my gosh, Laura! Laura, where are you? Are you okay?"

For some time, there was no answer. Ryan could tell Laura was struggling to speak. "I-I'm…I'm so sorry," she let out sniffling.

"Laura, don't you ever apologize to me. Don't. I am sorry. I am going to get you out of this, okay? Everything is going to be alright. Where are you? Where is Kayleen?"

"List-listen," Laura stammered. "Leave, Ryan. Get out of here. Get out of New York City. Get out of the state. Just go! DO NOT listen to them, you hear me? Do not do what this man says. Leave, Ryan!"

Her voice ventured off, and Ryan could hear her screaming in the distance.

"Well, hello again," Caine said, in a cocky, upbeat tone. "Long time, no speak."

Ryan didn't bother to say a word.

"You know," Caine stated, "it is pretty sad how you can just lie to her like that; how you have lied to her since the day you met her. Poor, poor girl…heads are really about to roll, aren't they, Ryan? Literally too. I will see you in, what would you say, thirty minutes? Be safe, unless you don't want to, of course. More importantly for you, be smart, especially if you ever want to see your family alive again."

CHAPTER SEVENTY-SIX

Jayren Raymond stepped back from his computers and television screens and hung up his telephone. He let out a long, heaving breath. He felt accomplished. He felt important. He felt extremely satisfied with the work he had put forth. J.R. entered his kitchen and wandered over to the sink. He splashed frigid cold water on his sweaty face. Using a red dish towel, he dried off his face. In the mirror positioned above the sink, Jayren Raymond stared at his reflection.

At first, he grimaced at the reflection of his face. The look of disgust didn't last long, as it soon grew into a smile. All traces of Jayren Raymond, the FBI technology and forensics specialist, were completely gone. The once black-haired, bushy-eyebrowed, small-lipped, button-nosed, shaggy-haired man was all but gone. J.R.'s hair was now a blonde-gray color, along with his eyebrows, which were now incredibly thin. His lips were overly large and puffy. His face had scattered wrinkles about it. Raymond now had a beak for a nose, which he wasn't particularly fond of. Not a single hair appeared on his face or neck, or ever would again.

The surgeries, he imagined, were out of this world expensive, but he didn't care, because he didn't have to pay for a single fraction of any of it. An even bigger smile spread across J.R.'s face as he stared into his own eyes. His eyes were the one thing on his face that weren't tampered with. He would've rather died before changing them. He refused to wear any sort of contacts too. His eyes were a gray color. They weren't an ugly gray like the gray of the city sidewalks, but they were a dreamy, cool, mesmerizing gray. His eyes were almost blue, but not quite. He was glad he kept his eyes the same, and he was happy with where he was now in life. Life had never been so good and stress-free.

J.R. left the kitchen and seconds later entered back into his bedroom. As he casually flipped on the lights, he stopped dead in his tracks and took two staggering steps backward. Sitting in a rolling chair in front of J.R.'s various computer and television screens was Kuron Taylor. Raymond's stomach dropped as he watched Agent Kuron Taylor spin the chair around and point a Glock in his direction. It was aimed right at J.R.'s chest. His gray eyes stared at the large man. He couldn't move. Kuron Taylor smiled. Jayren Raymond didn't like this. He didn't like it one bit.

CHAPTER SEVENTY-SEVEN

"Real convenient of you to leave your windows unlocked," Kuron said. "I mean, it wasn't easy for someone my size to squeeze through them but thank you. Jayren Raymond, what in the world did you do to yourself?"

J.R. said nothing. He remained frozen in place.

"It really is a shame what you've gotten yourself into. Did you think you'd get away with all of this? Really? How else did you think this would end for you? What benefit were you really going to get out of this? Because now, guess what? You are either going to end up in prison, or dead, depending on how cooperative you are with me, right now." Kuron stood to his feet and approached Raymond.

J.R. took three quick steps back but didn't get far before Kuron outstretched his long arm and grasped J.R. by the throat. Kuron threw Raymond down onto the living room floor like he was a rag doll. Raymond's head slammed hard into the back of the couch.

"You are one slinky, heartless, back-stabbing rat," Kuron said, gun still aimed in the direction of Jayren Raymond. "It was you that put together bugs in Mauer's home, *my* house, Kyle's, and, of course, Ryan's home. You have been spying on us and keeping tabs on us. You pathetic, filthy…" Kuron controlled his breathing. "If you were wondering, your eyes gave you away. But, I mean, even if you had done something to change them, you're not very good at playing dumb. You pissed your pants the second you saw me. You're pathetic, man."

J.R. still said nothing, avoiding eye contact with Kuron. "Where is Caine? I know you are working for him. Where is Ryan's daughter, Kayleen? What do you know?"

It took a while before J.R. replied, "I am unaware of anything pertaining to the whereabouts of Cybris Caine, Ryan Turner, or Kayleen."

Kuron cringed at the sound of the man's nasal, British accent. He always hated it; especially now.

BANG!

A bullet from Kuron's Glock exploded into the sofa next to J.R.'s head. J.R. screamed and covered his ears.

"Wrong answer," Kuron said. "This trusty Glock 21 has twelve shots left, and it wouldn't hurt my feelings to put every single one of them in you."

J.R. put his hands up in the air, and cried, "I can't! I can't. You don't understand."

"I'm fed up with you. I'm done. You have no idea how close I am to blowing your head off, right now. You have no idea, J.R.!"

Jayren's face was pale as he muttered and mumbled, "On the spot, I received in the near proximity of half a million dollars. How could I reject a massive sum of money such as that? Aside from this fact, how could I say 'no' to *the* Cybris Caine? Money or no money, how could I defy him?"

Kuron was fuming. "You selfish jerk. You're sick. Defy Caine? How about betraying your country? Has loyalty, or the security of your fellow men ever meant anything to you? Protecting and serving? That means nothing to you? Wow. Defying Caine…? How about stabbing your fellow Americans, colleagues, and friends in the back? Huh?"

"He will kill me. My life will be no more," J.R. whimpered. "If I speak a word, he will undoubtedly kill me."

Kuron glared at J.R., an apparent look of disgust on his face. "I can't even believe you…so much selfishness. Listen, I am going to give it to you straight. I'm not going to waste the time repeating myself either. You have two very distinct options here, okay? One: you tell me what I need to know, and you leave this house alive. Two: you don't tell me what I need to know, and I'll gladly put a couple bullets through your skull. It's your choice. I'm fine with either option, because honestly, using the cute little system you have set up in your room, and making a few calls on your phone, I will ultimately get what I want."

Shaking, J.R. spoke up. "Harrison," he said.

"What?"

"Harrison," J.R. repeated. "You need to go to Harrison. That is the definitive answer pertaining to the questions you have. Kayleen Turner is currently being held captive there. That is where you will find Caine."

Kuron nodded slowly. "Where in Harrison?"

"Gondelton. Gondelton Farms."

"Gondelton…" Kuron pondered. "It's a big place, right? Pretty old, sort of run-down, been there for ages?"

"Yes," J.R. replied.

"Lead me there," Kuron said firmly. "I drive, you guide me."

"I honestly don't exactly know how to get there. On second thought, Caine may not even be there. Yeah, I don't know if he really is. Sorry."

Kuron shot another hole in the sofa. J.R. whimpered.

"Don't play games with me. I'll ask you once, can you guide me there?"

Solemnly, J.R. nodded his head, and finally stood to his feet. That was a good enough answer for Kuron.

"Guns. Does a freak like you happen to own any?" Kuron asked.

The beaked man nodded. "Yes, follow me." Once back into the master bedroom, J.R. motioned toward a big open closet at the back of the room. "Top shelf."

Kuron grabbed Jayren Raymond by the shirt and tossed him on the floor. "Stay there."

J.R. did as he was told and remained curled up in a ball on the floor. Keeping a close watch on J.R., Kuron dug around through the closet, and came across a handgun that was the spitting image of the one he already carried. He returned over to J.R. and removed the clip from the newly acquired gun.

"Well, look at that," he said. "Fully loaded and everything. Twenty-four rounds between the two guns will do, I believe. Don't you think?"

J.R. didn't say anything, and Kuron reached down and pulled the cowardly man up to his feet. Kuron stuffed one Glock into a pocket within the inside of his jacket, and the other in the waistband of his black slacks. He smiled a sly smile.

"Next stop, Gondelton Farms."

CHAPTER SEVENTY-EIGHT

Keeping close behind a solid black SUV, Ryan glanced into his rearview mirror. Trailing close behind him was another black SUV, occupied by two Anglo men in the front seats. He had never seen the two men before. Ryan returned his attention to the road before him. He was slightly grinning. He couldn't help himself; he couldn't contain it. The random smile could have partially been closely attributed to the stress, the situation, and feeling completely helpless. Thus, it could have been a smile that came up because there was nothing left for Ryan to do but smile. He honestly could've been going crazy. None of those reasons stood one-hundred percent true, however.

Cybris Caine had slipped up. The cocky, confident, Mr. Know-It-All had missed something.

As Ryan veered around a car, he pushed the sheathed blade he had received from Kuron deep into his drawers. Although it was as uncomfortable as almost anything he'd ever done, he didn't care. Cybris Caine had made a mistake. He had slipped up. Although slim, Ryan now had some form of hope, some sort of chance. It wasn't real probable that a single knife would change the inevitable outcome of things, but maybe, just maybe, it could help shake things up. Maybe he would get the opportunity to shove the blade through Caine's chest, and send the cold metal into the psycho's stone-cold heart. Or, maybe he could split open the evil man's throat and watch him bleed out. It was a long shot, but Ryan liked running the possibilities and scenes through his mind.

The thought gave Ryan a glimmer of hope and that is all he needed right now. He did know that the second he pounced onto Caine, he and ultimately his family, would get showered with bullets. He knew by attacking Caine, the next time he would see his family would be in the afterlife. He knew that, and he was okay with it. Once and for all, Caine's reign of terror would end. Once and for all, he would be nothing more than a bad memory. Ryan looked to the side of the road to see a large green sign that read, *"Harrison   14 miles"*. Ryan Turner blew out a breath. He had never felt so helpless, so alone. He had nowhere to turn.

CHAPTER SEVENTY-NINE

There was a reply on the phone after only the second ring.

"Kuron! Where are you?"

Kuron rolled his eyes at Kyle's pleasant greeting. "Take it easy, man. Up front, I want to apologize. I am deeply sorry that I did not meet you at Mauer's. I should have called you earlier but something huge came up. I got caught in the heat of the moment. Kyle, I came across something big."

"Go on," Kyle replied.

"Mr. Jayren Raymond," Kuron said, giving J.R., who sat next to him in the passenger seat of Kuron's car, a quick glare through his Oakley sunglasses. "He's dirty. He got some plastic surgeries, redid his entire face, and the freak has been spying on you, me, Mauer, and Ryan. He has cameras and bugs set up in all our houses. The supposed funeral was B.S. This guy is a piece of work."

"Wow," Kyle said. "I never would have expected anything like this from him. I thought the funeral was legit. I felt truly sorry for the guy."

"Me neither, man," Kuron said. "It is what it is though. J.R. and I are making our way toward Harrison as we speak to…"

"Harrison? For?" Kyle said, cutting Kuron off.

"That's where Caine is holding Kayleen. I haven't heard anything from Ryan, and I haven't been able to get a hold of Laura. I've heard nothing from her. Caine is at Gondelton Farms. I just hope I'm not too late…"

"Ryan really is innocent…I'm sorry I doubted you, Kuron. I'm truly sorry. We still have time to make things right. Where are you? How far out are you?"

"Well, we've really just left J.R.'s place. Where are you? You still at Mauer's?"

"I'm leaving now," Kyle said. "I should be able to catch up to you pretty quick. If not, I'll meet you at the farm. You're a good guy, Kuron…a better man than I'll ever be. We still have a chance to help Ryan and put Caine away once and for all. We've got this, man. We've got this. I'll see you in a bit. I'm on my bike."

"See you soon, brother," Kuron said. Kuron tossed his cell phone onto the dash. "I wouldn't be surprised if Kyle decides to break that over-sized nose of yours when he sees you."

J.R. smirked and stared out the window.

"You really are just a freak," Kuron said.

Kuron reached for his phone as it began to vibrate on the dash.

"G-Man!" he answered. "What do you have for me?"

"Make that two," G-Man oddly replied.

Kuron was confused. He lifted his brows. "What?"

"Two lives," Gary Richards began. "I've killed two people in less than twenty-four hours."

CHAPTER EIGHTY

"What...? What happened? What do you mean? G-Man, what happened?"

"I saw her reflection in one of my computer screens at Headquarters. She had a gun pointed at me and could've blown my head sky-high," G-Man said. "I could barely make her out as I stared at the screen. She was sneakily squeezing her way inside my door. I almost froze, I really did, but something inside of me, some instinct or something, pulled me through. I dove to the floor, and rolled behind a huge, steel supply case. She fired twice but didn't come close to hitting me. I pulled out my Glock and gazed into my computer's screen. The lighting was just right. I could still see her reflection in it, clear as day."

G-Man took a second to catch his breath. Kuron let him.

He continued, "She was approaching me, gun raised-a little too high I noticed- and before I could even think about it, I dove out from behind the case, fell onto the ground, and fired my gun like crazy. Probably due to her being just as inexperienced with a gun as me, for goodness sake she's an accountant, she didn't fire a single shot back at me. I killed her, Kuron. I killed her."

"G-Man," Kuron said. "Who is 'she'? Who are you talking about?"

"Stacianna Kampton. I killed Stacianna Kampton."

"Stacianna..." Kuron was stunned, shocked. He and Malaya had always been close with Stacianna. She had always seemed like the sweetest, most caring, down to earth person...similar to Aaron Castillo. He knew Malaya would be crushed by this news. Kuron's mind was really reeling now.

Who in this world can I even trust anymore?

"That's crazy…absolutely crazy," Kuron said.

"Well," G-Man said, "did you confront J.R.?"

"I have him right here. He is working for Caine. He had a system of cameras set up in my house, Kyle's, Mauer's, and Ryan's house too. He sounded the alarm when he saw that I was snooping around Mauer's house. That is why Castillo showed up. But yeah, I am headed to Gondelton Farms over in Harrison. J.R. said that is where Caine is, and J.R. better not be lying to me or I'll kill him myself."

"I see."

"But, G-Man, did you uncover anything?"

"Well," G-Man began, "I did. I sure, sure did."

"Gary?" Kuron said leaning into the phone. "What did you find? Come on, man, I'm on the edge of my seat."

"Have you met with Kyle yet?" G-Man asked.

"No," said Kuron. "I decided seeing J.R. was a priority. I am going to meet up with Kyle here in a little bit though. He's going to meet me along the way."

"Gosh...Kuron…" G-Man said, unable to finish the sentence.

His voice was shaky. For what seemed like forever, Kuron waited for G-Man to continue, but he never did.

"Yo, G-Man, talk to me. What's going on?"

"Kuron…Kyle Harrison killed J.J. Mauer."

Kuron felt as if he had been shot in the chest. His cell phone fell out of his grasp to the floor. His head was spinning. He felt as if he was going to vomit. He found it hard now to control his breathing. Kuron picked up the phone with a shaky hand.

"There must be a mistake," he said.

"The prints, the phone call from him in Castillo's phone, and above all else, I watched him put a bullet through the back of J.J. Mauer's head. I watched the film. I watched him do it, Kuron. I'm so sorry. I don't even know what to do. I don't even know what to say. The past twenty-four hours has been too much for me."

Kuron was speechless.

"Okay," was all he could muster.

"Turn around," G-Man said sternly. "It is not safe. It is way too dangerous to continue on. You cannot take this upon yourself. You can't do this on your own."

Kuron bit the inside of his cheek. "Ryan would do the same for me, and by the looks of it, the only way to approach this is on my own."

It was true. He was completely and utterly alone. His question to himself had been answered: *no one*. There was no one he could trust. Kuron had never felt so helpless, so alone. He had nowhere to turn.

CHAPTER EIGHTY-ONE

There it is.

Ryan pulled his car up in front of two big, sliding barn doors. The barn was enormous. Not too far away was a cozy-looking farmhouse, but other than that, there wasn't much else around, aside from a very large silo and dense trees and fields surrounding the area. As he cut off the ignition, the flip phone in Ryan's pocket began to buzz.

Reluctantly, he answered, "Yes?"

"How was the drive, Agent Turner? Also, you can get out of that cute little car of yours now. Don't be shy," Caine said.

Ryan stepped out of the car and slammed the driver's door shut.

"Where is my family?" he said, surveying the area around him.

Two men with cut off sleeves and thousands of dollars' worth of tattoos scattered across their bodies, appeared behind Ryan. They were practically breathing down his neck.

"My boys will bring you to me," Caine said. "I am really quite proud of this place, if I do say so myself."

Two more men with the same look about them stepped out of the SUV that had trailed Ryan. They walked over to the barn doors and slid them open. Ryan felt a gun of some sort nudge him in his lower back.

"Move," one of the men behind him commanded.

Ryan did so. He moved out toward the barn doors.

"Now that is a good, good boy," Caine said on the other end of the phoneline.

Ryan spun around, and with all his might, chucked the phone into the trees and the brush around him. His action was immediately followed by a knee smashing into his lower back. Ryan fell to one knee, but quickly pounced back up to his feet. After only two steps closer to the doors, he was pistol-whipped in the back of the head, causing him to momentarily lose his vision and dropping him down to both knees. Ryan jumped back up to his feet, his vision blurry and legs wobbly. As tough as it was, he continued to walk.

Ryan knew that Caine had the upper hand, and that there was no way out of the position he was in, but he wasn't going to show Caine any sign of weakness. Ryan wasn't going to fold. He stopped right before the open doors of the barn and gazed up at the sky above. As the grayish-black, afternoon skies released heavy drops of rain onto his face, Ryan said a silent prayer in his heart, asking, begging, that everything would be okay.

CHAPTER EIGHTY-TWO

The rain hitting the tin roof of the barn was near deafening. Ryan made his way up an old rickety spiral staircase, heading up to a plain white door. The base of the stairs was just inside the doors on the right.

BANG!

The steps beneath Ryan's feet shook violently. He caught himself on the handrails. His ears were slightly ringing. The lightning was close now and fierce. It wasn't long before Ryan had his hand grasping the knob on the white door at the top of the stairs.

"Open it," one of the men behind Ryan commanded.

He held his breath and slowly turned the handle. He had no idea what he was about to find behind the door. Ryan didn't know what to expect, he had no idea if Laura and Kayleen were okay or where they were at. Slowly, Ryan pushed the door open.

"Laura!" Ryan shouted just before he was shoved to the floor from behind.

He scrambled back up to his feet and was firmly grabbed by the back of his shirt by two pairs of hands. Ryan threw his head back. His head made contact with a nose, and two of the four hands on Ryan loosened their grip. With his left arm free, he sent his elbow crashing into the second man's head, causing him to completely lose hold of Ryan. The first man who had been struck, grabbed at Ryan but failed, as Ryan dropped down to his haunches, spun on his heels, and gave the man a hard right-uppercut directly between the legs. The heavily tattooed man fell to his knees and puked all over the floor. Ryan dodged the vomit and an incoming punch all in one motion.

Ryan jumped up, grabbed the throat of the man he had elbowed and punched him square in the left temple, knocking him out cold. As Ryan tossed the unconscious man to the floor, the remaining henchmen tackled Ryan and held him down on the floor. Ryan struggled and thrashed around, but these two men were much stouter than the previous two.

"Boys, boys!" a voice said. "Let the poor guy go. He is going through enough already. Ryan! It's so nice to see you. Come, come sit down. Make yourself at home."

Ryan was released, and he pulled himself up to a standing position. He hastily approached his pregnant wife. Laura sat in a wooden chair, hands tied behind her back, her feet bound together, and blood covering her mouth and chin. There were dark, heavy bags underneath her eyes, and her head hung low. She looked physically and emotionally drained. She was up against the wall to Ryan's left, and an ugly pink, wrap-around couch faced her. On it sat Cybris Caine, who was wearing a white tank-top, a pair of holey blue jeans, and black Nike tennis shoes. In his hand he held an empty shot glass. In his mouth, hung a pipe. Behind the couch was a kitchen-type area. At the end of the large living space were two closed doors. Ryan dropped to Laura's feet and placed a hand on her face.

"Laura, I'm here, Hun. I'm here. What did they do to you?" he said in a hushed tone.

She lifted her head up and her busted lip began to quiver.

"I love you," she said.

"Sweet. Just sweet," Caine said, pretending to wipe a tear from his cheek. "I am sorry to break it to you, but he sure doesn't love you, sweetheart."

He grinned while taking a couple puffs from his pipe.

Ryan clenched his fist that wasn't on Laura's face. "I love you too, Laura…I am so sorry for all of this," he whispered. "I am going to get you out of this."

"Despicable! Unbelievable!" Caine said, momentarily pulling the pipe out of his mouth. "It is just unbelievable how easily you lie to her. Ryan, I think I already told you to sit down. I highly recommend you do so."

Ryan pulled himself to his feet and out of the corner of his eye he searched the huge room for the four tattooed men who had escorted him there. Two of them could hardly stand and didn't look very happy. The four men were positioned around the couch. Each of them held some sort of firearm. He looked over at Caine.

"Sit down, Ryan," Caine said, motioning over to the opposite end of the couch from him.

Ryan kept his eyes low and did as Caine said. As Ryan walked past Caine, it took everything in his power not to pull out his knife and stab Caine in the chest, right there and then. He refrained from doing so and plopped himself down onto the couch. He knew he had to be patient.

"So," Caine started, as he set his shot glass down next to his feet, "how is life treating you?"

An evil smirk was upon on his face.

"I'm doing wonderful, actually. Thanks for asking. And you?" Ryan said.

Show no weakness.

"Never. Better," Caine answered.

Just then, Ryan heard a scream followed by giggles. Ryan looked over his shoulder toward the closed doors at the back of the living space. Caine was chuckling.

"Good ol' Shaka. He really has a way with the ladies," he said, gesturing toward the sight of the giggling. "We got those two fine young women in from Brazil last night. They are really something."

Ryan said nothing. Hearing the name "Shaka" took him back to his time in Rome. The selling and shipping of young women made him sick to his stomach. He knew Caine had a hand to play in it for a long time, and knew Caine liked to have women for himself too.

"How do you like my new couch, Ryan?" Caine asked. "I mean the color, it just, just really grabs you."

"Yeah," Ryan said, expressionless, "it's great."

"Shaka!" Caine called out. "Take a break! I believe it is time for the fun to begin!"

CHAPTER EIGHTY-THREE

Buzz. Buzz. Kuron Taylor's phone vibrated obnoxiously in his left pocket. Pulled over in a truck stop parking lot, Kuron removed the phone from his pocket. It was Kyle. Kuron tossed the phone in the backseat and turned his eyes back to the road. Waiting. Watching. One minute passed by, then another, and the phone began to go off again.

"You know, there is no way you are getting out of this, right?" the handcuffed J.R. said, breaking the silence.

"Nothing is impossible," Kuron stated.

J.R. shook his head vigorously from side to side. "You just don't get it. Some of the most dangerous people in the entire world are on that farm. Caine, Shaka Nukawa, Zarius Zaloma, even Kyle. They are *all* there. You don't realize what you are walking into."

"I know *exactly* what I'm getting myself into," Kuron spat out. "I'm going to save Ryan. Plain and simple. Tell me though, why is Caine doing this? What is the end game?"

J.R. stared out the window. "You'll see soon enough. I don't even know what all Caine has planned. I just know it is big. Now, specifically with Ryan and his family? Caine and Ryan go way back. Farther than you even know. Mr. Caine is toying with him; killing him inside. He is defeating him, breaking him, little by little, piece by piece. Now, he is at the conclusion of his little game."

Kuron looked over at J.R. "What kind of personal beef would he have with Ryan? More importantly, what now? What is going to happen at Gondelton Farms?"

J.R. smirked. "You never really know with Mr. Caine," he said, completely ignoring Kuron's first question. "I do know that by the end of today, Ryan Turner and his little family will be no more. Like I said, this is the conclusion of Mr. Caine's game."

Kuron looked at the time on the screen on the radio. *12:00 p.m.* Kuron shifted into drive. The car jerked forward.

"I would call my wife, if I was you, Agent Taylor. You're never going to see her again."

Kuron wanted badly to bust J.R.'s pasty white teeth, but instead put the car back into park. He reached into the backseat and grasped his cell phone.

"Yeah, you can't deny that I'm right, can you, Agent Tay…?"

With all his might, Kuron slammed his fist into the J.R.'s lower left ribs. J.R. screamed out in pain. Kuron could have sworn that he felt a few ribs break. He ignored J.R.'s whimpering and lifted his cell phone up to his right ear. After a continuous ringing, the other end of the line went to voicemail.

"Please leave a message after the tone…"

"Malaya," Kuron said into the phone, "thank you. Thank you for being you. You are the love of my life, baby. You are the best thing to ever happen to me. No matter what has happened in our lives, you have been there. You are the light of my life. You're my world, baby. I wouldn't want to go on this journey called life with anyone else. I love you, Malaya. I love you forever and always."

With that, Kuron ended the message.

"Well," Kuron said out loud, "Kyle passed by here a good five minutes, or so, ago. He was going well over the speed limit, weaving through cars. I think the window of time between his arrival and ours will be just right."

J.R. groaned.

Kuron smiled. "I'm glad that you agree."

CHAPTER EIGHTY-FOUR

From the corner of his eye, Ryan watched as Shaka
Nukawa exited the room he was in, and approached the pink,
U-shaped couch. Shaka wore nothing but a pair of sweats. He
stared down Ryan as he passed, and grinned as he did so.

"Since you two didn't necessarily get to meet face to
face before, I guess I should introduce the two of you. Shaka,
this is our dear friend, Ryan. Ryan, this here is Shaka."

Ryan stared down at the floor below him and said
nothing.

"Shaka here has quite the story," Caine said.

Shaka moved around the couch, blew a kiss in Laura's
direction, and sat down next to Caine. Caine looked up at the
ceiling and wiped an imaginary tear away from his face.

"Shaka, Shaka, Shaka…Shaka wasn't wanted. He was
thrown away, disowned, abused. For fifteen long years of his
life, he lived on the brink of death. Eleven years ago, it was,
that I had some business to take care of in Chad. Yes, that is
in Africa for any of you who were wondering. It was a very
small, desolate village where I first met Shaka. I was set up to
meet with a client in that village…"

Ryan was staring at his wife, anger growing inside of
him.

"What did you do to my wife?" Ryan said, cutting off
Caine's story.

Caine threw his arms up in the air, looking exasperated.
Caine looked Ryan in the eye, then locked eyes with Shaka.
He nodded to Shaka, and Shaka stood to his feet. He took a
step toward Laura and slapped her hard across the face,

leaving a nasty welt on her cheek. Laura winced, but didn't make a noise. Ryan leapt up to his feet.

"Get your hands off...!"

"Ryan! Sit down," Caine commanded, holding a handgun in his grasp now.

Ryan clenched his teeth together. Reluctantly, he sat back down. Caine now pointed the gun in Laura's direction.

"That's a good boy," he said. "Let's get some things straight. When I talk, you listen. Period. Now, where was I?" He tucked the gun back into his waistband. "Oh, yes! My client's name was Sal. Sal Rivera. The man was a major weapons dealer, expert, and manufacturer from Cuba. He, however, lived and did his work in Africa. Reason being, all other excuses aside, he had endless amounts of laborers in Africa, who would do anything for clean water, food, clothing, and medicine. At fifteen years old, Shaka was one of those many laborers. I entered into Rivera's tent one day and found him sitting in a chair with his feet in a small bucket of water. At his feet, hunched over, was a scrawny African boy, who I guessed to be around eleven or twelve years old.

"The boy had his hands placed inside of the bucket and was washing and massaging Rivera's feet. 'Sit down. Sit down, my friend,' Rivera told me, in his thick Cuban accent. I did exactly that, placing myself in a rickety wooden chair positioned directly across from him. As I sat down, my eyes were immediately drawn to the boy. A shiver went down my spine as I looked down at him. The only thing he wore was a thin cloth around his waist. His back was exposed and looking at it sent shivers down my spine."

Caine's body shook, and he took a drag from his pipe. "I can take a lot. Not very many things bother me or get under my skin. I don't know why, but that day, for once in my life, I felt sympathy. I felt compassion. The boy had a giant 'X' on his back. It stretched from his shoulder blades all the way down to his pelvis. This 'X'? It wasn't paint. It wasn't even a tattoo or a burn, but it was sliced flesh. The 'X' had been carved into the boy's back by a blade. The deep cuts were infected and oozing puss. Sal must have noticed that I was staring down at the boy, because he said, 'They are my football playbook. My x's and o's,' Sal snickered. I didn't find the humor in what he said. I kept my eyes on the child. For a split second, the boy stopped scrubbing Sal's feet, and he looked over in my direction. I locked eyes with him and felt an instant connection with the little boy. Suddenly, Rivera lashed a whip across the child's back. 'Did I say stop?' he roared.

"Anger raged through my veins. Something inside my head clicked. I leapt out of my seat, reached out my arms, grabbed Rivera by the head and neck with both hands, and with little to no effort, I snapped his neck. I honestly expected the little boy to be frightened at what he had just seen, or at least look somewhat surprised, yet he looked calm. He removed his hands from the bucket of water, looked up at me and simply said, 'Thank you.' Little did I know that child was actually fifteen years old, going on sixteen. The boy went by the name of Shaka."

"Mr. Caine, here," Shaka spoke up, "is a father to me. The father I never had. I wouldn't look the way I do, or even be here alive and breathing if it wasn't for him."

Caine smiled. "Although only twelve years apart, he is the son I never had."

Caine placed a hand on Shaka's left shoulder. "You will never meet a more loyal, trustworthy, grateful man."

Ryan scratched his scruffy chin. "Wow, what a story. It reminds me, you're really starting to get some years on you now, huh? You should be closing in on being labelled as an official senior citizen, right?"

Caine chuckled to himself. "Well, let's see here, Agent Turner. I was, what, seventeen or so when I left? You were about six?"

Ryan said nothing.

Caine continued. "That was twenty-two years ago, believe it, or not; therefore, using your exceptional math skills, it would be easy to determine that I am at the wonderful age of thirty-nine. Senior citizen? Ryan, I am in my prime."

Ryan's skin tingled at the way Caine spat out his last sentence. Caine spoke up again. "It's just a surprise that it has taken so long for us to be where we are sitting now...so, Laura, now that we somewhat touched on the topic of mine and Ryan's past, let me ask you a question. Has your dear husband ever spoken about me?"

Weakly, Laura lifted her head and looked in Caine's direction, but instantly dropped her head back down, saying nothing.

Caine cleared his throat. "Excuse me, Laura, dear, I didn't hear you. You might have to speak up."

"He has," she said plainly.

"Oh, has he?" Caine asked, leaning back in his chair. "Please, do tell me more."

Ryan stared at Laura and watched as a slight smirk appeared on her face.

"He's actually mentioned your name quite a few times. He's said that you're a dirty, worthless scumbag. He's described you as a pig…and now looking at you, I definitely see the resemblance. You certainly match the description."

Ryan was astonished by his wife's bravery and wittiness. *Gosh, I love that woman.*

"Quite the feisty one, aren't you?" Caine said, glaring at Laura.

His seriousness turned into laughter. "This is why I'm strongly considering keeping you around. You'll be so much fun."

Ryan clenched his teeth together but kept his composure.

"So, Ryan," Caine said, "I take it that you haven't really spoken to this feisty woman about you and me? I'm pretty sure you know what I am getting at."

Ryan shook his head.

"No, you know exactly what I mean. Now, for once, tell Laura the truth. First things first, let's make it easy. Baby steps. Pull up your pantleg, and show us all that beautiful tattoo of yours…have you never seen this masterpiece of art on your husband?" Caine asked, looking in Laura's direction.

Her eyes were locked on Ryan and she shook her head.

"Don't be shy, Ryan," Caine said. "Let's see it."

Ryan pulled down his sock as far as he could, revealing a tattoo. It wasn't just any ordinary tattoo either but was a human skull with a "C" in place of each eye socket. It was nothing elaborate, but there was meaning behind it. Lots of meaning. It was a trademark; the identification of Cybris Commodus Caine's ever-growing empire.

CHAPTER EIGHTY-FIVE

"Isn't it fabulous?" Caine asked no one in particular.

He then reached down his dark blue pant leg, and pulled it up, revealing a very similar tattoo. The skull on his ankle was identical to the one on Ryan's, but this tattoo was slightly different. The skull was backgrounded by the earth. The earth was encircled by fierce, realistic flames of fire.

"I am the only person alive with this work of art on my body," Caine said. "All of my followers, like Ryan here, just have the plain skull."

Laura's eyes darted from Caine to Ryan. Her eyes were questioning, pleading, and confused.

Ryan looked his wife in the eye. "It isn't what it looks like."

"He has a very good point," Caine cut in, "because he really wanted to have a tattoo like mine. I mean he's an important piece of my empire, but not that important."

Ryan leaned forward in his seat. "Shut up! I swear…"

"Hey, hey! You need to work on not getting so riled up. Seriously, you…"

"I was twelve years old when I got this tattoo. Twelve years old. And, no, it wasn't by my own accord, want, or doing. Not even close."

"Yes!" Caine said, clapping his hands together. "Finally, the doors to the past have opened wide. Please, do let me tell a story, Ryan. You know how much I love to tell a good story."

CHAPTER EIGHTY-SIX

"It was 1996, and my goodness was life good. No, it wasn't good, it was great!" Caine said. "There was no tension in my family, we were all of good health, Dad and Mom were never fighting, I and my sister, Cindy, were on the best terms that we had ever been on. School was even great! I was making straight A's and was the captain of the high school basketball team as a sophomore. Mom and Dad, they were, by no means, wealthy. They didn't have much at all, really. They got by though and spoiled me and Cindy. One place Cindy and I had always dreamed of going to was Disneyworld. Even as a high schooler that dream held strong. I wanted to attend a Five-Star basketball camp too. Those were two of my lifelong dreams.

"It may not seem like that big of a deal, but being a family with no money, it was a big deal to Cindy and me. We had a collective savings going on as a family, and we were right there on the verge of having enough to fund a trip to Disneyworld, and possibly able to afford going to the Five-Star basketball camp. My parents were already planning the trips. Just when we had enough money though, Mom and Dad decided to use the money for something else. Adoption.

"Obviously, Cindy and I weren't enough, and my parents weren't already poor enough. They got word of two little brothers from Italy who needed a home. They had been discovered on the side of the road, next to a ditch. They were found a year or two before my parents found out about them. To that very day, they hadn't found a home. Our parents, of course, fell in love with the children the second they heard about them. Consequently, soon the two of them became a

part of our family. However, my father lost his job and there
wasn't enough money to adopt both. My parents decided it
would be impossible for them to support both boys. Honestly,
they weren't even going to be able to support me and Cindy,
let alone the boys too. Yet, no one ever accused my parents of
being the smartest people in the world.

"Now, the boys, their names were Alexander and
Johnathan. Alexander was six. Johnathan was four. Thus,
Alexander was ten years younger than me and Johnathan was
ten years younger than Cindy. We accepted them, I guess, to
an extent. We at least acted like we did, because really, right
off the bat, we had some ill feelings toward the two of them.
They were both with us for about a month, and Mom and Dad
finally made a decision. They decided to keep little
Alexander. They were shattered they couldn't keep both, and
that they had to split up the two boys, but they felt that if they
could give one of them a good life, they were going to.
However, they made it known to everyone, that if Dad got his
job back, and that if we got more money, our family would
adopt Johnathan too. So, there went any hope of me attending
the camp or all of us taking a family trip to Disneyworld.

"Al became Mom and Dad's pride and joy. He was their
little angel, their little trophy. Me and Cindy? We were
chopped liver. Rarely, did our parents ever make it to my
basketball games anymore. Instead, they were much more
interested in taking Al to karate, or to little league basketball,
or the park, or playdays, you name it! Four months. Four
months we put up with it before we finally had enough. The
little white kid had taken away our dreams and tore our
family apart. Our financial status had only gotten worse too.
Most days we were eating crackers, ramen, and bread. I was
an athlete. I mean, seriously. I can't live like that. I guess all

of it wasn't really Alexander's fault, but we did know who's it was. I still clearly remember the date.

"It was a week after the state championship basketball game. For the record, we won of course. It was March 17, 1997. Cindy and I prepared dinner that night and made some special accommodations to Mom and Dad's drinks. Mom, who was a wine lover, guzzled some of the wine right down. Dad though? He did not. My heart pounded while I sat at the dining room table, urging my father to try the wine. He never did.

"The sounds my mother made in response to the poison taking its course, were gut-wrenching, and still send chills through my body. Dad bounded across the table and lifted Mom into his arms. He screamed at her as he wept. Saliva and foam poured uncontrollably out of her mouth. We saw it in Dad's eyes as his mind clicked, realizing what had just happened. He stared at me and my dear sister in disbelief. Let's just say that we were prepared. We knew exactly where Dad kept his firearms, so I had one handy…"

Caine paused and looked around the room. Ryan looked over at Laura, who's chest was heaving in and out. Ryan wiped away the tears streaming down his face and shielded his eyes with a hand.

"We left after dinner. We booked it out of the house, Cindy and I did. We left for Canada in the family car. We removed the license plate, and on our way we took one off a junkyard car to replace it. It took a while to get there. We had to rob many people and businesses along the way, but in time, we made it there. We snuck our way across the border, and that was the start of it all. Right there. We had the taste for blood. We had the taste of the thrill of being on the run. We had the taste of feeling unstoppable. Now, here I am today."

Sick to her stomach, Laura spoke. "And the little boy? What happened to him?"

Caine felt that she already knew the answer. Instead of saying anything, he stared at Ryan. Ryan took the cue.

"Laura," Ryan said, locking eyes with his wife, "you're looking at him."

CHAPTER EIGHTY-SEVEN

Ryan shook his head. "It was the worst day of my life. I was only six, but I remember it like it was yesterday. Since that day, the nightmares have never stopped. My brother, and the closest thing I ever had to a family were suddenly gone. That night left a permanent scar that'll be with me as long as I live. I went back into the adoption system. I was never reunited with my brother; I assumed he had been adopted by a family, or else I probably would have been searching for him. Anyone I asked would either ignore me or tell me they didn't know where he was.

"Once again, I wasn't ever found a home. I was too mentally scarred. I wasn't lovable, social, lively. I had no emotion. Finally, when I was eight, an elderly couple took me in as their own. Although I was never reunited with Johnathan, I had a home again. I had a life. They were amazing, down to earth, hardworking people. They named me Ryan, and they raised me on a farm in South Dakota. They taught me and raised me right. I owe them everything. They gave me a second chance at life; a second chance at being something. However, I was twelve when Cybris and I crossed paths again.

"How had he found me? I have no idea. I really don't know. I was in the barn one day, feeding and milking the cows, when out of the blue he stepped into my view. I stepped back from underneath the cow I was milking, and my heart stopped. He grabbed me, and he took me. He took me to this trashy, run-down building far away from the farm.

"Now that I look back on it, the little shack Cybris took me to was a half meth lab, half tattoo shop. I was drugged and placed onto a table. The next thing I remembered, I was lying on my back in the middle of the barn at the farm. My leg felt like it was on fire."

Ryan glanced down at his left leg. "And there it was on my ankle, this evil, skull tattoo. I thought, why? What was the point? The answer became clear as I grew older, and as Cybris Caine's name filled news headlines. He was becoming dangerous, powerful, popular. He was being publicized, and many people loved him. Even many of my high school classmates adored him, honored him even. 'CCC' gangs popped up everywhere. So did the signature skull tattoo.

"Arrest warrants were put out for all those who had the tattoo. I consequently, had to drop out of high school. My guardians home-schooled me. For college, I also did home study. In my second year of college-I was twenty at the time-I still lived on the farm. My guardians were very old and couldn't hardly care for themselves or for the farm any longer. They needed me.

"That year, Cybris showed up again. I found him sitting at the kitchen table in our house as I awoke and walked into the kitchen for breakfast. He had a sly smirk on his face. His arms were crossed over his chest, and his legs were propped casually on the top of the table. With a gun in his hand, he had me sit down. He laid out five large stacks of cash on the table. Fifty-thousand dollars' worth. He then tried convincing me to work for him. He tried convincing me that it was the only way that I would get anywhere in life. He said it was the only way I could ever be anything, and not have to hide.

"Honestly, I almost gave up. I almost gave in. I almost did, but I couldn't. Long story short, he left just like that, and I found my guardians, Ben and Annie, lifeless in their bed. They had been poisoned. A trickle of dried blood was on each of their necks. So, why did I end up with this tattoo? Because Cybris wanted my life to be as miserable and difficult as possible."

CHAPTER EIGHTY-EIGHT

Caine clapped his hands three times. "Beautiful story, Ryan, just beautiful! Now, are there any questions from our audience? Anyone? Let's see here…Laura! Please, do present us with a question."

Laura kept her eyes on the floor in front of her, and then gazed at Ryan. "How…how did you get into the FBI? I mean how didn't the tattoo keep you from that?"

Caine jumped to his feet, obnoxiously clapping his hands together. "Muy bien!" he said, before kissing Laura on each cheek.

"Just perfect!" he said. "Now isn't this just fun? That is a wonderful question, I do say."

Caine sat back down on the pink couch and spoke up again. "And I do have the answer. You see, Ryan was smart. He really was. So, by his twenty-first birthday, he had a degree in criminal justice. Still living on the farm, one day a man stumbled onto the ranch. He was bloodied, hurt bad. He had been shot, and men were tracking him down. Those men worked for me. The man who stumbled onto the farm? He was an FBI agent. Ryan, would you like to take it from here?"

Ryan did. He swallowed. "He walked into my house as I was at the kitchen table eating some cereal. It was right before midnight. The guy looked bad. His name was Stefan Carter. He could barely stand. The moment he saw me, he fell to the floor. Wearily, I walked over to him, and rolled him over onto his back. He was bleeding from his chest and abdomen. I mean, I'm no doctor or medical specialist, so I didn't know what was going on internally with him.

"Anyways, I helped Stefan up to his feet, placed an arm around him, and helped him walk upstairs to my bedroom. I laid him on my bed and stopped the bleeding the best I could. All the while, he was mumbling things to me. He became more and more coherent, and I realized the things he was saying. He worked for the FBI, had been shot, and was being tracked down by a group of men. He kept telling me that I needed to run; that I needed to leave. I couldn't. I wanted to, yet I couldn't. I felt that the man's life was in my hands.

"Once I got his seeping wounds under control, I ran into my closet and grabbed an AR-15 rifle. It was semiautomatic, and it was my favorite gun. I used it almost every day hunting coyotes and rabbits, and target shooting. It was a beautiful gun. Still, Stefan kept telling me to leave. I refused. I opened the window in the bedroom to peer outside. That is when I saw them. My heart pounded. Then I started to think. How did I really know the man behind me worked for the FBI? I turned around and looked at the bloodied man. He must have read my mind, because in his hand he held an FBI badge. That was plenty of proof for me. I held my gun out the window and looked down the scope at the men approaching my house from the fields. I spotted out five of them.

"'Kill them,' Stefan said behind me. 'They won't think twice about killing you.' I didn't want to kill a man; however, it didn't bother me as much as one might think. I had seen lots of death in my life. I was a cold-hearted person, honestly, in a lot of ways. These men were bad. I didn't care if they died. I was willing to be the reason for their death too.

"As I held that AR out the window, all the built-up anger and hate inside of me that had grown throughout the years was coming out. It was resurfacing. As I peered through the AR's scope, I could see Cybris' face on every one of the men in the fields. Five shots were all it took. One after the other. They were coming toward the house in a perfect line. I didn't hesitate and dropped them all, left to right. I hit every one of them in the head. I was a very good shot. Always had been. I kept my attention on the men after I shot them, until I was for sure that they were all dead.

"I closed the window and turned to the FBI agent. I asked him how many of them there were. He said he had killed two and there were five more. I assured him that all five were dead. He was perplexed that I had taken them all out in just five shots. I reassured him that I was telling the truth. I called 911, and within about an hour, a helicopter arrived and took Stefan Carter to the nearest hospital.

"A week later he arrived back at the farm, thanked me, and offered me a job. With my degree, what he saw me do that night and the fact that I saved a federal agent's life, more than qualified me for the job. I opened up to him about the tattoo on my ankle and told him the backstory of it.

"He believed me. So did J.J. Mauer and Director Felix. Everyone understood, and contrary to Caine's wants and beliefs, I had made a life for myself. People like J.J. Mauer, Stefan Carter, and the FBI made that possible. I sold the farm and have been in the Bureau ever since. That is how, Laura. I did what is right, I always did, and it has always paid off."

"Yeah, yeah, yeah," Caine said, rolling his eyes. "Captain moral integrity junk over here. Just stop flattering yourself. 'Always take the high road, and if you do, your life will be set.' 'Everything will be okay.' 'The FBI is the greatest organization in the world.' That's all I just got from that, and that is all completely wrong. You did do a fantastic job telling the story; very intriguing. I applaud you. I was on the edge of my seat. However, you are so blind to some things. Even then, Ryan, the FBI was twisted. The FBI was dirty, even back then. At the time, yeah, Mauer was clean. It wasn't until about a year after that, that he decided to side with me…for dramatic effect, let me repeat that. *J.J. Mauer worked for me*."

Ryan was shocked. "What? No…you're a liar."

Caine placed a hand on his heart. "I put that on my dear mother's grave. There is a lot that you don't know. Your moral of the story earlier was, correct me if I am wrong, do the right thing and you'll be rewarded for it. Look where you are now? Look at the position you've put your family in? Yeah, real rewarding, right?" Caine snickered. "And for your beloved FBI, you are just finding out how dirty it really is. You had no idea all along who you really worked for, who you worked with, who you befriended. You now see that you knew absolutely nothing. *Nothing.* And it is amazing. This is really entertaining for me. I must be honest, it really is, and today is only going to get better."

Ryan shook his head. "No. No," he said. "I knew Mr. Mauer. He was odd, yeah, but he was a friend. He couldn't have…"

"Mr. J.J. Mauer worked for me," Caine said, cutting Ryan off. "So, did, or does, a very large number of the FBI. Honestly, I don't even have a number anymore on how many there are inside the FBI that work for me. That number is only growing too."

Ryan didn't know what to think. He didn't know what to say. He was completely speechless.

Is Caine just playing games with me?

Just then, the door leading into the living space from the barn, opened. Inside stepped a Caucasian man of about six feet tall and looks that the ladies faint over. Ryan locked eyes with the man. The man by the name of Kyle Harrison smiled.

CHAPTER EIGHTY-NINE

"And right here, ladies and gentlemen, is one of the most lethal of those FBI men and women. The one, the only, Kyle Harrison," Caine said, jubilantly.

"Surprise!" Kyle said as he approached the couch.

"How are things, Kyle?" Caine asked.

Kyle sat down next to Caine, and Caine wrapped an arm around Kyle's shoulders.

"Well," Kyle began, "we have a dilemma. Big, dark, and ugly is on to us. He should be here any second now. Oh, and he has Raymond."

"That Raymond guy..." Caine said, sounding annoyed. "I knew he could end up being a liability. All brains, no balls. Agent Taylor will be no problem. You four clowns," Caine said, motioning to four of the now eight tatted-up henchmen in the room, "we have intruders. You know what to do. Just kill them both, would you? Unless, our sniper doesn't take them out first."

Cybris popped his knuckles and leaned back in his seat. "So, Kyle, to get you up to date, we were just discussing the FBI and how it practically works for me, and how Mauer was one of us, so-on and so-forth."

"Oh, yes," Kyle said. "The old guy was wonderful for us. He was probably the key to expanding Mr. Caine's empire throughout the FBI. He was an essential asset; one of the greatest weapons we have ever had."

Ryan shook his head again and Kyle noticed.

"Ryan," he said, "just think about it. Think about some of the agents' deaths we have had. Think about some of the questionable 'missions' there have been, or some of the 'investigations'. Orders came straight from Mauer. Numerous cases, investigations, missions, arrests, and the agents on the cases? Fake. False. They were all to either to perform acts of terrorism, murders, drug exchanging, or any other Empire business; or, to get rid of agents like you, who ride the moral highroad and are impenetrable. Much of what we did was to remove agents who are actually clean. All the random, horrifying deaths within the Bureau last year? All those agents, specialists, and operatives who passed away? They were all set-up."

Caine nodded. "Beautiful, isn't it? Now that we are all here, how about we recap the last few days, just for fun? So! Actually...let's begin at Mongolies. That is a perfect place to start..."

CHAPTER NINETY

Sitting in his stationary car, amid trees and more trees, Kuron finished listening to J.R. explain the outline of the Gondelton Farm Headquarters.

"So," Kuron said, "this path up here that is going through all the trees? It loops around behind the big red barn? There, facing the back of the house, to the left, will be a farmhouse? To the left of that is a large white silo, that is sort of in front of the barn? The barn, house, and silo make a 'U' shape? There are fields, fields, and more fields surrounding the entire area?"

J.R. nodded. "That is all correct."

"Okay," Kuron said. "And Caine? Ryan? Where do you think they will be?"

"I honestly don't kn…"

"Where will they be, J.R.?"

J.R. sighed. "The house is slightly small, out in the open, and obvious. The barn; however, there is an installed living space at the top of the barn. The living quarters make up the upper, probably third of the barn. They may very well be up there."

Kuron nodded. He got out of the car, wrapped around to the passenger side, and threw open the shotgun door. Already his back was soaked from the pouring rain. He opened the glove box and removed a pair of handcuffs from the inside of it. He then clasped one end of the cuffs to the chain separating the cuffs already on J.R.'s wrists, and the other end onto the handlebar above the passenger door.

J.R. started to complain, but Kuron ignored him.

"I'll be right back," Kuron said, slamming the door shut.

He drew out the pistol from his waistband and turned off the safety, leaving his personal Glock in the holster on his hip. He started down the path through the thick trees, gun ready, and eyes and ears peeled, ready for anything.

CHAPTER NINETY-ONE

At the very top of the white silo, he laid there in the prone position with his head up. Watching. Waiting. With his left eye pressed against the end of the rifle's scope, he slowly moved the gun left-to-right-to-left-to-right. Back and forth he scanned the area. He moved the scope's sights through the trees, which engulfed a path. The rain had drenched him, and the constant strikes of lightning around him sent extra adrenaline coursing through his veins. The platform atop the silo was slick, along with the ladder that lead up to where he now laid. Lying there, he felt as if he were a sopping wet fish out of water and could slip off the side of the silo at any second. The rain; however, took little to no effect on the scope. It was a heated-interior, tactical waterproof scope.

After patiently watching and waiting…watching and waiting…he could see the shape of a man moving through the middle of the trees. The big man in the trees was moving fast. The man atop the silo then swung the rifle to the right, drew in a breath and held it. His finger on the trigger became heavy and still. At that instant, he was one with the rifle. He had been in this position plenty of times before, in even far worse weather than this. This was cake. This was nothing. The rain and trees no longer seemed dense. His target through the scope seemed clear as day.

Now.

He let out his breath and pulled the trigger.

CHAPTER NINETY-TWO

"I am just going to be straight up and honest with you. You were supposed to die that night at Mongolies. You were. Both you and Kuron Taylor were," Caine said.

Confused, Ryan glanced in Kyle's direction with a questioning look on his face.

"I was going to shoot you and leave you to die in that basement," Kyle said. "Paulie talking to Kuron ruined the entire plan. I was going to escape and shoot Kuron on the way out and let everyone in that building perish. Paulie Jr's dumb self screwed it all up. I decided killing you guys would have to take place another day."

Ryan heard everything Kyle said. His mind had wandered to another thought now. Laura seemed to read his mind and chipped in.

"Cindy...how could you do this to her?" Laura snapped.

Ryan nodded his head in agreement. Caine and Kyle both grinned.

"Yes," Caine said shaking his head from side to side. "Poor, poor Cindy. She is doing okay though. As a matter of fact, she is over at the farmhouse. She is watching her little niece-slash-stepdaughter. What is her name again? Kay-Kayleen, is it?"

Ryan was stunned, but once again, confused.

"Cindy..." he said, putting two and two together.

"Yes, Cindy!" Caine exclaimed. "Our beautiful sister!"

Ryan couldn't believe it. The bombshells just kept crashing down. Laura's eyes enlarged.

"Stepdaughter? What are you talking about, you freak?" Laura said.

Caine snickered. "I can't believe it never clicked with you, Laura. The dashing, charming Kyle Harrison never looked familiar to you? You just completely forgot about your in-depth past with good ol' Kyle?"

Laura stared at Kyle, then back at Caine, back at Kyle, and then back at Caine again. She shook her head.

"Honey," Caine said, "Kyle Harrison is the new and improved, 'post-plastic surgery-afied', Braxton Kyler Reddick-AKA the Invisible Man. The man who bombed the Smithsonian, who killed thirty-five U.S Congressmen, the man who suddenly disappeared out of thin air."

"What does that have to do with Laura? What does that have to do with any of this? What are you saying?" Ryan said.

"Braxton Reddick is my ex-husband," Laura said, staring off into the distance.

CHAPTER NINETY-THREE

"He was so hypnotizing, so manipulative, so dashing, so ugh…I was young, dumb, and fell hard for him," Laura continued. "He seemed like a good enough guy. We didn't waste time before getting married, so I guess I didn't give myself time to truly get to know him. I really thought he was a caring, sweet, hardworking, honest man.

"After I had Kayleen, I found that he was none of these things. The first time I became suspicious of him was the night I awoke with stomach pain and found him sitting on the couch in the living room. I had thought that he was working overnight as a business-man for Apple. Yeah, stupid, right? His torso was covered in blood, and he was whispering harshly into his cell phone. He was oblivious to me walking into the room.

"He saw me and quickly hung up the phone. He explained that he was talking to the police department and that he had been shot by some thugs as he was caught in the middle of a drive-by-shooting. Something told me, I don't know if it was the look in his eye, that he was lying. I offered to rush him to the hospital, yet he, for some odd reason, declined my offer. He said he had it taken care of.

"The final straw was when I found guns and drugs buried underneath the floor of the master bedroom's closet. Immediately, I called the police. However, he never came back home. I never heard from him again. Weeks later, his face appeared on a news station while I was watching the television one morning. He was being labelled as 'The Invisible Man'. My husband was a wanted murderer and psycho, and I had no idea. He had been in hiding under the roof of my house and I was completely oblivious to it all."

"And it killed you inside to think your new husband was a murderer too," Ryan chipped in, resting his face in his hands.

"Oh, love," Caine said. "Isn't it just a monster? Gosh, all this uncertainty, twisted and sketchy pasts, realizations, epiphanies, are just so entertaining. I am loving every minute of it…honestly, we should be broadcasting this. This is a grade A, award-winning type script. Really, it is just magnificent…now, back to the meat of our marvelous story. Mauer was getting soft. Soft doesn't cut it with me. He was bound to mess things up. So, we told him we had a master plan to finally put you away…"

"Before you continue to ramble on," Ryan interrupted, "can I ask you something?"

"Let me hear it," Caine said.

"Why now? Why do all of this to me now? You are going to kill me anyway. So, what makes right now so special when you could've put me away so many times before?"

"Great question," Caine replied. "I did try to end you a few times before, but you are slick. Also, I am actually happy I never did. Like Mongolies, you were supposed to die. At that point in time, my presence within the FBI was growing rapidly. You and Kuron Taylor were moral rocks. There would be absolutely no swaying you two, and being the huge assets that you are, I thought that it would be of my best interest to get you out of the way. Once you did get out of that situation alive, I saw the attraction that you and Laura drew toward one another. I realized there was no fun, no true justice, in just killing you. Kyle realized it too, especially with his growing hatred toward you. We needed to make you suffer.

"Ryan, there are several ways to kill a man, and everyone is different. I look at death in a whole other sense. I could've shot you dead multiple times. Really, I could've even tortured you, but there is no fun, enjoyment, or even significance in that. Not even close. No, killing you takes much more.

"Yeah, at Mongolies, I was tired of waiting around and just wanted you out of the way. But, like I said, I am glad you didn't die that night. To kill you, I had to kill you from the inside-out. I had to break you. Shatter you. Destroy you. To break a man like you, one must destroy everything he cares about: his loved ones, his job, his image, his credibility, his life.

"I know you. You couldn't care less about yourself, really. By tearing apart your life though? I kill you little by little until you are nothing. Until you have nothing. I tear you apart, from the inside-out. That is how to make you suffer. I never wanted to kill your physical self, Ryan. I wanted to destroy your inner self. Your soul. That is the point of all this. That is the answer to your question of 'why now'.

"It took a while, and several times I almost recklessly took your life easily and meaninglessly, but I guess fate has its way with things, thus here we are. You are probably thinking too, 'why me?'. Well, I'll tell you exactly why. You stole Kyle's spotlight in the FBI, and his woman. You took ownership of the only woman he had ever loved. You have it all, Ryan. And me? You already know that. You took my family's love from me. You ruined my life, even if you didn't know it at the time. Where we are now, has been the big plan ever since you entered the Bureau. It has been the plan ever since you shot down my men at your old farm."

Ryan nodded. "So, revenge is what this is all about, along with getting me out of the way for good. You want me gone, and you have been turning agents to your side. You have been working your influence into the FBI little by little. There is more to all of this. So, what is the motive? What is the bigger picture? There is something going on here that is bigger than just me."

Something in Caine's eyes changed. It sent a fear into Ryan that he had never quite felt before.

"Mr. Ryan Turner, you've seen the movies, the television shows, the video games...I plan to take control of the world."

CHAPTER NINETY-FOUR

Ryan Turner couldn't keep from smirking. "Oh, is that right?"

Caine smiled. "Go ahead, laugh, smirk, don't take me seriously. That sort of disbelief and lack of taking me seriously is what will ultimately lead to my success. It is what has led to my success thus far. You can laugh all you want. I want a global government. Globalism to the max; all run under me and my people. I plan to do so one country at a time. My influence is strong in every nation on earth, right now. It is only getting stronger. Therefore, I started with what I believe to be the world's stronghold, the world's powerhouse. The United States of America.

"This probably seems farfetched to you. It probably seems bizarre and irrational. It's not. So, how could so many people follow and respect me? How has my Empire grown so fast? How could I have it in my mind that taking over the world is even a possibility? I think you underestimate me and misjudge the people of this world. People treat world government and world domination like it is impossible. That is why it is in the film and entertainment industry. It is supposed *'non-fiction'*. That is what people have in their heads.

"What individuals like you fail to realize is that there are so-o-o many around the earth that have the same mindset, the same dream as I do…a world where everyone lives 'the dream', where everyone makes a living happily, easily, and wealthily; and those who can't compete or don't want to take part in this dream, are killed off due to the wonderful theory of natural selection. That is why people follow me. That is why my Empire is growing each and every day. People see my vision. They want my vision. I have given people hope. I have given them hope they never thought was possible. That is enough though. I will stop right there. I won't spoil it all."

Ryan said nothing. Caine's plan seemed offset, irrational, improbable, insane. However, Ryan believed Caine. He knew what he was capable of. He knew how powerful he had grown.

"Back to our dear friend, Mr. J.J. Mauer," Caine said, breaking the momentary silence. "The day he died, he truly believed that we had a plan to kill you once and for all. I explained to him that he was no longer needed at the Bureau, and that we had a plan for you, and needed you in his position. He fell for it. After being diagnosed with cancer, he seemed to be getting soft and starting to feel guilty about what he had become. I knew…"

"Let me stop you again," Ryan interrupted. "I don't care what you think, Cybris, but this world, especially this country, is good. There are parts of this Earth that aren't, but the good, the light? It always prevails. *Always*. This has been the case throughout all of history. You are going to start with the U.S.? You won't come close to what you're trying to achieve. It's not going to happen. This land of the free was built on amazing, good people. Strong, moral, freedom-loving people cannot be beat or broken."

Caine broke into a fit of laughter. "You…ha-ha! You really don't believe me? It's quite comical. You really don't think I can achieve the feat I speak of? I mean, it's okay, it really is. It's perfectly fine that you don't. Ryan, I have the strongest, most wide-spread army in the world. Unlike any other military on this earth, my empire expands over every country on this planet.

The pathetic U.S.? The United States of America is filled with so many ungrateful, lazy, and pissed off individuals. It is full of so much behind the scenes evil, contention, hate, and anger. I have ins with every U.S. military branch and every branch of the U.S. government. Hell, the majority of the FBI now works for me. It'll be easy, Ryan. *Scary easy.*

To be honest with you, you are a pretty big speed bump. I'll give you some credit. You are very dangerous when it comes to us trying to achieve our goals, which is the main reason why you need to be terminated. Once you are out, the FBI is mine, which means even closer ties to the government are mine. Once the government is practically in the palm of my hand, I have the White House-where I already have men and women working closely to-completely in my grasp. With the White House in my control, and the citizens of the United States on their knees, I won't be stopped. I will have the keys that I need. The codes that I need. I will have complete and utter control over the United States' nu..."

"Nuclear arsenal..." Ryan said, finishing Caine's sentence, his voice trailing off.

CHAPTER NINETY-FIVE

"Bingo," Caine said, smiling ear to ear. "We will put countries at war, weakening them all. Destroying them. Tearing them all apart from the inside-out. That is when we come in. The world will need me. My people will be ready. We will take action and we will pick the world up out of its own ashes. Taking power will be nothing but a walk in the park."

The room was completely silent.

Caine smiled. "Now, are there any more comments or questions?"

No one said a word.

"No? Okay, good. Where was I...yes! Your meeting with Mauer that night was the beginning of the mayhem we threw you into. It was the start of all this. Right before you got to his house, Kyle gave J.J. a visit. The poor lad wasn't expecting what came to him. Kyle shot him in the back of the head with the gun he retrieved from your place. He left in a hurry, but didn't go far, of course. You showed up, Mauer didn't answer the door, so you let yourself in. You walked inside the house to find Mauer dead, with a Glock lying next to him that you believed was yours. That is when Kyle arrived onto the scene again. So, your fingerprints were on the doorknob, your gun with your prints on it, which was used as the murder weapon, and Kyle Harrison, one of your best friends, there to witness it. The perfect scene. You knew it too. So, you ran. I think you had a feeling something big was going on too. And who took care of the investigation at Mauer's? Kyle and *our* men in the agency. With J.R.'s help, we tracked your cell to the hotel you hunkered down in the night Mauer died. Anyways, we knew where you were. I have no idea why you stayed there, but that is another story. Kyle, continue." Caine nudged Kyle.

"While you went to the outskirts of New York City to sulk, I gave the Shamble's a little visit. I had to. I loved those people, always had. I loved you too, Laura."

Ryan clenched his fists. Anger raged inside of him as he started to shake. He wanted to kill Kyle right there and then. He knew he had to compose himself, and let the conversation continue in order to prolong his and Laura's lives. The longer they talked, the more of a chance they had of getting out alive. As slim as that chance was. Caine and Kyle were pushing him to his limits though.

"I had to take Gerald and Shirley out," Kyle said. "As much as I didn't want to, I had to. They saw me get in and out of your home that day. They were witnesses. They would have said something. Killing them meant cutting off any possible loose ends. So, I knocked on their door and explained that I had been shot and needed their help. They believed the story. They took me in, and I took them out. Laura, that letter to you? Gerald scratched that down for me. Honestly, it helped putting dirt on Ryan, but it was to kill you inside too. It was to erase as close to all thought from your mind that Ryan might be innocent. It was to break you."

Laura kept her head low and said nothing.

"As I was leaving their house, ex-agent, Johanson Chame, tried to be a hero and attacked me. He is their trusty housekeeper-type guy and came in and saw me, I guess. He charged me, wielding a blade in hand. I killed him with the very blade that he attacked me with. That was that. The old guy did put up a decent fight. I will give him credit. Once I left the house, I got a room at the same hotel you were at. The

Hilton Airport Hotel. A few of our guys trashed your car. At this point in time, we decided last minute that we wanted you caught. So, we brought in some of the clean FBI agents, including Kuron, and some NYPD officers. At that point in time, Caine had also ordered me to kill you, Laura. Just to add to Ryan's pain."

Ryan lost his cool. "I swear on my life! You sons of bit…"

"Sit. Down," Caine said, using his gun to fire a shot in Laura's direction. The bullet smashed into the wall directly to the right of Laura's head.

"She is still here, isn't she? For now, at least," Caine said. "I called it off. Killing her just like that wouldn't have had the effect that I wanted. It wouldn't have made the same impact on you. The new and improved way? Much better. Much more effective. However, like I said, she is alive. I called it off, Ryan, so you can thank me."

Ryan said nothing.

Caine cleared his throat. "Maybe I wasn't clear. You can *thank* me, Ryan."

Ryan glared at Caine but refused to speak.

Caine shook his head, lifted his Glock in the air, and fired two rounds in Laura's direction. Ryan gasped, and Laura flinched. One bullet hit the wall directly above her head, causing small bits of debris to shower her head. The other shot hit the wall, just to the left of Laura's skull.

"Let's try this one last time, Ryan. I called off Laura's death. She is alive and well right now. What do you say?"

"Thank you."

"You are so very welcome. It is my absolute pleasure."

"How many times do I have to say, she has nothing to do with this?" Ryan asked, pleadingly.

Ignoring Ryan, Caine ushered Kyle to continue the story. "Like Mr. Caine said, the idea to kill Laura was put aside. We did not expect you to weave your way through traffic and run the mile, or half-mile, to the airport and manage to catch a flight out of the city. That was a clever move. Kuron and I still went after you and followed you to Los Angeles. We were right on your tail yet couldn't ever get close enough to you."

"Why did you let me get all the way there?" Ryan interrupted, "That makes no sense? If you knew where I was going, you could've easily bagged me. You let me get all the way to LA, no pilots, no airports, no LAPD, no one was aware of what I allegedly did and that I was being hunted."

"We called it off. We told the media that it was a fluke, and that Mauer was killed by a thug," Kyle said. "The White House Press Secretary gave the news nationally for us to clear things completely up. We didn't want anyone outside of the Bureau to know."

"Why?" Ryan asked.

"Well from the FBI's side of things, it was a bad look on the Bureau. Plus, we kind of wanted to let things play out. We wanted to see where things would go. We wanted to protect you but keep you in close watch. It was all a game. You threw us a lot of loops, honestly. When you reached California, we decided that we wanted to go ahead and take you in ourselves. We didn't want you in prison. Kuron and I would arrest you, Kuron would call it in, then Palino and Z would kill Kuron and we would have you. We wanted you for ourselves.

We then would get Kayleen and Laura, and be in the position we are in now, but just earlier. However, plans changed again as you avoided Z, Palino, myself, and Kuron."

Kyle coughed into his hand. "You left for Rome, which gave us the idea that you were hunting Caine."

"Yup," Ryan said.

"You did a pretty decent job," Caine said. "Killing X, that wasn't cool. That infuriated me. Pissed me off. You made me lose my cool. I'll admit it. In a way, you broke me for a second. So, I didn't want a game anymore. I wanted you dead, yet once again I somewhat underestimated you. You took out all our guys aside from Shaka. I regained some control of my emotions, rethought some things, and called Shaka off.

"I set up a meeting at my beautiful restaurant. There, your drink was drugged, and it kicked in fast. Once you went to sleep, I contacted Kyle, and shipped you to NYC to sit in a cold prison cell. We decided to let you rot in a cell, while we took your family. You couldn't do anything about your situation and couldn't help them. It killed you, didn't it? It drove you insane."

Ryan said nothing.

Kyle spoke up again. "The original plan was to kill Laura and Kayleen, or at least make you think we did. I was then going to break you out of prison, and we were going to go in guns blazing and take out Caine together." Kyle chuckled. "Kuron; however, beat me to it. Once again, our plans had to change. We had to be flexible. We no longer had you in our sights. You were MIA. We did know you would go home at some point. We told many of our operatives that you were on the loose and would be trying to hunt down Caine and find Kayleen.

"We made it known to all of our men that we were going to take Laura too. I decided to let Shaka do the honor of abducting her. Mr. Caine agreed to let him do so. We knew at some point that you would go home. You, of course, did. J.R. informed Mr. Caine of when you did so, and Mr. Caine called the house's landline and then called the cell phone Shaka left for you. Here we are now. In the end, everything worked out for the best."

There was a dead silence before Laura broke it.

"What now?" she asked.

There was a terrified look in her eyes. Ryan couldn't believe how frail and defeated she looked.

"Well, that is a good question," Caine said putting his arms out. "Ryan here gets to decide who goes first. The beautiful wife, or the little girl?"

CHAPTER NINETY-SIX

Kuron was drenched. The rain was deafening. Yet he could have sworn he heard gunfire. Not once. Four times. Four separate shots. It made him move out faster, that's for sure. The gun shots, along with the ominous lightning crashing all around him. Soaked from head to toe, he entered the large barn, keeping his gun held out in front of him as he surveyed the area. Kuron's eyes ventured to the opposite end of the barn, toward the two huge front doors. To the side of the doors were inclining stairs.

There.

He followed the pathway of the stairs with his eyes to find that they led up to a white door. Kuron trotted over to the stairs and began to ascend them. Step by step, closer and closer to the door he came. As he came closer to the door, he could hear voices.

They're here.

Pressing his ear against the white door, Kuron could make out some words that were being spoken.

"Great idea!" Kuron heard a deep, eerie voice say. There was a pause, and then the same voice started up again.

"Hello, Cindy…oh, it is going quite wonderful. Bring little Kayleen up here…yes…okay…okay, make it snappy, sis."

Kayleen! Someone by the name of Cindy is bringing her here!

Kuron swiftly, but quietly descended the stairs. At the very bottom was an old wooden door just to the left of Kuron. It was positioned laterally to the large double-doors. He assumed Kayleen would be brought in through either the door at the back of the barn that he had entered through, or by the means of this old wooden door. In front of the big double-doors was a large, green tractor. Kuron decided it would be a good hiding spot. He rushed over to the tractor. Just as he began to crouch behind one of its large tires, he overheard the creaking of a door being opened. It was the old wooden one.

As he heard the door shut, there was a flash of light followed by a ferocious roar of thunder. He peeked around the tire and was taken by surprise. At the base of the stairs stood little Kayleen. She was shivering and sobbing quietly. However, it wasn't Kayleen that surprised Kuron. It was the person with her that did. It definitely didn't look like a "Cindy". This person was a man. The man looked to stand at around average height, and as he threw off his hood, he revealed a head of dark hair. He was young and looked nothing like a "Cindy", *or* the usual person who worked for Caine.

Maybe Cindy sent someone to bring Kayleen.

Kuron remained poised and alert. He kept his Glock tightly enclosed in his hand. He kept his eyes on the pair at the base of the stairs.

The man with Kayleen crouched down and grabbed the little girl by the hands. He spoke to her, but Kuron couldn't make out the words he said. The rain was too deafening as it pounded on the barn's rooftop. Kayleen's crying slowed until it came to a complete stop. The man hugged her, and then lifted her up into his arms as he turned toward the stairs. Kuron took this as his opportunity.

"FBI!" he yelled, just loud enough for the mystery man to hear him over the rain pounding down on the barn's rooftop. "Turn around where I can see you! Nice and easy!"

Kuron approached the man from behind, and the man set Kayleen down on the ground as he slowly turned around.

"Hands in the air! Now. And I said nice and easy!"

Sitting on the floor, Kayleen hugged her knees and hid her face. The guy very slowly turned around with his arms extended above his head.

"Come here, Kay," Kuron said.

Kayleen didn't hear him.

"Who are you?" Kuron asked.

"I am the person who just might have saved this little girl's life, and I just might have saved yours not too long ago too."

"What are you talking about?" Kuron asked.

Kayleen crawled over to Kuron, and he pulled her up against his leg.

The man with his hands in the air cleared his throat. "You came out of that nice black car. You were the big guy moving through the trees. You're Agent Kuron Taylor, right?"

"How do you know me?" Kuron barked.

"I've done my research."

Kuron looked the man up and down.

"Wait, the four gunshots…" Kuron said in deep thought.

"Yeah, that was me," the man said, cutting Kuron's sentence short. "Four armed men came running out of the barn toward you. They scattered out through the trees and were headed straight for you."

"How did you know I was going to be here? Were you following me, or?"

"Well," the man began, "to be honest with you, I sat on top of that silo out there with my rifle hoping to get a chance to kill Caine and end all this madness once and for all. I have been trailing Ryan Turner for several days now. I got into the farm's perimeter; a little luck, a little bit of skill. I had to take out some guys here and there; a few watchmen and guards. I killed the man who was perched on top of the silo and decided up there would be a good spot for me to position myself. Like I said, I waited up there for an opportunity to hopefully kill Caine. I didn't exactly know where he was. I assumed in the barn or in the house, but I knew if I went in by myself, it was almost certain I would be killed. I just had the feeling I needed to go atop that silo, so I did.

"I had heard that Kayleen had been taken too. I assumed she was here also. Anyways, it all worked out. I saw you and then saw four oafs come out of the barn. I wasted all four of them. Then, I decided to run after you and knew we could help one another. As I climbed to the bottom of the silo, a woman exited the house along with a man. She was carrying a little girl that I thought could've been Kayleen. The girl was kicking and screaming. The man and woman were running as fast as they could toward the front of the barn. They were in quite the hurry and not once looked in my direction. I dropped my rifle, drew my Beretta, and ran after them. I shot the man in the back of the head and pistol-whipped the woman in the head. Honestly, I might have killed her. I didn't waste time checking for a pulse, but her head was bleeding pretty good and she dropped instantly. I grabbed Kayleen off the ground. Now, here we are."

Kuron nodded. He bit his lip and shoved his Glock into his waistband.

"So," he said, "what's our plan now?"

CHAPTER NINETY-SEVEN

Ryan's mind was racing. He couldn't think straight. He couldn't find a solution to the problem he was faced with; the living nightmare he was currently in. Caine broke the silence.

"Kyle, Shaka, have you heard anything from those four clowns? They should've been back by now. And where is Cindy?"

Both Shaka and Kyle shrugged as they shook their heads.

"Kyle," Caine said, "give them all a few more minutes and if they don't return, go find them and see what is going on. Cindy, she should be here any second now."

"Yes, sir," Kyle said. "I don't want you having fun without me here, if I do have to go. I want to see everything."

"Oh, don't you worry about that," Caine said. "The party won't start without you."

"Cybris. Caine. Freak show. Whatever they call you," Laura said, "there has to be some good in you. There must be. There is in everyone. Please. Please. I beg of you, don't do this. If anything, just spare my little girl. Don't let her see all this. You can torture and kill me. That is great, but don't let her be here, and please don't kill her too. She is innocent."

Caine laughed hysterically. There was a crazed look in his eyes.

"There is much good in me, Ms. Laura. Lots and lots of good! I know that what I do, what I plan to do, is what is best. It is *all* good. I am not the corrupt or sick one. I'm not. Now, the selfish, ruthless, two-faced leaders and politicians? They are the problem. Even people like you. You doctors, lawyers,

teachers, architects, the list goes on…you don't care about
those who are barely getting by. You don't give two cents
about those who have nothing. You don't care about those
who are living in poverty. You don't care about the real
dream of people. While there are those of you sit around
eating steak and lobster in your nice little houses, with your
spoiled children, there are others out there who spill sweat
and blood and tears just to stay alive, just to wear a raggedy
old shirt on their backs. They are struggling. They are
slinking around in the shadows trying to make it.

"These people don't know what it is like to be able to
have true happiness or have a life without pain. They can't
even begin to fathom what life is like without worry, without
restraint, without constant and continual hardship. The dream
of true equality and true freedom, the perfect world? That is
what I am shooting for. That is the goal. Plus, don't get me
wrong, having the immense, undeniable power that'll come
with all of it will be incredibly nice too. So, you see, there is a
lot of good in me. Lots. And it is up to Ryan whether Kayleen
will have to watch either of you suffer. It is up to him who we
have fun with first. That decision is out of my hands."

Ryan began to speak up but was interrupted by his
furious wife.

"Screw you, Cyberius! Whoever, whatever you are!" she
spat out. "You power hungry freak. We 'selfish' people
worked to live in peace and happiness. We worked hard to
get to where we are now. We, through sweat and tears, got to
the point we are at in our lives. It takes work to be successful.
It isn't just given to you. Us doctors, teachers, lawyers,
businessmen? I'd like to see the world without us."

Caine smirked. "Be careful what you wish for…woman,
you are full of so much fire. I love it," he said, staring into

Laura's eyes. "I swear, so badly do I want to keep you around. I would if I could. I love me a feisty girl."

Caine stood up and approached Laura. He stood over her and put his face as close to hers as possible. He caressed her neck and face with his fingers.

"And so beautiful you are. The two of us would have some fun together."

Ryan stood up. "Get your hands off her!" he yelled.

With one step, and the swipe of his arm, Shaka threw Ryan back into the couch. He stood over Ryan and shoved the muzzle of a handgun against Ryan's head. Meanwhile Caine leaned his head to the side and kissed Laura's neck. As he did, she screamed out, and headbutted Caine. He jerked back and grabbed at his face. Blood began to trickle out of his nostrils.

"You witch!" he said, drawing a knife out and poking it against Laura's stomach. "You know what? I think I have an idea. While we wait for Cindy, how about I try to give Laura here a C-section. I think it is time for the baby to be welcomed into this glorious world. I think it deserves an invitation to the party too, don't you all think so? Maybe that is why Laura here is so moody. Okay, beautiful, hold still, Dr. Caine's got you."

Laura's face became paler. She began to weep, begging and pleading with Caine in between sobs. With his knife, Caine horizontally cut Laura's shirt. A small incision formed across her abdomen, just below her belly button. Caine placed a hand through the opening in the shirt and placed it on Laura's skin. He slowly ran it up and down from her bloodied belly to her chest.

"I am going to enjoy this," Caine said. "I am going to enjoy this very much."

CHAPTER NINETY-EIGHT

The front door of the living quarters creaked
open. Inside stepped a young, hooded man. In his arms, he
held a screaming little girl.

"This little demon is giving Cindy fits. I brought her
over. Ms. Cindy should be here in a little bit," the hooded
man said.

"Interesting," replied Caine. He stepped away from
Laura. "Who are you, anyway?"

The hooded man kept his head low. "Jason. I am the new
guy here, sir. I am from New York City. Remember?"

Caine kept his eyes locked on the man. "Is that right?"

He started to approach the hooded man. Kayleen kicked
the man in the face. He cried out, spun around, and fell to his
knee, his back facing Caine. The man remained hunched
over, facing the half-opened door. Ryan wanted so badly to
charge Caine now. With his back to Ryan, and his attention
occupied, this was Ryan's chance. Shaka no longer had his
gun pointed at Ryan, and he too was facing the door now.
Ryan knew he had to go for it. His attention though, suddenly
strayed to the hooded man. He looked familiar. Too familiar.
Ryan couldn't shake the feeling. He snapped back into
reality, moving his attention back to Caine. Caine's backside
was still to Ryan. This was Ryan's shot and he knew that had
to take it. He quickly reached for the knife inside of his pants.
It was now or never.

CHAPTER NINETY-NINE

All chaos broke loose. Everything seemed to unravel in slow motion. Suddenly the hooded man spun around with a gun in his clutch. Gunshots erupted inside the room.

Ryan could no longer see Kayleen. Caine dove behind the couch and screamed out, grabbing at his left shoulder. Ryan pulled out his knife. He glanced over at Shaka, who jerked back, and dove for cover behind the couch too, leaving a streak of blood on the pink couch. Ryan felt as if he was in a dream. He moved his attention to the left to find Kyle swinging his Glock toward the doorway, where Ryan could see the hooded man standing alongside a large black man.

Kuron.

Ryan's instincts kicked in, and he threw himself into Kyle, knocking him to the ground. Kyle fired his gun as Ryan hit him, sending a bullet crashing into a wall. As Ryan and Kyle fell to the floor in a heap, the gun fell from Kyle's grasp and clattered across the floor. Kyle's strength and flexibility surprised Ryan. He alligator rolled himself out from underneath Ryan's weight. Ryan was now underneath Kyle. Kyle began to throw punches, one after the other. A few blows met their target, and somewhat dazed Ryan. Ryan lifted his hands in front of his face and as he did, Kyle ceased punching and reached for his gun.

Bad move.

Ryan took advantage of this and shoved his blade into Kyle's chest. Kyle never saw the blade. He didn't even know Ryan had it. He never saw it coming. Kyle screamed out in pain. Ryan threw Kyle off him and threw him down onto his back. Ryan rolled himself onto Kyle, keeping his hand on the knife's handle. Blood gushed out of Kyle's chest as Ryan jerked the blade out of it. He knew Kyle was done for. The blow was too close to his heart for him not to die. Ryan stabbed Kyle once more, this time in his abdomen. Ryan jerked the blade downward before removing it from Kyle's body. Blood gushed out of the wound. Kyle wasn't going anywhere anytime soon.

Ryan dove away from Kyle's body and grabbed the gun up off the floor. He slid his back up against the backside of the couch. Scanning the room, he couldn't find any sight of Caine or Shaka. He turned his attention to Laura and Kayleen. His heart pounded. He spotted Laura, who still sat in the chair. Her head was stooped down low, but she looked to be unharmed.

He still couldn't find Kayleen.

Where is she?

Ryan moved his attention to the doorway, where Kuron and the hooded man stood, the two using the door as cover. To the right of the doorway, in the corner of the room, one of Caine's men was pulling himself up off the ground. He was bloodied and battered. He initiated lifting his gun toward Kuron and the man in the hood. They were completely unaware of him. Ryan immediately fired two rounds into the man's chest, who jerked back from the bullets' impact and crashed back down to the ground.

Ryan again ducked down next to the couch and peeked around the corner of it. He watched as Kuron stepped into plain view, both of his hands holding a Glock out in front of him. He swung his pistol to his right and fired two shots over Ryan's head. Ryan looked over his shoulder to see one of Caine's henchmen fall flat onto his stomach. Just like that, the gunfire ceased. Just as suddenly as the chaos started, it was all over.

CHAPTER ONE HUNDRED

The only noises Ryan could hear were the sound of Kyle's coughing and gurgling, and Kayleen whimpering. He could hear her, but he still couldn't see her.

"Kayleen? Where are you?"

"She's safe," Kuron said as he walked over and put an arm around Ryan. "We've got her man. Kay, you can come out."

Kayleen came running through the door from the stairway. Ryan met her halfway, bent down, and threw his arms around her.

"Are you okay? Are you hurt?"

"No, daddy," she replied. "I'm okay. Just scared."

"You're safe. Everything is going to be okay," Ryan said, hugging her tightly. "I've got you."

To the left of him, Kuron and the hooded man were crouching around Laura, unbinding her from the chair. Ryan set Kayleen down and approached Laura. Now untied, she weakly threw herself into Ryan's arms.

"I love you," Ryan said. "I am so sorry for all of this."

Laura was pale. She could hardly keep her head upright. Blood from her belly seeped onto Ryan's shirt.

"Are you okay?" he asked.

Laura nodded her head, and kissed Ryan's cheek. A series of horrific noises broke out inside the room, drawing Ryan's attention back to Kyle.

How is he not dead yet?

Ryan pulled away from Laura's hug, and Kuron placed an arm around Laura's shoulders.

"I've got you," he told her before leading her to the sofa and sitting her down.

Kayleen quickly scampered onto the couch and cuddled against her mother. Ryan walked over to Kyle and crouched down next to him. Blood covered his chest and seeped out of the corners of his mouth. Ryan placed a hand behind Kyle's head and tilted it upward.

"Look at you," he said, glaring down at Kyle. "Look where all of this has gotten you."

Kyle said nothing. His eyes remained shut. He coughed hard, and blood flew from his mouth onto Ryan's shirt.

"You were my friend, Kyle," Ryan said softly. "I loved you, man. Now look where you are."

Kyle's chest heaved in and out, and his eyes attempted to flutter open, but failed to. A wretched gurgling sound came from deep inside Kyle, and his body went limp. Ryan let Kyle's head fall to the floor and he looked away from the man's lifeless body.

CHAPTER ONE HUNDRED ONE

Ryan leapt to his feet.

"Where is Caine? Where is he?"

Ryan hurriedly searched the room for bodies. There was no sign of Cybris Caine. Next to the couch, he spotted Shaka, who's shot up face was hardly recognizable. In total, there were six dead bodies in the room. One was Kyle. One was Shaka. None of them were Cybris Caine.

"Where is he!?" Ryan exclaimed.

Kuron redrew his gun and shook his head. "He must have gotten away. My man over here shot him but didn't kill him, I guess. The snake must have crawled away and found a way out. We didn't really keep an eye on him. We were taking heavy gunfire."

Ryan was perplexed, frustrated.

"There has to be a back way…another way out," the man wearing the hood said.

Ryan looked over at him, trying to piece together who the man was. The hooded man grinned.

"Still can't put together who I am, huh?"

Ryan shook his head. "Still working on it."

"You two," the man said, "go find Caine. I'll stay here with the girls…and hurry! We probably don't have much time before he gives us the slip."

Ryan and Kuron exchanged glances while a roar of thunder erupted outside.

Kuron rolled out his neck. "Let's go get him."

CHAPTER ONE HUNDRED TWO

Ryan threw open the wooden barn door that was parallel to the huge sliding doors. As he stepped outside, he was instantly hit with rain, hail, and wind. To his left he could make out the outline of two bodies lying between him and the farmhouse. One of the bodies looked to be that of a woman. He guessed it was Cindy.

"Where to Ryan!?" Kuron yelled through the sound of the roaring storm.

Ryan leaned in closer to Kuron, and a bolt of lightning crashed a short distance in front of them. The ground shook beneath them.

"He obviously didn't take either of the cars!" Ryan yelled, motioning to the black vehicles parked in front of the barn. "He must have another way of getting out of here, or he is hunkering down in the house!"

Ryan ran toward the farmhouse. He stopped next to two bodies that were lying on the ground, and Kuron stopped next to him.

"What do you think he is planning!?" Kuron asked. "I don't see Caine as someone who is going to hole up in a house and wait to die."

Ryan rolled the woman over onto her back. It was Cindy Caine Harrison. She was soaked and covered in mud. Ryan checked for a pulse. She was alive. Her head was bleeding, but she was alive. Slinging Cindy's limp body over his shoulder, Ryan answered Kuron's question.

"Helicopter, jet, private plane! He has had that kind of transportation at his disposal before. On as big of a place as this, it wouldn't surprise me if that's the case!"

The two sprinted to the nearest door of the upcoming house. Kuron threw the door open. Drenched, they stepped inside. Ryan laid Cindy on the floor of the living room area they had just stepped into. Across the room, through windows that were above the sink in the kitchen, Ryan spotted Caine's means of escape. It was a helicopter.

Just behind the house, the helicopter was beginning to lift off the ground. Ryan broke into a dead sprint, running through the living room, the kitchen, and out the back door of the house that was positioned to the right of the refrigerator inside the kitchen. Ryan stared up at the ascending chopper.

In the cargo area of the helicopter was Cybris Caine. Madly, Ryan began to fire rounds at the helicopter, but his fire was immediately followed by bullets flying back at him. The bullets flew in his direction and showered the ground all around him. Quickly, Ryan dove back into the house, bouncing into Kuron.

"Ryan…he is slipping away," Kuron said, ducking behind a counter.

Ryan peeked around the half-opened door that was under gunfire. He knew Kuron was right. The helicopter was lifting off the ground, higher and higher into the air. Along with the pouring rain bullets continued to shower the ground and house. Ryan removed the clip from the gun he had acquired from Kyle. One single bullet occupied the clip.

CHAPTER ONE HUNDRED THREE

Kuron was speaking, but Ryan couldn't hear him. He closed his eyes. He pictured Laura. He could hear her helpless voice and see her bleeding face and abdomen. He remembered his first parents. He remembered the elderly couple who raised him on the farm. The horrible past week replayed through his head. Then he could see Caine's smiling face. He could picture him slapping Laura and kissing her neck. His heart began to feel as if it was going to beat out of his chest. He took a deep breath, and halfway through it, he busted through the door and into the pouring rain.

Gun raised high above his head, Ryan kept his arms steady, his eyes focused. The only thing on his mind was Caine. He kept his eyes locked on him. He narrowed his focus, ignoring Kuron's screaming behind him, ignoring the rain and lightning, ignoring the bullets flying all around him. He was one with his Glock. He could almost see Caine's grin through the thick film of rain. Ryan's finger tightened on the trigger. He took in a breath, held it, and fired the gun.

Time stood still.

At first nothing happened. He could almost see the bullet spinning toward Caine. He was sure he had missed. Caine stood firm, a smile still on his face. Ryan knew he had missed. A bullet suddenly soared through Ryan's thigh.

Ryan fell backwards, and as he fell to the ground, he kept his eyes on Caine. Caine's demeanor had changed. A smile no longer existed on his face. Ryan felt Kuron's strong hands grab him from behind and start to drag him into the house. As he was pulled backwards, Ryan watched as Caine staggered around, high above in the aircraft.

The incoming gunfire from men inside the helicopter came to a stop. Ryan watched intently as Caine ceased from stumbling, reached for his now bloody throat, and started to fall out of the side of the helicopter. His fall was stopped short though, by one of his own men, who quickly reached over and grabbed Caine out of the air. He pulled Caine back into the chopper before he fell out of the sky.

Kuron finished pulling Ryan into the farmhouse, and the sound of the helicopter ventured off into the distance until it was no more. Ryan leaned his back against a set of cabinets and peered down at his thigh. Kuron pulled Ryan's cut-off pants up a tad and nodded in a circular-like motion. Ryan grimaced at Kuron's touch. Kuron's eyes went wide.

"You are lucky, fool. Somehow the bullet missed the femoral artery. The bullet looks like it went right by it; in one side, out the other. Just skimmed you. You aren't bleeding too horribly either. I mean it's bleeding, but it isn't just gushing out of there. Let me find something to cover that up."

Ryan let his shoulders go lax. He laid his head back against the cabinets. He blew out a breath, trying to keep "Emotional Ryan" away; or what Kayleen liked to call "Crybaby Daddy". She often used his words against him, for he called her a crybaby anytime she fussed. It was hard to hold back. A tear or two squeezed past his eyes. All the emotions, all the fear, the pain, everything Ryan had kept cooped up inside of him was suddenly surfacing. The tears that fell now were tears of relief. It was over. Just like that, it was all over. The living nightmare was no more. Ryan could stop running. He could stop hiding. He could stop living in fear. Kayleen was safe. Laura and the baby were safe. Cybris

Commodus Caine was gone. Possibly forever. It was finally over.

CHAPTER ONE HUNDRED FOUR

Kuron returned to Ryan's side, having retrieved two long dish towels.

"Let me cover this up really quick," he said, placing a towel around the wound, and tying it onto the leg with the other towel.

Ryan grimaced as Kuron pulled it tight.

"Let's go get my family and get out of here," Ryan said.

As Kuron helped Ryan off the floor, the front door of the house flew open and in stepped the hooded man holding Kayleen in one arm. His other arm was wrapped around Laura. Ryan limped over to his little family. He stepped around a half-conscious Cindy and embraced his wife. He tried hard to keep his emotional self away again. He felt Kayleen beneath him wrapping her arms around his bad leg. Pain shot up his leg causing him to grunt and cringe, but he embraced the hug.

It was maybe the greatest moment of his life. He could hold them again. They were finally safe and in his arms. Ryan kissed his wife and helped her over to the living room sofa. Kuron remained close to Cindy, keeping a close eye on her.

"Here, sit down, honey," Ryan said.

"No, no," Laura said. "I have been sitting around tied to a chair for way too long. I can stand."

Ryan nodded in approval. "So," he said looking over at the man he couldn't recognize, "FBI? CIA? NYPD? Vigilante? Neighborhood watchman?"

The man pulled of his hood and chuckled.

"Actually, CIA," he said, crossing his arms in front of his chest.

Ryan cocked his head to the side. "CIA, huh? What brought you here?"

"I have been keeping an eye on you for a while, Mr. Turner. I followed you when you were in Rome. I was in disguise, but I kept a really close eye on you…."

"No way," Ryan said, placing a hand on the man's shoulder. "You were the guy that helped me in Rome! John, right? John Drexel?"

John smiled.

"Yes, sir," he said. "I had a guy help me track you down. I was currently undercover in Rome. Lucky for me, that is where you ended up, and I trailed you while I was there. I lost track of you after the shootout at the hotel, and then found out you had been imprisoned."

"At the hotel!" Ryan exclaimed. "You helped me take down that group of men. You're the one who killed a bunch of those men! *You* are the one that helped me."

"Yeah, I took out a few of them."

Ryan grinned, shaking his head from side to side. "Unbelievable. You've saved me twice now. How did you end up back here? I mean, why? And what was your purpose all this time?"

"I beat myself up over losing track of you," John said. "I really, really did. I found out that you were being held in New York City. Without permission, I made my way here. I was going to do whatever it took to help you, or at least try to. About the time that I arrived, I find out that you had escaped from prison. I did some research to find out where you lived, knowing that you would try to get home at some point. I got to your house, and the moment I did, you left in the Prius. I was suspicious of the cars leading and trailing close behind you. I had an uncomfortable feeling about all of it.

So, I followed close behind. I tried to get right behind you a couple times, but the black car kept cutting me off. I knew something was up. You led me here. When you followed the SUV and turned at the sign to enter Gondleton Farms, I knew it was too dangerous to follow. I could see armed men stationed at the sign. I knew they wouldn't be the only ones, and I knew you were in a dire situation.

I passed by the turnoff and parked a distance down the road. I used my rifle to take down the two guards at the sign. Shot them from a distance away. I knew that getting you back by busting down doors and going all hero-like wouldn't work but would only get us both killed. I figured that wasn't going to be the way to approach the situation.

So, I stealthily made my way into the farm's perimeter, killed two more men, and then shot the watchman off the top of the silo. I think the rain has been a blessing. It helped silence the gunshots and helped camouflage me in a way. I climbed to the top of the silo and waited for an opportunity to help you. I knew Caine was involved and hoped I would get a chance to take him out, once and for all. I saw one man pull up behind the barn on his motorcycle. Yeah, real smart of him in this kind of weather.

It turned out to be the guy you stabbed and killed. I never got a shot at him. I didn't know who he was anyway. I then saw Kuron running toward the barn through the trees. I looked through my scope, and knew it was him. Then, I noticed four armed guys running out of the barn. They split up and were going toward Kuron. I knew they couldn't possibly be good guys. I mean, I guess there could have been a chance that they were, but it was unlikely to me. So, I took a chance and shot every one of them dead. Then, I saw this woman here."

He motioned in Cindy's direction. "She was running toward the barn carrying a little girl. I assumed it had to be Kayleen. I had seen news reports that she was missing. A man was with her too. I took off after them and they never saw me coming. I killed the man and knocked the woman out. I carried Kayleen into the barn. We wouldn't all be here now if it wasn't for Agent Taylor showing up. I didn't know what I was going to be able to do alone."

John and Kuron exchanged glances and nodded at one another.

"I cannot thank either of you enough," Ryan said gratefully. "But, John, I am still curious, not complaining, just curious...why? Why get involved in all of this? Why were you tracking me in the first place, and so set on defending and protecting me? You left your station in Rome. You went MIA on your Agency, man. You probably lost your job because of it. You did it all to help me. Why?"

Ryan looked on at John, who looked to be getting somewhat emotional. It took Ryan by surprise. However, Ryan would never forget John's next words. John looked into Ryan's eyes.

"Ryan, it has been over twenty years...I'm Johnathan. Your brother."

CHAPTER ONE HUNDRED FIVE

Six Days Later...
November 24, 2017.

It was 5 p.m. Ryan sat at his new desk inside his newly acquired office, left leg crossed over his right, and his arms folded across his chest. He kept his eyes shut as he spoke on the phone with the FBI Director, Trey Felix.

"I am very impressed with all of you, Mr. Turner. Very impressed. What Johnathan Drexel did too? I'm extremely impressed with him. I talked to Director Danley at the CIA, and he said he was furious about John. He thought he had gone rogue. Technically, he could be arrested and sentenced for leaving his station without informing anyone, but I am very happy he did. I explained to him everything John did. Danley is okay with it, and completely understands. To the sound of it, none of this would have been possible without Mr. John Drexel. We wouldn't be speaking to one another right now."

He was right. Ryan knew that if it wasn't for John, he wouldn't be sitting there now in the Head of the Bureau chair. He knew he and his family would be dead. Caine's plan would have continued to grow, and the evil, dirty agents within the FBI never would've been uncovered until it was too late. Instead, with the help of Jayren Raymond, Ryan had worked alongside Director Felix to uncover the corruption within the FBI. It had only been a few days since the incident at Gondelton Farms, and already hundreds of FBI, CIA, and military leaders had turned up guilty, and charged with the highest degree of treason. Ryan knew there would be plenty more arrests. Even if they didn't bust all the dirty agents and military personnel, he imagined that those who weren't caught would change their ways after seeing all the arrests being made and Cybris Caine's Empire losing ground fast.

"Yeah, I wouldn't be here if it wasn't for him," Ryan answered. "That is for sure."

The Director coughed.

"So, he is your brother? You're blood brothers? Do I understand that, correctly?"

"Yes, sir," Ryan replied.

He still couldn't believe it himself, really. Little John. Ryan and John had a few times to sit down and talk, and Ryan still felt almost ashamed and guilty for not putting forth the same amount of effort to find John as he did to find Ryan. Ryan had given up. He admitted it. He had accepted long, long ago that he would never be reunited with his brother. He accepted he would never see him again. He'd pretty much convinced himself that John had been adopted into a family living in another country, or something.

Ryan had always felt that John wouldn't remember him due to how young he was when he and Ryan were split up. He was certainly proven wrong. John explained to Ryan that he always had dreams about the two of them together, and that those dreams always comforted him. As he grew older, the dreams never went away. They continued to occur every night. John had been adopted at the age of five by a family in Nebraska. They were unable to have children of their own and adopted John. They treated him like royalty. Although they spoiled him, John said that they taught him manners, respect, how to work hard, and how to love. They were still alive, and Ryan hoped to meet them someday. John also had a memory of the deceased Caines, who had taken he and Ryan in as their own for some time. He also remembered Cybris and Cindy Caine as children.

"I never liked those two," he had told Ryan when they spoke of the matter.

After high school, John specialized in combat, and enlisted into the U.S. Army, and was accepted into the 75th Ranger Regiment. He was an Army Ranger for five years. After his time in the Army, he applied to work for the CIA. He got in easily. That was when he really began his research to find Ryan. Now, after two and a half decades of being apart, John lived in New York City, fairly close to Ryan and his family. After very little discussion about it, it was decided that John would stay in NYC and work alongside Ryan in the FBI.

"He will make a stellar agent for you, Mr. Turner. Director Danley has attested to that," Felix said.

"For sure. He's a great asset, and he is an even better man," Ryan replied.

"Tell me," Felix stated, "how are you doing? Your family?"

"For the most part, we are all doing okay now."

It wasn't a lie. It had only been six days, but life was finally returning back to normal. Whatever "normal" means. Ryan really didn't know anymore. He had gotten his leg fixed up and it was feeling good. His shoulder had all but healed. The hospital had also gotten lots of fluids into him through IV's. Finally, he was back at home with his wife by his side every night. To have that again, made Ryan's heart full. Laura hadn't suffered any serious injuries, just a busted lip, bruised face, and an incision on her abdomen that wasn't very deep and didn't really require much attention. The baby was healthy too. Kayleen had been completely unharmed. Her and Laura's biggest setbacks were psychologically. Laura wasn't too bad, but Kayleen was.

Kayleen couldn't sleep at night. She spent her nights in Ryan and Laura's bed, and would wake up from nightmares, screaming and crying, which wouldn't cease for hours at a time. It had only been a few nights, so Ryan hoped things would gradually get better. Ryan had a friend who was a well-known psychiatrist, and already had dates set up for him to meet with Kayleen. Ryan felt horrible that Kay had to go through the things she went through and see the things she did. He prayed every night that she wouldn't be mentally scarred and affected long-term.

"I am very glad to hear that," Felix said. "And again, I am deeply sorry for what you had to go through. No one should have to be put through what you did, especially someone like you who has done so much for our country."

"It's really okay," said Ryan. "It is fine, Mr. Felix. It's done and over with."

"Well," the Director said, "I am just saying, it was a bad deal for you. It's sickening to even think about, and I am sorry for not having more faith in you, and sorry that I didn't look harder into what really happened. It was a sickening and horrible situation you were in."

Ryan could picture Director Trey Felix as he spoke. He was tall, wiry, six-foot-three, maybe six-foot-four. He had a small nose, beady eyes, and thin, gray hair that was always combed back. Trey Felix was probably in his early fifties. His back was messed up and he had to walk with the assistance of a cane. Felix had a full set of pearly white teeth that accompanied his genuine smile. Trey Felix was one of the good ones. He was a beloved figure to the entire nation.

Everyone knew who he was. Unlike many past directors, he had a true connection with the nation's citizens. He was someone Ryan always had the deepest respect for. He was genuinely a great man. Ryan uncrossed his arms, and gently rubbed his injured thigh. It was still tender to the touch, but the doctors had done a respectable job of caring for it.

"I definitely can't disagree with you there," Ryan said. "I never want to relive any of that again."

"However, like you said," Felix stated, "it is all over and done with, and thank the good Lord that it is."

"Amen," Ryan said in reply.

CHAPTER ONE HUNDRED SIX

"So," Felix said, "Cindy Caine and Jayren Raymond? What was made of them? They got locked up, right?"

"They are awaiting trial, but yeah, there is no doubt in my mind that they will be locked up for good," Ryan replied, nodding. He grabbed a pen off his desk, and simultaneously clicked it. "Jayren Raymond was taken to a hospital. Kuron broke a few of his ribs. It caused him quite a deal of pain, and I'm surprised nothing too major was wrong with him. I mean, his ribs were broken bad, but nothing life-threatening. Even being in the hospital, he was able to help us bag dirty agents, and he gave us leads on many of Caine's hideouts and right-hand men. Anyways, he is at Guantanamo Bay. That is where we have all been contacting him in the last few days, or so. The people there have been very helpful in getting us in contact with him when we need him. The freak will get roughed up there, but I won't lose any sleep over it. He deserves every bit of it. Cindy? I think you know, but she is pregnant. So, she'll be held here at the Ryker's Island facilities until she has the baby. After she does, we'll send her to Guantanamo too."

"Sounds good," Felix said. "Cindy is pregnant?"

"That's correct. The baby is Kyle's. The two were married. She got some plastic surgery and was married to Kyle, living under the radar. All these years, I never recognized her to be Cindy Caine."

Ryan could picture the Director nodding while in thought.

"The baby? Is it healthy? What will become of it? Just go into the adoption services? Find a foster home?"

"Well, we have a plan concerning that," Ryan said. "Laura and I plan to take the baby in as our own. We are expecting a baby boy too, and the two should be born very close to the same time. They can grow up together as brothers."

"Wow!" Director Felix exclaimed. "That sounds wonderful!" He sounded very sincere. "It will probably be best that the kid never knows who his parents really were. He'll have an amazing home. That is really great of you and Laura."

"Agreed," Ryan said, "and thank you, Mr. Felix."

There was a momentary pause in the conversation before Felix continued.

"And Cybris Caine?"

Hearing that name still made Ryan's skin crawl.

"He's gone. I killed him," Ryan said.

"Is that your gut feeling?"

Ryan thought about the question. He let himself think for a second. He wanted to say that he knew for a fact that Caine was dead. He wanted so badly to feel that Caine was gone forever, but he would never be one-hundred percent sure until he saw Caine's dead body himself. That is just how it would always be.

"It's Cybris Caine."

That was all the answer Ryan had. The Director made a clicking noise with his mouth.

"Point taken." Felix coughed before speaking up again. "So, Ryan, are you for sure up for this position? I know you are just the sitting-in Head of the Bureau as of now, but when the time comes, are you ready for this to be official?"

Ryan let the question sink in. He had thought about this quite a bit lately. He still wasn't so sure what his answer was.

"I don't know, Mr. Felix. I'm still not sure yet."

"Hmm," the Director said pondering, "I don't want to push you into any kind of decision, but I strongly believe, with all my heart, that you would be perfect for the position. My own bias, I'd love to work alongside you. There couldn't be a better person to fill Mauer's spot. Everything that you have seen, done, and experienced, and being at the head of unravelling all this corruption? You took down two of the most wanted men out there. Ryan, you took out the Invisible Man and *the* Cybris Caine. Honestly, I feel like you are not only destined for the job, but the Bureau needs you there. I'm not saying that to put pressure on you, but I am just being straight with you. That is how I feel. You are a great man, Ryan Turner. One of the very best."

Ryan was touched by Felix's words. "Thank you, Mr Felix. I just…I don't know. I have been a field agent for so long and have had much success. I feel like it is who I am and who I am meant to be. I still feel like I can contribute as a field agent. I've been effective for so many years. I feel like I still have much left to give."

"I totally see where you are coming from," said Felix, "but, you could do both. That is an option. Really. You can stay in the field still, until you get in the groove of being 'the man'. Then once you are ready, the position is yours when available. Or, you can remain in the position you are in for as long as you'd like, while holding the position as Head of the Bureau. If anyone can handle doing both, it is you, my friend. Like I said, I am not going to pressure you into any decision. We still have plenty of time, so continue to think about it all, and continue to talk with your wife about it. I want what is best for you. Although there is no one I'd rather see in this position, above all else, I do want what is best for you. I do want you doing what you want and living how you want to. So, please, take your time in making a decision."

Ryan nodded and scratched his freshly shaven chin. "I'll certainly give it some thought."

"Well, Caine is gone. It has been three days since the whole ordeal," Director Felix said. "Things are finally getting back to normal, so?"

Ryan had a feeling something interesting was coming next.

"So?" he asked.

"So…" Felix continued, "people in Washington DC have been getting brutally murdered. All the murder scenes are practically identical…it is unlike anything that I have ever seen before."

Ryan leaned forward in his desk.

A case.

This is what he lived for. Felix had his attention.

"Go on," Ryan said.

"These murders have been going on over the space of the last two weeks. There are three recorded deaths thus far. All committed by the same person, we believe. They were all killed in a very unique way, to say the least. Like I said, it is unlike anything I have ever seen before, and I have been alive and in this business for a very long time. The scenes are gruesome, horrific. They make your skin tingle and your stomach churn. Already, DC detectives and agents of our own have died trying to uncover the person responsible. With this murderer's unique way of killing, he's been given a very fitting nickname."

Ryan said nothing. He waited for Felix to continue. Director Trey Felix cleared his throat.

"Agent Turner? Have you ever heard of *The Crucifier*?"

The following is the first chapter from the next riveting novel in the Ryan Turner series: *Turned Around*.

TURNED AROUND

CHAPTER ONE

He shivered violently. Not from the cold December night, but from the fear and excruciating pain he was experiencing. His chin rested on his chest. No longer able to hold his head up, Dominic Montez was bloodied and battered, still oblivious of where he was now. His legs dangled freely in the air. His ankles were tied together with thick rope. All around him, it was pitch dark, keeping him from seeing the large pool of blood beneath his body. He couldn't move his arms. His hands and wrists throbbed with pain. His head hurt, and he could feel blood pounding behind his ears. He wore nothing but his underwear. The cool air continuously rushed against his bare skin.

"How is it going up there?" a voice asked out of the darkness.

Dominic attempted to lift his head. He could see nothing in front of him. His eyes failed to adjust to the complete darkness surrounding him. He said nothing.

"Oh, Montez?" the voice called out. "Are you still alive? Please tell me you're still alive and breathing?"

Again, Dominic Montez said nothing. Pain surged through his entire body. He felt as if he was on the brink of death. Suddenly, a small flame began to flicker amid the darkness. The flame moved in the dark and came to a stop. It then moved atop a tall candle stick that sat upon a gold base. There were now two flames. The first flame moved again, this time to Montez's right. It then stopped shining, and another candle, identical to the first, began to flicker. Montez forced himself to lift his head. He looked toward the light to find a figure sitting in a chair. On the floor, a candle was positioned on each side of the chair. The figure before Montez was dressed all in black, and wore a white mask, covering all but two beady eyes. A big gold cross hung from a necklace around the individual's neck. Finally, Montez spoke.

"Who are you?" he muttered. "Where am I?"

The figure in black stood up from the chair and picked up the candles off the ground. Holding one in each hand, the individual approached Montez. The person moved with robot-like motions, walking one slow step at a time toward Montez. After a few steps, the figure stopped in front of Montez, and dropped to the floor into a kneeling position. The person in black set the two candles down on the floor, a few feet apart from one another. Dominic's body seized up at the sight of blood.

He could now see the pool of blood beneath him. He could now see that his feet were a foot or two off the ground, tied against a wooden object. A renewed wave of fear surged through his body. He began to yell and tried to move but failed to do so. Aside from his head, he couldn't move a single part of his body. He cried out again.

"Hush, hush," the masked individual said while softly caressing Montez's legs. "Just relax. Breathe. In and out. Everything is going to be just fine."

Shivering, Montez stopped yelling, but quietly began to sob.

"What have I done to you? I don't know you. I am a good man," he cried. "Why am I here? Where am I? Who are you? Please...PLEASE!"

"Easy," the figure in black said. "Easy now. You have so many questions, and so little time. Please, one at a time."

There was complete silence for a moment, then Montez quietly asked, "Where am I?"

Now holding a long, jagged blade, the individual answered, "You, Dom, are where you are meant to be. You are where you are supposed to be. You are hanging from a cross. A beautiful, magnificent cross. You are in a place that is of no concern to you. Now, breathe. Deep breaths. In and out. Everything is going to be just fine. You were meant for this moment."

Montez struggled to lift his head high enough to look over at his outstretched arms. The mysterious being in front of him wasn't lying. His hands were nailed to the wood of what he now knew was a cross. He now realized the direct source of where the pain surging through his hands and arms was coming from and began to thrash around.

"Who are you? PLEASE! Why am I here? I do not deserve this! I don't."

Tears streamed down Montez's cheeks. Stroking the knife's blade, the individual dressed in black peered up into Montez's pleading, fear-filled eyes.

"I am *The Crucifier.* You are right, Dom. You do not deserve this...which is why it must be you."

Before Dominic Montez could mutter another word, The Crucifier shoved the long blade deep into the man's side. Montez whimpered, but no longer had the energy to cry out. Although still breathing, he was already a dead man. It was only a matter of time now before he bled out, or before shock killed him. He no longer had the will to live. He knew he was helpless.

Still holding the blade into Montez's side, the Crucifier whispered, "You are not the first, Dominic Montez. You are not. You are part of something big, something great. This, Dominic Montez, is only the beginning."

The Crucifier then jerked the knife out of the dying man's side. Blood instantly gushed out of the wound. Watching Montez breathe his last breaths, the Crucifier stepped back, and smiled beneath the white mask. Dominic Montez's head went completely limp. His chest no longer heaved in and out. The Crucifier moved back toward Montez and using the dead man's cell phone that had been retrieved earlier, dialed "911", reported the scene, ended the call, and tossed the phone onto the floor. It clattered onto the concrete ground and slid next to the large pool of blood. Then, bending over slightly, The Crucifier removed the mask and kissed Dominic Montez's feet.

The Crucifier took a step back, pointed a finger into the air, turned away from the body, and then exited the cold, dark basement that held Dominic Montez's bloodied, lifeless body.

Made in the USA
San Bernardino, CA
18 January 2019